The Irish Stories of Sarah Orne Jewett

THE Irish STORIES

of
Sarah
Orne
Jewett

Edited and
with an Introduction
by JACK MORGAN and
LOUIS A. RENZA

Southern Illinois University Press
Carbondale and Edwardsville

Library of Congress Cataloging-in-Publication Data

Jewett, Sarah Orne, 1849–1909.
    The Irish stories of Sarah Orne Jewett / edited and with
an introduction by Jack Morgan and Louis A. Renza.
       p.   cm.
      1. Irish Americans—Social life and customs—Fiction.
    2. Ireland—Emigration and immigration—Fiction.
    I. Morgan, Jack, 1939– . II. Renza, Louis A., 1940– .
    III. Title.
    PS2131.M67   1996
    813' .4—dc20   96-7719
    ISBN 0-8093-2039-8 (alk. paper)   CIP

To our parents,
and to
Jennifer,
Brendan,
and Shayne

The lovely weird songs of the ancient Irish, how old they are, how sweet they are . . . but now and then a listener of the new world of the western seas hears them with deep delight, hears them with a strange, golden sense of dim remembrance. . . .

—*Sarah Orne Jewett*,
"A Little Captive Maid"

Contents

Illustrations

Preface

Sarah Orne Jewett originally published these eight collected Irish stories in contemporary magazines. She subsequently published five of them—"The Luck of the Bogans," "Between Mass and Vespers," "A Little Captive Maid," "Where's Nora?," and "Bold Words at the Bridge"—in three of her story collections: *Strangers and Wayfarers*, *A Native of Winby and Other Tales*, and *The Queen's Twin and Other Stories*. She made only minor revisions between the original and the collected versions of these five stories.

We have corrected only three instances of egregious typographical errors. Two entail an unnecessary quotation mark—in the priest's dialogue (section 6) from "The Gray Mills of Farley" and in Patrick Quin's dialogue in "Where's Nora?" The other occurs in a sentence from "The Luck of the Bogans" (toward the end of section 2). This sentence in the magazine version reads, "Someone came in unconscious of the pitiful scene and impatiently . . . " whereas in the collected version it reads, "Some one came, in unconscious of the pitiful scene, and impatiently . . . ." Assuming that Jewett intended to include the comma, we have changed this sentence to read: "Some one came in, unconscious of the pitiful scene, and impatiently . . . ."

Aside from her likely acquiescence to the typographical

exigencies of different publishers (e.g., printing "'Tis" or "'Twas" in her magazine versions as "'T is" or "'T was" in the collected versions—we have decided to use the former typography), Jewett occasionally changed punctuation (most often replacing comma splices with semicolons); Americanized spelling (e.g., "travelers" for "travellers"); hyphenated or de-hyphenated words ("church door" for "church-door," "hill-slope" for "hill slope," "farmstead" for "farm-stead"); and occasionally replaced words ("looked" for "seemed") or inserted new ones ("a few feet of clean pine boards" for "a few clean pine boards"; "'he has a fine, steady job'" for "'he's a good, steady job'"). With the same infrequency, she altered the position of phrases within sentences (as from "'There was Bogans when I first come here living down by the brick mill'" to "'There was Bogans living down by the brick mill when I first come here'"), turned two separate sentences into one, or more often, separated a relatively long sentence into two separate ones.

Seldom, if ever, do such changes alter the significance of the passage in question. It appears that they were changed simply to make the text read more clearly, more fluently, or more grammatically. Or, in the case of several excisions, for instance one in the last paragraph of "The Luck of the Bogans" ("A terrible sea of wickedness was near to dragging him down," which originally appeared in *Scribner's Magazine* after the second sentence), and one three paragraphs from the end of "A Little Captive Maid" ("It was like a miracle, he could scarcely speak"), they work primarily to reduce editorial redundancy. The same kinds of reasoning hold for the one or two lengthier revisions Jewett added. In the first section of "The Luck of the Bogans," for example, such an addition, although here yielding to a comma-spliced sentence, helps clarify the formerly misleading elision of Irish "times" solely with the weather: from "As for Mike, the times never seemed very different—it was sometimes rainy but usually pleasant weather" to "As for Mike, the times always seemed alike, he did not grudge hard work and he never found fault with the good Irish weather." Very rarely does a notable change serve to underline a story's thematic motif. Thus, the enduring friendship between the two neighbors in "Bold Words at the

Bridge" and its relevance to an otherwise obliterated, cultural memory gets stressed by Jewett's changing the timespan from twenty to thirty years since a mother and daughter, both common acquaintances of the neighbors, died in the same year.

In some cases, the captions at the bottom of the original illustrations differed slightly from the actual lines in the stories they were taken from. Where there were such discepancies, the caption lines have been modified to bring them into agreement with the story text.

Finally, Jewett made certain changes in dialect representation in revising these five stories. Sometimes she apparently sought to emphasize such dialect (substituting "after" with "afther"), sometimes to de-emphasize it ("praste" with "priest"), and sometimes to stress its visual as opposed to phonic appearance ("l'ave" for "lave," "wit'" for "wid'," "b'y's" for "by's") or vice-versa ("aich" for "'ach")—sometimes she tried ambivalently to retain the value of both ("meself" for "mesilf"). Jewett did not always practice the same style of representing Irish dialect between stories—she will use "after" or "any one" in one, "afther" or "anny one" in another, and even occasionally shift dialect formats within the same story.

For this volume, we have used Jewett's revised versions of the five stories—although the selected illustrations that accompany them first appeared, along with others not reproduced here, in their magazine versions. For the other three stories—"A Landlocked Sailor," "The Gray Mills of Farley," and "Elleneen"—we have used the texts and selected illustrations (with the exception of "A Landlocked Sailor," which lacked such illustrations) as they appeared originally in the respective magazines.

Acknowledgments

We wish to thank a number of people who have contributed toward making the present collection possible: Jim Simmons and Carol Burns of Southern Illinois University Press for their supportive cooperation in executing this project; Charles Fanning, Dennis Perry, Deborah McWilliams, Phil Sittnick, and Michael Davitt Bell for their encouragement and valuable suggestions in the project's overall construction; Carleen Humphreys for typing the basic draft of our manuscript in the face of much typist-unfriendly material; Margaret Sinex for reading and critiquing early drafts of the introduction; and Crista Rahmann Renza, one of the editors would add, for her steadfast personal support.

For help in tracking down references and texts, we acknowledge appreciatively the invaluable assistance of the Baker Library reference librarian at Dartmouth College, Cynthia Pawlek, and the research staff of the Curtis Law Wilson Library, University of Missouri-Rolla. For permission to use as well as advice on photographing the included sample of illustrations from the magazine texts of Jewett's stories, we thank, respectively, Dartmouth Library Circulation and Philip Cronenwett from Dartmouth Special Collections. Dartmouth Humanities Computing, directed by Susan Bibeau, effectively donated to us computer-scanned versions of the five stories appearing in both the magazines and later Jewett collections, which facilitated our being able to compare these versions.

It would be remiss of us, finally, not to mention the importance that our common upbringing some years ago in an immigrant neighborhood of the south end of Hartford, Connecticut, has had in leading us to coedit this volume.

Introduction:
Imagining the Irish in the Works of Sarah Orne Jewett

Charles Fanning, in his *Exiles of Erin*, notes that our historical knowledge of nineteenth-century Irish immigrant life in America has traditionally derived from three sources: "demographic records, reports by members of the host American culture, and . . . the immigrant press" (1). Sarah Orne Jewett's Irish stories clearly exemplify imaginative "reports" of the second kind and can be, therefore, ethnographically problematical, as the following discussion suggests. Though perhaps not as immediately compelling as some of her more well-known fiction—"A White Heron" or "The Foreigner" or *The Country of the Pointed Firs*—these stories still represent, at a minimum, the first serious treatment of the Irish in America by an important literary figure and a prescient engagement with what today we would term the issue of multiculturalism. Yet, despite the current interest in Irish and ethnic studies, these stories have been curiously overlooked. Among past, influential American critics, only Van Wyck Brooks took brief notice of them while discussing the Irish in *New England: Indian Summer* (1940): "Some of Miss Jewett's best stories were tributes to them, and certainly Miss Jewett knew the Irish . . ." (413).

Originally published in *Scribner's*, *The Cosmopolitan*, *McClure's*, and *Lippincott's*, Jewett's stories about Irish immigrant figures constitute a neglected corner of her oeuvre, though she herself entertained the possibility of collecting them "into a volume called *Transplanted Shamrocks*" (Blanchard 319). Altogether, they would have made up a collection at least as long as some of those published during her lifetime. These tales include "The Luck of the Bogans" (1889), "A Little Captive Maid" (1891), "Between Mass and Vespers" (1893), "The Gray Mills of Farley" (1898), "Where's Nora?" (1898), "Bold Words at the Bridge" (1899), "A Landlocked Sailor" (1899), and "Elleneen" (1901).[1]

All these stories were written after a visit to Ireland, which was part of her first European trip with Annie Fields in 1882. While in Ireland, Jewett wrote her grandfather, Dr. William Perry, telling him not only of her attraction to Dublin, that "beautiful old city," but also of the high value she placed on this phase of her trip:

> It is worth crossing the sea if it were twice as wide, just to have had these ten days in Ireland—and Mrs. Fields and I have enjoyed every day and only wish we could stay longer. . . . In the time we have been ashore we have been at Cork, Glengariff Killarney, Enniskillen, Portrush and the Giants Causeway and a night in Belfast beside two nights here. . . . Tell Elizabeth I liked Enniskillen very much. It is really a most beautiful place. (Letters, ed. Cary 48)

The concluding reference to Elizabeth, Dr. Perry's Irish cook, typifies Jewett's friendships with the Irish domestic help with whom she grew up. Along with her travel in Ireland, these friendships undoubtedly helped motivate the writing of her Irish stories.[2]

Two socio-literary conventions become apparent in reading these tales. As might be expected, they occasionally indulge in the late nineteenth-century "mystique of Irishness" (Seamus Deane's phrase), sometimes to the point of sentimentality. In the story "A Little Captive Maid," "an old, wealthy, and embittered curmudgeon" serves as a "good uncle" figure to his young maid Nora, who, in effect, comes to represent for him a still pastoral Ireland. She herself nostalgically recalls her homeland in picturesque terms, with its "familiar little group of thatched houses . . . pink daisies underfoot . . . golden gorse climbing the hill . . . figures of the blue-cloaked women who went and came, the barefooted, merry children . . . ." Another example is apparent in "The Luck of the Bogans," when Mike and Biddy leave a prosperous little farm where, idyllically, they have been "on good terms with their landlord the old squire . . . a generous, kindly old man. . . ."

Such romanticized views of an Irish "peasantry blessed by refinement, an aristocracy free from decadence, [and] both distinct from the crude citizens of the towns . . ." (Deane 57) also accord with Jewett's well-known, local-colorist ideology. That is, her attitude toward the immigrant Irish in the eight collected stories seems very much akin to her sympathetic attitude toward her rural characters in general, which Hyatt H. Waggoner claims consists "of a small remnant of class feeling—social condescension—and a larger portion of genuine affection and admiration" (376). One senses such affection simply in the way Jewett attempts to depict with precision the manners and dialect of her Irish immigrant figures.

More importantly, her Irish stories effectively perform a kind of specific cultural-historical work. Not least, they serve to undo the "Paddy" stereotype of the Irish favored in nineteenth-century Yankee discourse. If anyone needed to be disabused of the old notion that great writers are necessarily moral paragons or seers, an examination of the distinctly uncharitable characterizations of the Irish in the works of Emerson, Thoreau, and their otherwise enlightened New England contemporaries—Hawthorne among them—might do the trick.[3] Although such an examination is not Dale T. Knobel's main undertaking in *Paddy and the Republic*, he gives several examples of how these writers uncritically voiced popular Yankee prejudices, often grounded in the period's pseudoscientific texts on phrenology and physiognomy. In his *English Traits*, Knobel notes, Emerson, in all seriousness, "insisted that all one needed to do was to look at Irishmen, 'deteriorated in size, the nose sunk, the gum exposed,' to know that they operated with 'diminished brain'" (120). Thoreau, a good example, given his fervent abolitionism, of Emerson's dictum that love afar is often spite at home, wrote with consistent condescension toward the Irish in *Walden*. He described one Irish neighbor, for instance, as "born to be poor" and with his "boggy ways" fated "not to rise in this world, he nor his posterity, till their wading webbed bog-trotting feet get talaria to their heels" (260).[4]

Critical readers committed to the discipline of "cultural studies" would likely regard Thoreau's ethnic reductions of Irish figures as evidence of his inability to transcend the "boggy ways" of his own Yankee-cultural setting. *Walden*'s "transcendentalist" and "self-reliant" project leads him to perceive Irish immigrants as transparent examples of Americans having bought wholly into a United States culture's materialist (read: spiritually bankrupt) ethos. But considering the contrary examples of Jewett and Margaret Fuller (see n. 4), both of whom, roughly speaking, shared important aspects of Thoreau's cultural milieu, one cannot simply excuse his mean-spirited references to the Irish as symbolically benign, social representations "addressed to other socially constituted subjects immersed in historical circumstance" (Stam 253).

The immigrant circumstance became more rather than less evident to Emerson's and Thoreau's genteel intellectual progeny as the century progressed.[5] The continued influx of Irish immigrants into New England coincided with increased labor unrest throughout the country in the 1880s, growing Hibernian political clout in major cities like Boston, and, in general, perceived threats to American notions of cultural self-identity during the postbellum period (Altschuler 41–49; Zagarell 41). Such social "problems" produced an environment hardly conducive to later nineteenth-century Yankee literati questioning the prejudicial examples set by Emerson and Thoreau. Indeed, even Mary Baker Eddy, at the turn of the century, was still given to using the Irish, much as Thoreau had done, as handy foils in anecdotes like the following:

> I am afraid you are like the Irishman that used to work on my father's farm. He was so useless about the place that my father finally called him and said, "Mike, I shall have to let you go. You're not earning what I am paying you. . . . The Irishman pleaded to be kept in my father's employ. He said, "If you'll only keep me sir, I will work for my week's board." "But," replied Mr. Baker, "you don't earn your board in a week." "Well sir," he said, "if I can't earn it in one week, I'll do it in two." (Powell 224)

The Irishman here, of course, occupies the shiftless, dim-witted role that a Negro would in the same kind of tale told in the South of the period.

All the more noteworthy, then, is Jewett's acknowledgement of the Irish "other" in her fiction, breaking new topical ground in American literature. For example, in one story in the present collection, "The Luck of the Bogans," she depicts the Irish community with noticeably greater understanding than her New England precursors and contemporaries had done:

> Who of us have made enough kindly allowance for the homesick quick-witted ambitious Irish men and women, who have landed every year with such high hopes on our shores. There are some of a worse sort, of whom their native country might think itself well rid—but what thrifty New England housekeeper who takes into her home one of the pleasant-faced little captive maids, from Southern Ireland, has half-understood the change of surroundings.

Showing a keen interest in Irish diasporic psychology, Jewett proceeds astutely to analyze the changed surroundings the Irish faced in emigrating to New England. Life in Ireland, she notes, had been one

> of wit and humor, of lavishness and lack of provision for more than the passing day—of constant companionship with one's neighbors. . . . The beauty of Ireland is little hinted at by an average orderly New England town—many a young girl and many a blundering sturdy fellow is heartsick with the homesickness and restraint of his first year in this golden country of hard work. To so many of them a house has been but a place of shelter for the night—a sleeping place: if you remember that, you do not wonder at fumbling fingers or impatience with our houses full of trinkets. Our needless tangle of furnishing bewilders those who still think the flowers that grow of themselves in the Irish thatch more beautiful than anything under the cover of our prosaic shingled roofs. ("The Luck of the Bogans")

Such an analysis displays an ethnographic sensitivity that compares favorably with the studied observations of a contemporary historian like R. F. Foster, who in his *Modern Ireland, 1600–1972* remarks on the "psychic disruption" that nineteenth-century Irish immigrants underwent. At odds with their rural background, the new American locale "conflicted sharply with the high value that Irish country people put upon communalism, kinship and a sense of place" (351).

Jewett's informed Irish ethnography, as previously noted, parallels and extends her sympathetic rendering of the communalistic, rural New Englanders whom she also regarded as often patronized by the new breed of American urbanites: "When I was, perhaps, fifteen, the first city board-ers began to make their appearance near Berwick, and the way they misconstrued the country people and made game of their peculiarities fired me with indignation" (qtd. in Cary 23). But the extension of that affinity in her tales to foreign-ers (French-Canadian as well as Irish) was hardly inevitable. Even with its insistence on the values of village community, folkway traditions, and local-color vernacular, Jewett's par-ticular disposition as a New England regionalist writer was to ward off, if not altogether deny, the complex and largely urban-oriented realities of postbellum United States society. Commercialization, industrial growth, large-scale immigra-tion, and the ugliness endemic to urbanization were often viewed as interchangeable expressions of a single, and sus-pect, new order (Altschuler 42). F. O. Matthiessen assumes that point of view when describing the New England of Jewett's girlhood:

> Throughout New England the invigorating air that Emerson and Thoreau had breathed was clogged with smoke. A mile away from Sarah's house the textile mills at Salmon Falls were employing larger and larger numbers, and rows of drab rickety houses were growing like mushrooms overnight. The native village folk were crowded out by Irish immigrants. (20)

Jewett therefore could just as easily have rendered her fictional Irish immigrants as synonymous with American ex-pansionist policies or with the cultural sea change threaten-ing New England's supposed societal homogeneity. This was how some of Jewett's friendly literary peers, like Thomas Bailey Aldrich, typically regarded the influx of such immi-grants (Zagarell 41). Yet she chose to treat her Irish figures neither with Thoreauvian derision, nor reactionary appre-hension. Jewett's social, and not merely imaginative, Irish sympathies appear all the more conspicuous when viewed in the context of a New England culture that forty years ear-lier had been a center of anti-Irish and anti-Catholic nativism.[6] Such sympathies are evident, for example, in a May 1897 let-ter to her friend Louise Imogen Guiney. Her sister having recently died, Jewett mentions a condolence visit from a lo-cal South Berwick Irish priest and the fact that she had been reading the Irish nationalist poet, James Clarence Mangan: "I have wished to tell you what help I found in a visit from Father Gorman and how glad I was to find he knew you. . . . I have had illness as well as sorrow to fight against lately. Somehow these poems of Mangan's have touched me more than I could have believed" (Lucey 62).[7]

But it is especially how her relations with Irish culture and Irish-Americans get refracted through her fiction that will most likely interest readers of the present collection. Jewett recognizably represents the Irish as regionalist allies, with many stories clearly illustrating, often with more explicitness than her other fiction, the binary themes usually associated with her particular brand of regionalism.

In the American-Irish context, such a binary theme is implicit in the distinction between the connotations of the words "immigrant" and "emigrant" drawn by Matthew Frye Jacobson in his *Special Sorrows*. Jewett's Irish characters are sometimes the one and sometimes the other—"immigrants" when they are drawn toward American possibility and promise, "emigrants" when the former belief falters and the values of "home" come to the fore. If, as Jacobson argues (after Kirby Miller), American scholarship has tended to privilege Emma Lazarus's "golden door" motif to the neglect of the immigrant-as-exile (1), Jewett, by contrast, captures both sides of the equation. Thus, the family and social values of an old rural Irish community collide with those of a materialistic American culture in the story "Between Mass and Vespers." Dan Nolan falls victim to corrupting American influences at odds with the Irish village/family traditions carried over, as best the immigrants were able, into a Massachusetts mill town. His father's source of pride, he was also treated like a son by the local priest in whose church he had served as an altar boy. Attracted by American fame and fortune, however, he traveled out west and while away became arrogant, ambitious, and mean—a con-man willing to dupe past friends and even family members in fraudulent investment schemes. Jewett pointedly describes him as dressed in "smart, dirty, city-made clothes" and looking "as sharp and ugly as a weasel." Dan now scorns the values of the Irish community he has been reared in, as seen when he gets collared by his old parish priest and Dennis Call, a friend of Dan's father. Having become a communal apostate, Dan bristles at Call's "aggravating sense of honesty, his narrow experience of a stupid mill town."

Jewett's priest, Father Ryan, a tirelessly concerned and selfless worker for the community—he cares for Dan as a family member ("'I've a warm Irish heart in me, and there are times when I'd like a brother's young child, or one of my sister's that I left long ago in Kerry, or to see my old mother shake her head and have the laugh at me'")—ends up "saving" Dan Nolan from his American fate by bringing him to account. He accomplishes this feat, which from Call's perspective must seem all but a miracle given Dan's recent past and his physical aggression against the priest earlier that day, "between" Sunday Mass and Vespers—in other words, beyond the call of official duty. Yet in the end, the story swerves from depicting Dan's full-fledged communal redemption. If he sits at the priest's late supper, "hungry, crestfallen . . . abashed by all the light and good cheer," it is still only some vague "golden hopefulness" persuading Father Ryan "that the look of his own young brother had come back again into Danny Nolan's eyes."

Another priest, Father Miles, fails to save the day (and Irish communal values) at all in "The Luck of the Bogans." Mike and Biddy Bogan leave behind a "well to do" farm around Bantry, owned by a likable old Anglo-Irish squire, and emigrate to the United States with the blessing (that later becomes a curse when the Bogans forget to send her Christmas money) of a shamanish old beggar-woman named Peggy Muldoon. They dream of affording their son Dan an opportunity for upward social mobility, which would have been denied him in their homeland: "'Dan will be a fine squire in Ameriky'" ("The Luck of the Bogans").

Thanks to American economic opportunity and an enterprising will, Mike eventually becomes successful in business, owning a "clean and wholesome" drinking establishment. However, "the luck of the Irish" deserts him, in large part, the narrative intimates, because of his son's exposure to American ways: "Dan was put to school and came home with a knowledge of sums in arithmetic which set his father's eyes dancing with delight, but with a knowledge besides of foul language and a brutal way of treating his little sisters when nobody was looking on." The very social means to his wealth and success as a town citizen—the story here equally functions as a propaganda piece for the temperance movement of the time (see n. 15)—ironically leads to Mike Bogan's physical and mental breakdown: his son becomes a drunk, hangs around with bad friends, and finally gets killed in a fight.

Both "Between Mass and Vespers" and "The Luck of the Bogans" implicitly criticize the social choices available in late nineteenth-century American culture that tragically attenuate Irish immigrant (a.k.a. regionalist) values. This critique becomes, as much as it ever would in Jewett's fiction, quite direct in "The Gray Mills of Farley." In an earlier story, she had already suggested the deleterious effects of mill work on hard-working Irish Americans:

> They were a contented, pleasant-looking flock . . . ; they might have lost the gayety [sic] that they would have kept in the old country, but a look of good cheer had not forsaken them, though many a figure showed the thinness that comes from steady, hard work, and almost every face had the deep lines that are worn only by anxiety. ("Between Mass and Vespers")

In "The Gray Mills of Farley," the Irish mill workers are victims not only of American industrial activity, which has resulted in an environment that shows "all its poverty and lack of beauty, at one glance," but specifically of its abstract sponsor, a capitalist system that owns the village and effectively transforms it into its own impersonal image as the "Corporation."

Jewett's venture into "proletarian" fiction portrays the corporate system as turning its immigrant Irish and French-Canadian workers into anonymous "operatives," in other words deracinated, ethnic figures.[8] The narrative designates the sensitive and successful manager of the Farley textile mills as the "agent" and suggests that his presumably dead mother, a former worker for the Corporation, herself lacked a determinable, ethnic identity: "Even Mr. Kilpatrick, who was a walking history of the Corporation, had never known his mother's maiden name, much less the place of her birth." Despite or because of this lack of social identity, the agent's loyalty lies primarily with the workers. In this sense, he assumes the communal role played by the priests in the two previously mentioned stories: "He was part of Farley itself, and had come to care deeply about his neighbors, while a larger mill and salary [that he had been offered] were not exactly the things that could tempt his ambition." The mill entirely shuts down, as it has done periodically before, for reasons concerning stock manipulation and despite the hardship the shutdown will visit upon the workers. This occurs against a background that is surreal even when the plant is functioning: "There were always fluffs of cotton in the air . . . drifting down out of the picker chimney. . . . [T]he Corporation homes looked like make-believe houses . . . they had so little individuality. . . ."

The shutdown makes explicit the system's infantilizing effect on the mostly Irish mill workers, for their "make-believe houses" also "looked as if they belonged to a toy village, and had been carefully put in rows by a childish hand." Appropriately, the story focuses on a particular child victim with whom the agent especially identifies, a waif, Maggie, one of the children who tend the bobbins in the mill's weaving room. She lives with whatever Irish family will take her in from day to day. "When Mrs. Kilpatrick spoke to her she answered in a hoarse voice. . . . You felt that the hot room and dry cotton were to blame for such hoarseness; it had nothing to do with the weather." Maggie embodies the more tragic side of the Irish immigration story (a side analyzed by Kerby A. Miller in *Emigrants and Exiles*). Even in normal times, the Farley textile workers barely survive from one paycheck to another. They are typically no better off than were Maggie's father and grandfather, who "had left no heritage but work behind them for this orphan child; they had never been able to save so much that a long illness, a prolonged old age, could not waste their slender hoards away."

The irony of the story's ending is the pathetic joy and relief with which the citizens of Farley greet the news that the mill is ready to resume operations. So ingrained is the Corporation routine, and so dependent are they upon the meager salaries it doles out, that the workers can only perceive the resumption of deadening labor as a merciful and "blissful satisfaction." But "The Gray Mills of Farley" focuses less on the egregious fact of class conflict or exploitation of the immigrant proletariat by capital, than on the agent's anxious concern for and attempt to ameliorate the plight of these workers. Does he therefore suggest a human side still available to the American capitalist system? Even if so, one feels here the real vulnerability of Irish-American, New England communities to the postbellum, American *Gessellschaft*.

At the very least, all three preceding stories expose the fault lines that threaten Jewett's regionalist ideology. In their use of Irish-American or Irish immigrant figures, the other five stories also reveal, perhaps because of Jewett's *displaced* identification with these figures, her willingness to question regionalist ideology as a possible critical alternative to the country's invasive, federalist, and materialistic culture. On the one hand, she insists on the value of a stable and traditional community life, which she associates with "old Ireland" in "A Little Captive Maid." She would thus have rural Yankees and Irish immigrants alike resist "the demon of change, that restless American spirit which has spoiled the beauty of so many fine and simple old houses" ("A Little Captive Maid").

On the other hand, each story includes an undercurrent of social anxiety, as if the appearance of "that restless American spirit" had already made moot any commitment to Irish or regionalist communal values: "This was not the first time that the honest pair [Mike and Biddy] had felt anxiety creeping into their pride about Dan" ("The Luck of the Bogans"); Dennis Call's niece "looked poor and anxious," as do the town's Irish workers whose faces, as already noted, "had the deep lines that are worn only by anxiety" ("Between Mass and Vespers"). In a comical but still apprehensive vein, Patrick Quin asks about Nora's whereabouts in "Where's Nora?" Having just come from Ireland, she has immediately gone out to see the American town: "'Maybe she's strayed beyond and gone losing in the strange place,' suggested Mr. Quin, with an anxious glance."

Jewett's Irish stories, in short, do not appear to fix on any discernible portent, like an epiphanic white heron, that might consecrate or confer the status of enduring myth on

the communal or regional place. With possibly one exception, neither do the stories project any community of women
without men, such as the matrifocal society, Dunnet Landing, in *The Country of the Pointed Firs*. There, what one could term
Jewett's "folk aesthetic," clearly affirms community or "com-
monplace rather than middle-class values," particularly in relation to "female experience" (Mobley 11, 61, 18). Even as an
imagined setting, such a community could still represent her
critical alternative to an urban and predominantly patriarchal American society, as some of her recent feminist critics
have contended.[9]

A possible illustration of this vision is "Bold Words at the
Bridge," in some ways the most arresting of Jewett's Irish
stories.[10] Bringing to mind the more elemental tales of the
Gaelic writer Mairtin O'Cadhain, stories in which little action
or plot occurs, this three-part story concerns the daily rites
and rituals that define community life as such. (Comprised
entirely of women characters, the story may also reflect a
sociological fact peculiar to Irish immigration, namely that
an unusual number of Irish women typically preceded their
male relatives to the United States. Cf. n. 17.) The first part is
spoken to an anonymous "listener, with simple interest" by
Mrs. Dunleavy, who recounts a quarrel that she has had at
the bridge with her erstwhile friend, Mrs. Connelly. Though
set in a small New England mill town, the tale occurs on the
rural side of the bridge that separates the town from its country outskirts where the two women reside in houses next
door to each other.

The occasion for the argument is the fact that Mrs.
Dunleavy has planted some pumpkins in her garden patch.
This distresses Mrs. Connelly, who thinks they will interfere
with the melons she herself has planted on the other side of
the fence.[11] The squabble becomes fierce, even a bit physical
in the end, as the two women play to the crowd "that was
passing by with their grins, and loitering and stopping afther
they were behind her back to hear what was going on betune
us.'" The women call on all their verbal acuity as the fight
becomes more heated. When Mrs. Dunleavy puts up her
basket between them, ostensibly to defend herself from Mrs.
Connelly's rage, "'she being bigger than I, and I getting no

chance . . . herself slipped and fell, and her nose got a clout with the hard edge of the basket, it would trouble the saints to say how.'"

The dispute, at first comically rendered by Mrs. Dunleavy's Irishisms, ends in bitterness: "'I'd no call for her company anny more . . .,'" she concludes, "'and I took a vow I'd never spake a word to her again while the world stood.'" In the second part of the story, Mrs. Dunleavy, whom a third-person narrator now describes as "large and noisy, but generous-hearted," soon shows discomfort with the situation, primarily because she feels alone: "'I've nobody to have an honest word with, and the morning being so fine and pleasant.'" She also feels "estranged and solitary" because she has no one else from the same Irish background with whom to converse:

> Mrs. Dunleavy sighed heavily and stepped down into her flower-plot to pull the distressed foxgloves back into their places inside the fence. The seed had been sent from the old country, and this was the first year they had come into full bloom. She had been hoping the sight of them would melt Mrs. Connelly's heart into some expression of friendliness, since they had come from adjoining parishes in old County Kerry.

Her nostalgia for a communal bond then becomes uncannily embodied in the figure of a stranger, when "a fellow country-woman," who, dressed "'very decent, but old-fashioned,'" comes along the road carrying "a large newspaper bundle and a heavy handbag" and asks if someone named Ann Bogan lives nearby. When Mrs. Dunleavy informs her that no such person lives in the area, the stranger departs: "Mrs. Dunleavy could hardly bear to let the stranger go away. She watched her far down the hill to the bridge before she turned to go into the house."

As it turns out, the stranger, looking for a lost friend, ironically helps recreate the bond between Mrs. Dunleavy and Mrs. Connelly, who in her cottage has overheard the exchange "and for the first time in weeks looked with friendly intent toward her neighbor's house." The estrangement over, "the reunited friends" together piece out that two Ann Bogans resided in the town thirty or so years earlier. In the third part of the story, the women learn that the "weary and disappointed" stranger had once worked in America and had met Ann Bogan at a mutual friend's house. She had then gone back to Ireland "'to mind me old mother'" but "'was always homesick afther America, so back I come to it, but all me old friends and neighbors is changed and gone. Faix, this is the first welcome I've got yet from anny one.'" Mrs. Dunleavy and Mrs. Connelly, "the great feud . . . forever ended," treat the stranger as one of themselves, "talking over old times," and walk, "one on either hand, to see the town with her that evening," happy that no one sees them crossing over the bridge together so as to remind them that they once "'had bold words at the bridge.'"

"Bold Words at the Bridge" plays on a dialectic between narrow self-interest and our gregarious pull toward other people. Human relationship is, in the story's course, broken and repaired—revitalized. Separated by their anger, the two women have had to experience and meditate upon the reality of aloneness, and what saves them from permanent separation seems to be a mythic or "folk" sense of community. For one thing, the story's simple setting—the neighboring cottages and their small gardens, the road, the bridge separating the two women from the mill town—bespeaks a region associated with the pre-industrial or agrarian ethos of an old Irish community. For another, the mysterious stranger responsible for the two friends reuniting resembles an archetypal figure of place, a transplanted *genius loci*—"'She'd the looks as if she'd lately come out; very decent, but old-fashioned'"—someone who herself has lost but again found friends *here*, in this town of otherwise departed or dead Ann Bogans. Moreover, the stranger's *re*-immigration to the American place where Mrs. Dunleavy and Mrs. Connelly reside metaphorically equates their present communal bond with their Irish place of origin. Perhaps, too, the image of the lone stranger on the road with her bundle stirs up racial memories, embodying the plight of dispossessed, Irish refugees who had historically suffered confiscations, evictions, and famine.

A certain mythological energy thus quietly informs this Jewett story, in effect serving to sacralize its represented regional space. The aura of folk myth possibly occurs in at least two other ways as well. The pair's rapprochement is celebrated when the wayfarer returns later and is invited to tea by the two neighbors. Gathering for tea resonates with Irish folk-cultural significance: a ritual marking recovered, rediscovered kinship.[12] Analogous to the haunting world-tree motif of "A White Heron," the garden in "Bold Words at the Bridge" also alludes to vegetative/fertility myths that include an ancient, celebrative pattern such as described, for instance, in *Finnegan's Wake* (both the book and the song that inspired it): the fall or breakage, the partaking of the water of life (here tea), and finally rebirth. "'This is the first welcome I've got yet from anny one,'" says the stranger at the gathering; "''Tis a beautiful one to.'"

A similar pattern is evident in "A Landlocked Sailor." Mike Dillon, a sailor who has met with a career-ending accident, finds a haven (and a family) in an out-of-the-way New England farm. At the time of the narrative, Mike unexpectedly meets and shares his story with the ship's doctor (who had previously mended his injury), while both happen to be fishing a no less out-of-the-way brook. Here suggesting the very antithesis of work (which for both men is associated with shipping on the ocean), the watery body of this brook also evokes for the narrator a sacred, pastoral communing with nature—"a Sunday rest to all one's activities": "In it alone one may 'listen to the voices' and receive what nature has to give and what himself is hardly ever fit to receive."

"Bold Words at the Bridge" and "A Landlocked Sailor" also rely heavily on Irish dialect. In a written text, the foregrounding of dialect often signifies an occurrence of oral discourse, which in turn subliminally invokes the presence of an enduring folk-cultural tradition. Mike Dillon, for instance, has in effect returned to his "folk" roots with his recently (rediscovered) vocation as a farmer, for he grew up in Ireland as a farmer's son in "'County Wexford, sir, parish o' Duncannon.'" A similar folkish restoration underlines the moment in "Bold Words at the Bridge" when Mrs. Connelly puts her bundle down on the bridge, the better to address her adversary, at which point the latter hits her with the jibe, "'Clane the mud from your shoes if you're going to dance.'" We have here the ancient "gaber" tradition, from which "gab," identified by Huizinga as the folk-traditional slanging match or, like "the dozens" in African-American contexts, a contest of skill in mockery and derision (67–71).

Jewett's deployment of Hiberno-English dialect, archetypal allusions, narratives reliant on oral storytelling practices, and, as in "Bold Words at the Bridge," the theme of Irish female experience grounding a renewed sense of community, illustrates her recourse to a "folk aesthetic" explicitly evident in a work like *The Country of the Pointed Firs*. At the same time, such speech invokes the continuity of a folk tradition as a strategy to resist the quicksilver mores, or the pressures of displacement and assimilation, associated with a dominant, urban-oriented American culture.

Yet, can one really make such "bold" thematic assertions about Jewett's Irish stories? Just as with her other fiction, her mythic allusions arguably remain tentative or "minor," as suggested by the very images of a small garden, tea, and a brook (as opposed to the sea).[13] Similarly, Jewett's endorsement of feminist communitarian values as here perhaps only evidenced in "Bold Words at the Bridge"—assuming the two rural women and a stranger do, in fact, constitute community writ small—are countered by her projecting affirmative patriarchal ones as well. In "The Luck of the Bogans" and "Between Mass and Vespers," for example, she implicitly criticizes the Irish patriarchal rule of primogeniture, whereas in "A Little Captive Maid" and "Elleneen," she uncritically represents the strong loyalty and devotion of Irish immigrant women to the men they have left behind in Ireland.

An even stronger example of Jewett's sympathies toward men occurs in "A Landlocked Sailor." There, as narrator, she transparently identifies with John Hallett, the doctor, in his effort at "being alone in a piece of well-known country long unvisited": "Solitary and undisturbed, we are now and then aware of ourselves: not the person the world takes us to be, not the ideal person our hopes and ambitions are trying to evolve, but the real man." On one level, we could interpret the Sunday fishing excursion of Hallett and Dillon as a veiled critique of a patriarchal work ethic—escape from the onerous rigors of shipping or farming. Jewett, however, ends this story with Dillon's both acknowledging to Hallett his good life with a "beautiful wife" and supportive mother-in-law *and* affirming the special value of his former male experience: "'But I made bowld to slip away from [the farm] for a while the day; 'twas thinkin' of salt wather and the gay old times wit' the b'ys I was whin I caught sight of yourself comin' t'rough the brush.'"

A similar critical ambiguity marks Jewett's use of Irish-English dialect, the labored "realism" of which could as well distract us from, rather than attract us to, its folk-mythic significance. Her use of New England Yankee speech patterns is typically restrained and skillful, "without the excess of eye-catching vernacular that doomed most of the local-color movement to quick oblivion" (Cary vi). By contrast, her attempts to render the Hiberno-English of the New England Irish immigrants are sometimes undercut precisely by the kind of excess she managed otherwise to avoid.

Her Irish characters, that is, frequently speak a west-of-Ireland dialect that seems too rich and overdrawn: "'Twas afther picking it I was before breakfast . . . Himself was the b'y that loved a melon,'" says Mrs. Dunleavy to Mrs. Connelly in "Bold Words at the Bridge." Or in "The Luck of the Bogans," there would surely be enough Irish flavor if Biddy Bogan had said "mark me words now" instead of, as she does, "marruk me wuds now." Characters, moreover, are too often "after" doing this and "after" doing that, this immediate past, present-perfect Hiberno-English idiom occurring with greater range and higher frequency than would be the case naturally. Nor is the accent consistently represented. "Boys" is written "B'ys" in one story, for instance, but "I" is not rendered as "Oy." "Try" is written "thry," but "thinkin'" is given with the initial "th" intact, not as the familiar Irish "tinkin'." And in "A Landlocked Sailor," Mike Dillon pronounces "sea" as "say" on one occasion, as "sea" on another.

One can, of course, choose to overlook such mimetic misdemeanors.[14] Jewett's Irish-English vernacular must be favorably distinguished from the stage-Irish brogue that contemporary writers and journalists employed for caricature. Granted its shortcomings, her Irish dialogue appears comparatively studied and considered, the product of long familiarity with Irish speech both in the United States and Ireland. And she clearly attempts such dialogue in good faith.

Still, the issue here concerns more than Jewett's dialectal accuracy. Does her use of it undergird the stories' folk-cultural significance, and do her "folk" allusions pose a viable, regionalist alternative to the abstract, capitalist culture of late nineteenth-century American society? As we have seen, these stories at best adopt a qualified critical stance toward mainstream American society. Indeed, one could argue that they often expose the *weakness* rather than the strength of such regionalist alternatives.

Jewett's use of the "bridge" metaphor in "Bold Words at the Bridge" is a good illustration of this last surmise. The bridge separates the town from its regionalist environs and at the same time suggests the potential (American) isolation the two regionalist-immigrant women *could* experience, not only in relation to themselves, but to their nearby "urban" society. Notice, for example, Mrs. Dunleavy's sense of shame before the town crowd as the two women shout at each other: "'I'd no call to have tark with Biddy Con'ly before them idle b'ys and gerrls, nor to let the two of us become their laughing-stock.'" This sensitivity reminds us of Jewett's own indignant response to how city people "misconstrued the country people and made game of their peculiarities." The stranger, too, experiences a sense of social disorientation, less as the result of her immigration to America per se than of the social changes—the emigrations of acquaintances to other towns—doubtless propagated by the materialistic values of American society.

"Bold Words at the Bridge," however, hardly fires "bold words" at late nineteenth-century American society. No permanent crisis occurs in the story. The two women reestablish communication with each other. The stranger finds compensatory friends and so no longer suffers absolute isolation. And the three women go out on the town as the story ends, showing that the bridge between town and region maybe, as its very size surely suggests right from the start, not so difficult to cross.

Such bridgings, which one can regard as ideological tropes, also inform the way Jewett alludes to other "Irish" issues in the stories collected in this volume. One such issue concerns the social conflicts Irish immigrants experienced with American cultural assimilation, which the stories sometimes allegorize as virtually impossible to resolve. As we have seen, in "The Luck of the Bogans," Mike Bogan gains socio-economic success in America, but at the price of losing Irish family cohesion through the temptations offered his son by new American ways. In "The Gray Mills of Farley," the threat to an Irish-American community's very survival is only precariously overcome, and with the suggested likelihood of this community's inevitable cultural deracination at the hands of the American corporate system.

But most of the stories frame the problem of translation between Irish and American cultures as finally negotiable. We see Nora's nostalgia for and unproblematic return to Ireland in "A Little Captive Maid," or the successful Irish homecomings and goings of Nora in "Where's Nora?," or the Irish lover in "Elleneen" happily transported to his girlfriend in America—or simply the direct declaration of American assimilation by Ellen's sister: "'I never saw the half day I wanted to go back'" to Ireland. Even the ironically titled "The Luck of the Bogans" points to a similar cultural resolution. Dan Bogan's perverse, egocentric exploitation of the unhealthier aspects of American society or his Irish parents' displaced social investment in him are as much to blame for the destruction of the Bogan family in America as is some unresolvable difference between Irish and American cultures. In fact, the story's narrator at one point views the American scene as positively reinforcing the best Irish traits, suggesting their symbiotic relationship: "The climate makes the characteristics of Cork and Kerry; the fierce energy of the Celtic race in America is forced and stimulated by our keen air."

Do such ideological bridges suggest Jewett's ultimate complicity with the dominant culture? On this account, even her deployment of Irish dialect may signify precisely the obverse of a "folk" or "regionalist" assertion against the values of mainstream American society. Indeed, it may not even indicate a wish to defend or to maintain Irish ethnic identity in the face of American "nativist" demands for ethnic deracination or assimilation. This is not simply because, as

Thomas J. Ferraro observes, many "dialect stories . . . remind us that the tight-knit communities of the immigrants were insular and restrictive. . . ." Rather, if we regard Jewett's Irish as representing, so to speak, rehabilitated immigrant figures safely removed from the desperate Irish refugees of the 1840s and 1850s, they could easily serve as "attractive," Americanized versions, as Ferraro proceeds to argue, of an "immigrant community [when it] is no longer a force to be reckoned with and therefore can be invoked as a model for establishing interdependence among middle-class individuals, couples, and nuclear families" (198).

Undoubtedly, the most apparent theme of Jewett's Irish stories is her already remarked regionalist opposition to American urban industrialism, whether advanced with utopian hope or resigned fatalism. Yet it might also be emphasized how the stories encode the message of American "family values," still heard today and perhaps with a very similar political valence. The Bogans stand or fall on such values, as do the economically beleaguered families or substitute families (e.g., Mrs. Kilpatrick and "little Maggie") in "The Gray Mills of Farley." In "Between Mass and Vespers," Dennis Call leaves behind his own family gathering to help Father Ryan, the community's paternal figure, bring Dan Nolan back into familial reference.[15] Nora finds a similar figure in Captain Balfour, and through his posthumous generosity returns home to Ireland where she "married the lad she loved, and was a kind daughter to his mother" ("A Little Captive Maid"). A different Nora becomes financially successful in America and returns to Ireland specifically to see her mother, leaving behind a loving Irish-American husband who expects her to come back ("Where's Nora?"). Even in "Elleneen," the formerly fickle Ellen has the value of heterosexual romance dramatically brought home to her by her sister Mary Ann, herself a happily married wife and mother.

One could claim, then, that Jewett here, as elsewhere in her fiction, tends to privilege "the traditional family as an institution" and thus "defines the community within the parameters of a conservative structure" (Zagarell 45). If only in this sense, her emphatic representation of Irish family values perhaps covertly works to support mainstream American social agendas—whether belief in a certain class mobility *or* the perceived need to counter the alienating effects of postbellum, capitalist culture on individuals—rather than, as in the more critical regionalist position, to resist or oppose such agendas.[16] To be sure, several of Jewett's Irish stories, as we have suggested, appear to criticize a post-agrarian United States too often unable to offer its immigrants any immediate semblance of unalloyed health and prosperity: "Alas [Irish immigrants] sail away on the crowded ships to find hard work and hard fare," the narrator in "A Little Captive Maid" apostrophizes, "and know their mistakes about finding a fairyland too late, too late!" The Irish figures in "The Gray Mills of Farley" at best struggle to maintain, despite the numbing influence of mill work, the vitality and dignity fostered in them by their essentially rural homeland.

Nevertheless, many of Jewett's main Irish characters combine a willingness to do hard, enterprising work and the desire to preserve the values of family or community associations to better themselves American-style. Mike Dillon, the main character of "A Landlocked Sailor," represents a classic rags-to-riches American success story, ending up happily prosperous on a family-run farm. Nora, the delightful and energetic "grasshopper greenhorn" of "Where's Nora?," quickly sees the dreary promise of manufacturing work for what it is: "'I was looking at the mills just now, and I heard the great n'ise from them. I'd never be after shutting meself up in anny mill out of the good air. I've no call to go to jail yet in thim mill walls.'" Yet her entrepreneurial gifts and native vitality—her continual one-step-ahead movements (hence "where's Nora?") that exemplify an instinct for social mobility—allow her not only to escape but also to transcend the stultifying routine mill work would have had in store for her. She therefore typifies the young, bright, and independent Irish woman, such as studied by Hasia R. Diner in *Erin's Daughters in America*, able quickly to adjust to life in a new country, as opposed to the nineteenth-century, stereotypical representation of the Irish immigrant woman as mere "servant."[17] Moreover, she has great success selling cakes and tea to railroad hands and travelers. This uncomplicated scene of economic exchange suggests, if anything, the compatibility of a small cottage industry with the railroad, a signifier of the major mode of nineteenth-century American industrialism and cause of class divisions. Such socio-economic optimism can even infect how one perceives "Old Ireland." As the ultimately successful Nora goes on her way toward her mother's house near the story's end, "it seemed as if the return of one prosperous child gave joy to the whole landscape."

Richard Cary feels such an ending "portrays America as the pot at rainbow's end which is to be ransacked and left to rust" (128), but in fact, these Irish "success stories" appear to adopt an American chauvinistic slant themselves. If nothing else, as Werner Sollors has suggested in another context, they associate Jewett's Irish immigrant figures with the "widely shared [American] bias against hereditary privilege" that "has strongly favored *achieved* rather than *ascribed* identity . . ." (37). These figures do shy away from representing the corollary to such ideological bias, namely that it has traditionally "supported 'self-determination' and 'independence' from ancestral, parental, and external definitions." However, this is arguably because their familial and communal values also proffer strong models for a wider social union. Put another way, Jewett's Irish figures constitute metaphors for the country's desired, if self-contradictory, nationalist ethos in the postbellum period: the putative union between entrepreneurial self-determination *and* a social orientation around family values.

One might perceive a further "reactionary" slant in the stories collected in this volume. According to some of her recent critics, Jewett imagined characters and situations, such as the Bowden reunion in *The Country of the Pointed Firs*, through certain "racialized and nationalist . . . categories . . ." (Howard 4). One such category was, in effect, anti-immigrationist, in the sense "that the best of America [to her] was Anglo-Norman." In *The Story of the Normans* (1887), a book written for children, she appears quite openly to express this sense of racial hierarchy, linking "the traits she celebrates in Normans with England's expansionist world leadership" (Zagarell 42).

Such a view, however, would not for Jewett necessarily exclude the Irish, especially since Ireland had a significant Norman period itself. That is, one can at least speculate about whether her Irish figures signify *acceptable* immigrants in comparison with "the more 'foreign'" peoples from southern and eastern Europe emigrating to the United States in the late nineteenth century who were causing "class tensions with new ethnic strains" in the cities (Brodhead 146).[18] Besides being hard workers and showing signs of social mobility, Jewett's Irish characters are all English-speaking.[19] Irish immigration, it should be pointed out, had begun in the Revolutionary War period (see Shuffleton 178) and, if only in this sense, may have signified for Jewett a long and, in the end, successful tradition of American assimilation.[20] Thus, compared with the "other" new immigrants to the United States, the Irish, to Jewett, could easily have seemed more compatible with the social ideal of (eventual) Yankee homogeneity. In "The Gray Mills of Farley," for example, one is permitted to wonder about Dan's own possibly Irish-American origins, given the narrative's ambiguous reference to his mother's, his own former status as a Farley mill worker, and not least, the special sympathy he shows toward the little Irish girl Maggie. In that case, the successful and talented manager represents a transitional, assimilationist figure serving to mediate the two otherwise extremely divided cultures.

Using such evidence, it might be argued that Jewett's Irish and local-color stories alike traffic in a nostalgia for a racially homogeneous, Anglo-American society, just as her works overall, according to Susan Gillman, tend to enshrine "the Civil War and the history of slavery in order to defuse their fratricidal energies and underwrite a new era of national reunion—and of new racial and ethnic divisions" (103). Of course, one still needs to ask how her Irish figures in particular could symbolically track such a "reunion," especially given Ireland's own contemporary—this designation being itself colonialist—"fratricidal" conflict with Britain. Jewett, however, was not only aware of this conflict, she was inclined to side with the British perspective on it, as indicated in an 1884 letter to Annie Fields:

> The [Anglo-Saxon and Celtic] races were antagonistic, and England could not have said "no matter, she may plague me and fight me as she pleases." . . . Ireland is backward, and when she is equal to being independent, and free to

make her own laws, I suppose . . . she will be under grace of herself, instead of tutors and governors in England. Everybody who studies the case, as Mr. Arnold has, believes that she must still be governed. (Letters, ed. Fields 22–23)[21]

As this letter suggests, if Jewett's Irish stories at all trace an imaginary, ideological prescription for a (re)unified American nation, they do so by adopting an Arnoldian position on the supposed antagonism between Anglo-Saxon and Celtic cultures such as expressed in his *On the Study of Celtic Literature.* Jewett mentions having read Arnold's views in "Celtic Poetry," and as Richard H. Brodhead has argued, she also adhered to his notion of "high literature" (155, 156). More importantly, Arnold wanted to bridge the two cultures, something we have seen Jewett analogously try to effect in different registers. Interpretable as a cultural extension of British colonialism, he wanted to bring together Anglo-Saxon and Celtic cultural traits, for according to his argument, "neither Celts nor Anglo-Saxons can in themselves represent a complete state: both are fragmentary by virtue of their differentiation out of a common root, the Indo-Aryan race" (Lloyd 7, 11).

This assimilationist, cross-cultural motive, based on a supposedly common racial identity, could help explain why many of Jewett's Irish figures depend on an "Anglo" sponsor to convey their value to others.[22] Captain Balfour serves as the socially redeeming foil for Nora in "A Little Captive Maid"; the Americanized Dan in "The Gray Mills of Farley" for the Irish workers; the narrative and nondialectal interlocutor, evident in the first section of "Bold Words at the Bridge," for Mrs. Dunleavy, Mrs. Connelly, and the Irish stranger; Doctor Hallett for Mike Dillon in "A Landlocked Sailor"; the insistently more-American-than-Irish Mary Ann in "Elleneen" for her sister. It might even be maintained that the many priest figures in Jewett's Irish stories satisfy a similar Anglo-assimilationist function. At the time, Irish prelates, after all, dominated the Roman Catholic hierarchy in the United States and in this capacity "often undermined [the] old country language and norms [of non-Irish Roman Catholic immigrants] by exhorting their parishioners to Americanize" (Altschuler 53).

Given the wide-ranging interpretations available to them, readers and cultural critics of these collected Irish stories might therefore ask, Where's Jewett? Do the stories adopt the perspective of persons from a subjugated culture either criticizing or, in effect, reluctantly surrendering to the subjugating culture's questionable values—America's or England's? Or, do the stories in fact subtly endorse such values, mitigating the otherness of Irish culture and opening the way for the Irish later to be conveniently cited at the expense of other ethnic groups?

But this last sort of interrogation is surely too skeptical. If such racialized traces are to be found in Jewett's work, they must usually be sought for. Far more evident in the present volume are its attempts to mediate between older New England certainties and the newer social contingencies of Jewett's own time, particularly her inclination to write about the nascent Irish-American culture around her, contemporary prejudices notwithstanding. And, of course, never do we find anything remotely like the xenophobia manifest in, for instance, Hawthorne's characterization of the Irish as "pauper dregs," and "the scum which every wind blows off the Irish shores." [23] Her Irish narratives reflect, rather, a warm and humorous interest in and concern for a people who had recently undergone a cultural devastation of major proportions—*An Gorta Mór*, The Great Hunger. Terry Eagleton has termed that dark occurrence "the greatest social catastrophe of nineteenth-century Europe," one that "continues to elude appropriate speech" (42). Jewett suggests this tragedy and the consequent diaspora in "A Little Captive Maid." "Poor Ireland," her narrator laments,

> who gives her best to the great busy countries over seas, and longs for the time when she can be rich and busy herself, and keep the young people at home and happy in field and town. What does foreign money cost that comes back to the cottage households broken as if by death? What does it cost to the aching hearts of fathers and mothers, to the homesick lads and girls in America with the cold Atlantic between them and home?

Such an apostrophe surely signifies Jewett's respect for Irish cultural otherness. Her considerable optimism about

Irish success in America is balanced by her recognition of their rootedness in the world of their native island and her respect for their own traditional view of themselves—as exiles. Hers, as we have noted, is no one-dimensional "saga of immigrants coming to America and ineluctably becoming American" (Jacobson 10). The above passage demonstrates awareness of the anguish and ambivalence Irish immigrants experienced in journeying from one cultural world to another. Moreover, the tenor of this address perforce applies to the situations of other nineteenth-century ethnic groups emigrating to the United States. It is as well the tenor of generosity that predominates in Jewett's fiction generally, typified, for example, by Mrs. Todd's mother's injunction to her regarding "the foreigner" in the story of the same name: "'She's a stranger in a strange land. . . . I want you to make her have a sense that somebody feels kind to her.'"

As noted earlier, Sarah Orne Jewett deserves credit for having represented the Irish in ways remarkably novel in her cultural context and at odds with its standard discourse. At the very least, the stories in this collection, written by a significant American writer, provide a valuable study of the post-Famine, New England Irish population, one all the more valuable since firsthand Irish accounts of the period are less than abundant. These stories carry out this study with obvious sensitivity and openness toward their ethnic subject, which they imaginatively engage as much as record. Michael M. J. Fischer has noted that ethnicity is a process of "inter-reference between two or more cultural traditions, and . . . these dynamics of intercultural knowledge provide reservoirs for renewing humane values" (201). Jewett's Irish stories demonstrate just such a renewal—redefining, questioning, and expanding cultural boundaries within concentrated American communities, her own New England area in particular. As such, they constitute important documents in the history of a country still engaged with the multi-ethnic as well as multi-individualist paradox of *E pluribus unum*.

Notes

1. As the Weber *Bibliography* indicates (40–47), the stories that
    came out in *Scribner's Magazine* were "The Luck of the Bogans" in
    January 1889, "A Little Captive Maid" in December 1891, "Between
    Mass and Vespers" in May 1893, and "Where's Nora?" in
    December 1898. "The Gray Mills of Farley" appeared in *The
    Cosmopolitan*, June 1898. *McClure's Magazine* published "Bold Words
    at the Bridge" and "Elleneen" in April 1899 and February 1901,
    respectively. *Lippincott's Magazine* carried "A Landlocked Sailor" in
    May 1899. Jewett included five of these stories in her other
    collections: "The Luck of the Bogans" in *Strangers and Wayfarers*
    (1890); "Between Mass and Vespers" and "A Little Captive Maid"
    in *A Native of Winby and Other Tales* (1893); "Where's Nora?" and
    "Bold Words at the Bridge" in *The Queen's Twin and Other Stories*
    (1899). Jewett makes favorable references to Irish figures in
    some of her other stories as well, for example, to "'Heron the
    Irishman'" in "The Courting of Sister Wisby," which appeared in
    the *Atlantic Monthly* in 1887 (collected in *The King of Folly Island and
    Other People*, 1888): "'He was a good-hearted creatur', with a
    laughin' eye and a clever word for everybody. He was the first
    Irishman that ever came this way'" (63).

2. Van Wyck Brooks states that Jewett also "had spent the greater
    part of a year among [the Irish], once at Bantry Bay" (413), but
    informed chronologies of Jewett's life, including Paula
    Blanchard's recent biography, make no mention of such an
    extended visit.

3. In *Passages from the American Note-Books*, published posthu-
    mously in 1868, Hawthorne records his experiences from an
    1837 summer visit to a friend in Maine, in the process of which
    he makes many disparaging remarks about the Irish and draws
    casual "Anglo" caricatures of them. A typical example is his
    observation of an Irish couple who, "after our departure . . .
    came to blows, it being a custom with the Irish husbands and
    wives to settle their disputes with blows; and it is said the
    woman often proves the better man" (48). In part, this
    observation instances a common reaction by native born,
    white males to what was perceived as the immigrant threat to
    American "manhood" throughout the nineteenth century and
    later. Michael Kimmel refers to these reactions in his *Manhood
    in America: A Cultural History* (New York: Free Press, 1996) 83. Jewett
    was very likely acquainted with Hawthorne's ethnic sentiments
    as expressed in the above volume, and not simply because
    of its "Maine" topic in the 1837 section. Hawthorne's wife,
    Sophia, held the copyright to the 1868 edition of his *American
    Note-Books*. She had been friends with Annie Fields (later, of
    course, Jewett's closest companion) who, with her husband,
    had written a biography of Hawthorne and, as noted previ-
    ously, with whom Jewett took her first trip to Ireland.

4. Not to tar all Yankee transcendentalists with the same brush, it
    should be noted that Margaret Fuller, as Frank Shuffleton
    points out, looked forward to ethnic mixture in New England

as a happy prospect, "a dynamic enrichment, bringing movement and newness to an otherwise static, inbred group . . ." (3–
4). Walt Whitman's view was likewise positive—see his poem
"Old Ireland." And at least on one occasion, even Thoreau
wrote compassionately of the Famine Irish. The *St. John*, an
immigrant ship bound from Galway to Boston, sank in a
violent storm off Cape Cod in October of 1849. In the first
chapter of his posthumously published *Cape Cod*, Thoreau, a
firsthand witness to the tragedy's aftermath, describes in
compelling and elegiac terms the recovery and identification of
the 145 drowned victims.

5.   Cf., for example, Henry James' characterization of Irish
immigrants in *Washington Square* (1880). Mrs. Penniman, the
romantic, go-between aunt who is trying to find a place for her
"interview" with Morris Townsend, is depicted by the narrator
as thinking "of the Battery, but that was rather cold and windy,
besides one's being exposed to the intrusion from the Irish
emigrants who at this point alight, with large appetites, in the
New World . . ." (82).

6.   Anti-Irish-Catholic sermons were preached in influential
New England pulpits, and virulent anti-Catholic literature
circulated during the period—the apocryphal *Awful Disclosures* of
"ex-nun" Maria Monk being but one example. In 1834, rioters
burned and sacked an Ursuline convent outside Boston, and in
the 1850s, "Know Nothing" crowds torched Catholic neighbor
hoods in Lawrence, Massachusetts. Yankee perception of the
Irish was somewhat less aggressively negative after the Civil
War, however, owing to the extensive Irish immigrant casual-
ties suffered in the Union cause. But even as late as the 1870s,
"such a civilized magazine as *Scribner's Monthly* [was] supporting
its shabby Irish anecdotes with threatening editorials" (Leyda
260).

7.   An Irish-American writer and poet, Guiney was Mangan's
American editor. James Joyce termed Mangan "the most
significant poet of the modern Celtic world" in a lecture, which
he gave in Italy, entitled "Giacomo Clarenzio Mangan," part of
which appears in *The Field Day Anthology*, vol. 3, 5–7.

8.   Jack Kerouac's *Maggie Cassidy* is a later study of the French-
Canadian/Irish-American dynamic in a New England mill town.

9.   See, among other examples, Marjorie Pryse's introduction to
Sarah Orne Jewett: 'The Country of the Pointed Firs' and Other Stories, ed.
Mary Ellen Chase (New York: Norton, 1981), esp. viii–xii, xix;
Sarah Way Sherman, *Sarah Orne Jewett: An American Persephone*
(Hanover: UP of New England, 1989), esp. 67–80, 176–77; and
Margaret Roman, *Sarah Orne Jewett: Reconstructing Gender*
(Tuscaloosa: U of Alabama P, 1992). For a different but still
"feminist" discussion of "communal or separatist feminism" (73)
in *The Country of the Pointed Firs*, see Michael Davitt Bell, "Gender
and American Realism in *The Country of the Pointed Firs.*" *New Essays
on 'The Country of the Pointed Firs'*. Ed. June Howard. Cambridge:
Cambridge UP, 1994. 61–80.

10. Richard Cary judges this story otherwise, claiming—mistakenly,

we would argue—that in it "she trades in surface qualities and fanciful dialogue," her "tone" in rendering the two women's conflict "strained" (128).

11. Battles arising from infringement upon somebody's garden are, of course, part of an old folkloric tradition. The theme is used, for example, by Faulkner in the "Barn Burning" section of *The Hamlet* and by the Uruguayan writer Horacio Quiroga in *The Roof of Incense*.

12. Cf. Blanchard's observation that "in Jewett's work generally, ritual serves to bring people together: through the small daily ceremonies of tea-drinking and calls and the larger ones of funerals and town celebrations, people acknowledge and strengthen their responsibility to one another" (92).

13. Richard Brodhead ascribes Jewett's "minor" mode of writing to her acceptance of Arnold's "high" cultural criteria for the great artist (as stated in our earlier discussion): "[T]he major-minor distinction maintained in Jewett's culture entered the thought of those [like her] who inhabited that culture and helped frame their personal understandings—of themselves quite as much as of others." Hence, "the renunciation of [any 'major'] ambitions formed part of the governing idea of her career . . ." (165, 166). Also cf. Louis A. Renza, *"A White Heron" and the Question of Minor Literature* (Madison: U of Wisconsin P, 1984), esp. 61–72.

14. There is, it would seem, an issue of intertextuality involved here too. In Jewett's representations of spoken Irish dialect, the abundant use of the interjection "faix" (faith) and the meticulous placement of an *h* after *t*—for example, "wather" for "water"—as well as frequently after *d*, suggest the influence of William Carleton's dialogue in the then very popular *Traits and Stories of the Irish Peasantry*, a book that is not without its own dialectal inconsistencies.

   A dictionary of Hiberno-English has long been lacking, but that situation is being remedied. Richard Wall (University of Calgary) and others are presently laying the groundwork for a major dictionary project, and Diarmuid Ó Muirithe's *A Dictionary of Anglo-Irish* is forthcoming from Four Courts Press, Dublin. In addition, Joyce scholarship has produced some work that can serve as introductory to Hiberno-English studies. See, for instance, Richard Wall, *An Anglo-Irish Dialect Glossary for Joyce's Works* (Syracuse: Syracuse University Press, 1987) and T. P. Dolan, "The Language of Dubliners," *James Joyce: The Artist and the Labyrinth*, ed. Augustine Martin (London: Ryan, 1990) 25–40.

15. The recurring priest figures in these stories, from Father Miles in "The Luck of the Bogans," Father Dunn in "A Little Captive Maid," to Father Daly in "The Gray Mills of Farley," often serve a similar function. In this regard, Jewett anticipates the "priestly comedies" (Mary Gordon's term) of J. F. Powers, as well as the parish life film genre of the 1940s and 1950s. Her Irish priests, that is, resemble later Hollywood stereotypes—acted by such notables as Barry Fitzgerald, Bing Crosby, Pat O'Brien, and Spencer Tracy—who also attempt to preserve Irish family values in a mode wryly humorous, compassionate, and

democratic. Cf. "The Foreigner," which originally appeared in the *Atlantic Monthly* (1900), where Jewett's Mrs. Todd refers to an ethnically unspecified Catholic priest who "'was a kind-hearted old man; he looked so benevolent an' I could ha' stopped an' told him my own troubles'" (*Uncollected Stories* 317).

Jewett also alludes to an actual Irish priest, "Father Matthew" (in fact spelled with one *t*), in "The Luck of the Bogans" to underscore the story's "temperance" motif. Father Theobald Mathew (1790–1856) was a temperance leader in Ireland—a statue of him stands in Cork and one in Dublin—beginning in 1838. He brought his anti-alcohol crusade (something heretofore associated with Protestant denominations) to United States Catholics in 1849–1851. He was an acquaintance of Frederick Douglass whom he met in Ireland in 1845. William Thackery, who met Mathew in Ireland in 1842, describes him in *The Irish Sketch Book*, chap. 5. See also John F. Quinn, "Father Mathew's American Tour—1849–1851," *Éire-Ireland* 30.1 (Spring 1995): 91–104.

16. Werner Sollors makes an analogous point about the ideological suitability of regionalist and/or ethnic communities in relation to more mainstream American myths: "If the codes of American exceptionalism identified the sacred rhetoric of religious redemption with the secular place of America, then the concepts of American regionalism identify that same language of typological ethnogenesis with the region, while ethnic thinking applies it to the ethnic group" (193).

17. "If nineteenth-century Americans thought at all about Irish women, they usually had in mind Bridget, the servant girl, who darted from one American kitchen to another, usually shattering the crockery as she went. . . . She emerged in American lore in the home of her employer, rather than in her own community or her own home. . . . she was generally depicted as a foil to American values and accepted American behavior patterns and not as someone of great consequence. Yet numbers alone take Bridget out of the parlor and kitchen and into historic center stage. In the decades after the Famine, more Irish women than Irish men immigrated to the United States; the Irish communities contained more females than males. . . . [T]hey were the only significant group of women who chose to migrate in primarily female cliques [cf. "Bold Words at the Bridge"]. They also accepted jobs that most other women turned down, and their rate of social and economic progress seems to have outdistanced that of women of other ethnic groups" (Diner xiii–xiv).

It might be noted that Irish domestics were also often at literary-historical center stage working in other New England writers' households besides Jewett's. The role of Katy Leary in running the Twain house in Hartford is well known. Concerning the significant Irish immigrant presence in the life and household of Emily Dickinson, see Aife Murray, "Kitchen Table Poetics: Maid Margaret Maher and Her Poet Emily Dickinson," *The Emily Dickinson Journal* (fall 1996).

18. In this context, note the glimmer of ethnic tension suggested
     between the French-Canadian and Irish-American communi-
     ties in "Between Mass and Vespers" and "The Gray Mills of
     Farley." One could even regard Jewett's marginal admission of
     French Canadians in these two Irish stories as an extension of
     her espousing an Arnoldian brand of "nineteenth-century
     European Hellenism" that privileged "northern Europeans, the
     British, the French" (Zagarell 54). Cf. Gillman, 112–13, on Jewett's
     French, as well as Anglo-Saxon, characterizations of the Bowden
     clan in *The Country of the Pointed Firs*—the two ethnic origins she
     also happened to claim as her own ancestral roots. Also see
     Blanchard, 6, concerning Jewett's actual English and French
     ancestral background.

19. It remains difficult to estimate the number of non-Anglo-
     phonic Irish speakers living in the New England area between
     the 1860s and 1890s. Still, "an unprecedented proportion" of
     1840s–1850s famine refugees "were traditionalist peasants, often
     Irish-speakers" (Miller 326), despite the fact that "[i]t was mostly
     the Irish-speakers the Famine carried off, since they were the
     poorest, most vulnerable classes" (Eagleton 43). (Even after the
     decimation of Gaelic-speaking natives by starvation and
     emigration in the 1840s, Ireland's 1851 census found that they
     comprised nearly 25 percent of the total population [O'Murchu
     27].) One can only speculate about whether Jewett ever
     actually encountered such speakers. The Irish domestic
     workers with whom she was most familiar undoubtedly spoke
     English. It is worth noting, however, that in 1837 Hawthorne
     registers the presence of Gaelic speakers (and not kindly) in
     Maine (Hawthorne 52; see note 3 above). More important to
     the issue at hand, a sizable community of them had settled in
     Portland, Maine, some forty miles from South Berwick
     (Jewett's home), in the early 1880s (Nilson 8). Cf. Shell's
     discussion of how non-Anglophonic immigrant speakers
     became (and become) "subsumed" by "anglophone Americans
     [who] often say they believe in the equality of all language
     groups, when they mean only the equality of language groups
     other than the definitively, if not officially, anglophone one"
     (127). The demoralized post-Famine Irish speakers in the United
     States were especially vulnerable to being thus subsumed.

20. On the other hand, exaggerated and therefore highly
     questionable "Anglo" criticisms of the Irish were also part of a
     long United States political tradition dating from the Revolu-
     tionary War period. For example, William Cobbett, an English
     journalist who temporarily immigrated to the United States
     after that war, wrote vitriolic pamphlets against the Jeffer-
     sonian Republicans, whom he considered to be not-so-
     closeted French Jacobins. One such pamphlet in 1798 was
     entitled "Detection of a Conspiracy Formed by the United
     Irishmen, with the Evident Intention of Aiding the Tyrants of
     France in Subverting the Government of the United States of
     America" (qtd. in Morgan 11).

21. Jewett had aired like-minded "Anglo" sentiments two years

earlier, during her first trip to Ireland with Annie Fields, in a passage from a June 1882 letter to her sister. Jewett recognizes that many Irish "have had their incomes cut off," and so "of course, as in all such questions there is wrong on both sides [i.e., England's and Ireland's]—but the Irish mob is a crazy headed one—we all know *that!*" (qtd. in Blanchard 139; Jewett's emphasis). In "The Luck of the Bogans," moreover, she twice alludes to the agrarian reform movement in Ireland—probably the Land League—in clearly pejorative terms. Thus, the narrative depicts Biddy Bogan as being "eager to join some successful members of her family who had always complained at home of their unjust rent and the difficulties of the crops. Everybody said that the times were going to be harder than ever that summer and she was quick to catch at the inflam-mable speeches of some lawless towns-folk who were never satisfied with anything." Also cf. how the old squire, on whose farm the Bogans worked, "suffered from the evil repute of some short-sighted neighbors. 'If I gave up all I had in the world and went to the almshouse myself, they would still damn me for a landlord,' he said, desperately one day."

One could argue that the passages from both the 1882 letter and "The Luck of the Bogans" reflect as much Jewett's class-bound biases—Blanchard claims that they show "the tunnel vision of [a] middle-aged, middle-class literary [lady]" (139)—as any specific ethnic prejudice toward the Irish. In any case, her Irish stories primarily concern the intercultural difficulties that late nineteenth-century Irish immigrants faced in the United States and, in this sense, circumvent the issue of Irish nation alist conflict—not to mention the issue of any uneasy United States cultural rapprochement—with Britain. One could even argue that Jewett's Arnoldian views of the Irish reveal a latent pull on her imagination to regard such immigrants in a certain politically peaceful light. In accord with a middle-class, liberal ideology that would resolve the social problems raised by the proletarian and/or immigrant "mob" in the United States at the time, these views, which at bottom provide a model for social accommodation, could have helped motivate the writing of her "Irish" stories. Some critics have also recognized Jewett's serious acknowledgment of the marginal, European "other" in her relatively late story, "The Foreigner" (1900). For instance, Zagarell cautiously claims that this story "seems to call into question the nationalism and Nordicism that . . . inform and help shape the earlier [and earlier written sections of her] narrative" (55) of *The Country of the Pointed Firs* (1896).

22. These "others" perforce included the *Atlantic Monthly* type readers to whom her stories were pitched—readers identified by their "cross-cultural cosmopolitanism . . . anxious nativism . . . acquisitiveness and sense of . . . rights to own . . . [along with] care for literary art" (Brodhead 149). In this sense, Jewett herself, under the present interpretation, would be assuming the role of Anglo-sponsor for her Irish characters.

23. The Hawthorne quotation is cited by Monica Elbert 69n. Also
     see Beth L. Lueck, "'Mediating on the Varied Congregation of
     Human Life': Immigration in Hawthorne's Travel Sketches," *The
     Nathaniel Hawthorne Review* 14.2 (Fall 1988): 1–7.

Works Cited

Altschuler, Glenn C. *Race, Ethnicity, and Class in American Social Thought, 1865–
     1919.* Arlington Heights: Harlan Davidson, 1982.

Blanchard, Paula. *Sarah Orne Jewett: Her World and Her Work.* Radcliffe Biogra-
     phy Series. Reading, MA: Addison-Wesley, 1994.

Brodhead, Richard H. *Culture of Letters: Scenes of Reading and Writing in Nine-
     teenth-Century America.* Chicago: U of Chicago P, 1993.

Brooks, Van Wyck. *New England: Indian Summer, 1865–1915.* Chicago: U of
     Chicago P, 1984.

Cary, Richard. *Sarah Orne Jewett.* New Haven: Twayne, 1962.

Deane, Seamus. *Celtic Revivals.* Winston-Salem: Wake Forest UP, 1987.

Diner, Hasia R. *Erin's Daughters in America: Irish Immigrant Women in the Nine-
     teenth Century.* Baltimore: Johns Hopkins UP, 1983.

Eagleton, Terry. "Feeding Off History." *The Observer Magazine* 20 Feb. 1994:
     42–44.

Elbert, Monica. "Nathaniel Hawthorne, *The Concord Freeman*, and the Irish
     'Other'." *Éire-Ireland* 24.3 (Fall 1994): 60–73.

Fanning, Charles, ed. *The Exiles of Erin: Nineteenth Century Irish-American Fiction.*
     Notre Dame: Notre Dame U P, 1987.

Ferraro, Thomas J. *Ethnic Passages: Literary Immigrants in Twentieth-Century
     America.* Chicago: U of Chicago P, 1993.

Fischer, Michael M. J. "Ethnicity and the Post-Modern Arts of Memory."
     Writing Culture: The Poetics and Politics of Ethnography. Ed. James Clifford
     and George E. Marcus. Berkeley: U of California P, 1986. 194–233.

Foster, R. F. *Modern Ireland: 1600–1972.* New York: Penguin, 1988.

Gillman, Susan. "Regionalism and Nationalism in Jewett's *Country of the
     Pointed Firs*." *New Essays on 'The Country of the Pointed Firs'.* Ed. June Howard.
     Cambridge: Cambridge UP, 1994. 101–20.

Hawthorne, Nathaniel. *Passages from the American Note-Books of Nathaniel
     Hawthorne.* Cambridge: Riverside, 1868.

Howard, June. "Introduction: Sarah Orne Jewett and the Traffic in Words."
     New Essays on 'The Country of the Pointed Firs'. Ed. June Howard. Cam-
     bridge: Cambridge UP, 1994. 1–37.

Huizinga, Johan. *Homo Ludens: A Study of the Play-Element in Culture.* Boston:
     Beacon, 1950.

Jacobson, Matthew Frye. *Special Sorrows: The Diasporic Imagination of Irish,
     Polish, and Jewish Immigrants in the U.S.* Cambridge: Harvard UP, 1995.

James, Henry. *Washington Square. Washington Square, The Portrait of a Lady, The
     Bostonians.* Ed. William T. Stafford. New York: Library of America, 1990.
     1–189.

Jewett, Sarah Orne. *The King of Folly Island and Other People.* Boston: Houghton,
     1888.

————. *Letters of Sarah Orne Jewett*. Ed. Annie Fields. Boston: Houghton, 1911.

————. *A Native of Winby and Other Tales*. Boston: Houghton, 1893.

————. *The Queen's Twin and Other Stories*. Boston: Houghton, 1899.

————. *Sarah Orne Jewett Letters*. Ed. Richard Cary. Waterville: Colby College P, 1967.

————. *Strangers and Wayfarers*. Boston: Houghton, Mifflin, 1890.

————. *The Uncollected Short Stories of Sarah Orne Jewett*. Ed. Richard Cary. Waterville: Colby College P, 1971.

Joyce, James. "James Clarence Mangan." *The Field Day Anthology of Irish Writing*. Ed. Seamus Deane. Vol. 3. Kerry: Field Day, 1991. 5–7.

Knobel, Dale T. *Paddy and the Republic: Ethnicity and Nationality in Antebellum America*. Middletown: Wesleyan UP, 1986.

Leyda, Jay. "Miss Emily's Maggie." *New World Writing*. New York: New American Library, 1953, 255–267.

Lloyd, David. *Nationalism and Minor Literature: James Clarence Mangan and the Emergence of Irish Cultural Nationalism*. Berkeley: U of California P, 1987.

Lucey, William L. "'We New Englanders . . .': Letters of Sarah Orne Jewett to Louise Imogen Guiney." *Records of the American Catholic Historical Society of Philadelphia* 70 (Mar.-June 1959): 58–64.

Matthiessen, F. O. *Sarah Orne Jewett*. Gloucester: Smith, 1929.

Miller, Kerby A. *Emigrants and Exiles: Ireland and the Irish Exodus to North America*. New York: Oxford UP, 1985.

Mobley, Marilyn Sanders. *Folk Roots and Mythic Wings in Sarah Orne Jewett and Toni Morrison: The Cultural Function of Narrative*. Baton Rouge: Louisiana State UP, 1991.

Morgan, Edmund S. "Pioneers of Paranoia." *New York Review of Books* 6 Oct. 1994: 11–13.

Nilson, Kenneth E. "Thinking of Monday: The Irish Speakers of Portland, Maine." *Éire-Ireland* 25.1 (Spring 1990): 6–19.

O'Murchu, Mairtin. *The Irish Language*. Dublin: Department of Foreign Affairs, 1965.

Powell, Lyman P. *Mary Baker Eddy: A Life Size Portrait*. New York: Macmillan, 1931.

Shell, Marc. "Babel in America; or, The Politics of Language Diversity in the United States." *Critical Inquiry* 20.1 (Autumn 1993): 103–27.

Shuffleton, Frank. *A Mixed Race: Ethnicity in Early America*. New York: Oxford UP, 1993.

Sollors, Werner. *Beyond Ethnicity: Consent and Descent in American Culture*. New York: Oxford UP, 1986.

Stam, Robert. "Bakhtin, Polyphony, and Ethnic/Racial Representation." *Unspeakable Images: Ethnicity and the American Cinema*. Ed. Lester D. Friedman. Urbana: U of Illinois P, 1991. 251–276.

Thoreau, Henry David. *Cape Cod. A Week on the Concord and Merrimack Rivers, Walden, The Maine Woods, Cape Cod*. Ed. Robert F. Sayre. New York: Library of America, 1985.

————. *Walden and Other Writings*. Ed. Joseph Wood Krutch. New York: Bantam, 1962.

Waggoner, Hyatt H. "The Unity of *The Country of the Pointed Firs*." *The World of*

Dunnet Landing: A Sarah Orne Jewett Collection. Ed. David Bonnell Green. Gloucester: Smith, 1972. 373–84.

Weber, Clara Carter, and Carl J. Weber. *A Bibliography of the Published Writings of Sarah Orne Jewett*. Waterville: Colby College P, 1949.

Zagarell, Sandra A. "*Country*'s Portrayal of Community and the Exclusion of Difference." *New Essays on 'The Country of the Pointed Firs'*. Ed. June Howard. Cambridge: Cambridge UP, 1994. 39–60.

The Irish Stories of Sarah Orne Jewett

The Luck
of the Bogans

1

The old beggar women of Bantry streets had seldom show-
ered their blessings upon a departing group of emigrants with
such hearty good will as they did upon Mike Bogan and his
little household one May morning.

Peggy Muldoon, she of the game leg and green-patched
eye and limber tongue, steadied herself well back against
the battered wall at the street corner and gave her whole
energy to a torrent of speech unusual to even her noble
powers. She would not let Mike Bogan go to America
unsaluted and unblessed; she meant to do full honor to this
second cousin, once removed, on the mother's side.

"Yirra, Mike Bogan, is it yerself thin, goyn away beyant
the says?" she began with true dramatic fervor. "Let poor owld
Peg take her last look on your laughing face me darlin'. She'll
be under the ground this time next year, God give her grace,
and you far away lavin' to strange spades the worruk of hapin'
the sods of her grave. Give me one last look at me darlin' lad
wid his swate Biddy an' the shild. Oh that I live to see this
day!"

Peg's companions, old Marget Dunn and Biddy O'Hern
and no-legged Tom Whinn, the fragment of a once active
sailor who propelled himself by a low truckle cart and two

short sticks; these interesting members of society heard the shrill note of their leader's eloquence and suddenly appeared like beetles out of unsuspected crevices near by. The side car, upon which Mike Bogan and his wife and child were riding from their little farm outside the town to the place of departure, was stopped at the side of the narrow street. A lank yellow-haired lad, with eyes red from weeping sat swinging his long legs from the car side, another car followed, heavily laden with Mike's sister's family, and a mourning yet envious group of acquaintances footed it in the rear. It was an excited, picturesque little procession; the town was quickly aware of its presence, and windows went up from house to house, and heads came out of the second and third stories and even in the top attics all along the street. The air was thick with blessings, the quiet of Bantry was permanently broken.

"Lard bliss us and save us!" cried Peggy, her shrill voice piercing the chatter and triumphantly lifting itself in audible relief above the din, — "Lard bliss us an' save us for the flower o' Bantry is lavin' us this day. Break my heart wid yer goyn will ye Micky Bogan and make it black night to the one eye that's left in me gray head this fine mornin' o' spring. I that hushed the mother of you and the father of you babies in me arms, and that was a wake old woman followin' and crapin' to see yerself christened. Oh may the saints be good to you Micky Bogan and Biddy Flaherty the wife, and forgive you the sin an' shame of turning yer proud backs on ould Ireland. Ain't there pigs and praties enough for ye in poor Bantry town that her crabbedest childer must lave her. Oh wisha wisha, I'll see your face no more, may the luck o' the Bogans follow you, that failed none o' the Bogans yet. May the sun shine upon you and grow two heads of cabbage in the same sprout, may the little b'y live long and get him a good wife, and if she ain't good to him may she die from him. May every hair on both your heads turn into a blessed candle to light your ways to heaven, but not yit me darlin's — not yit!"

The jaunting car had been surrounded by this time and Mike and his wife were shaking hands and trying to respond impartially to the friendly farewells and blessings of their friends. There never had been such a leave-taking in Bantry.

Peggy Muldoon felt that her eloquence was in danger of being ignored and made a final shrill appeal. "Who'll bury me
now?" she screamed with a long wail which silenced the
whole group; "who'll lay me in the grave, Micky bein' gone
from me that always gave me the kind word and the pinny
or trippence ivery market day, and the wife of him Biddy
Flaherty the rose of Glengariff; many's the fine meal she's
put before old Peggy Muldoon that is old and blind."

"Awh, give the ould sowl a pinny now," said a sympathetic voice, "'twill bring you luck, more power to you." And
Mike Bogan, the tears streaming down his honest cheeks,
plunged deep into his pocket and threw the old beggar a
broad five-shilling piece. It was a monstrous fortune to Peggy.
Her one eye glared with joy, the jaunting car moved away
while she fell flat on the ground in apparent excess of emotion. The farewells were louder for a minute—then they were
stopped; the excitable neighborhood returned to its business or idleness and the street was still. Peggy rose rubbing
an elbow, and said with the air of a queen to her retinue,
"Coom away now poor crathurs, so we'll drink long life to
him." And Marget Dunn and Biddy O'Hern and no-legged
Tom Whinn with his truckle cart disappeared into an alley.

"What's all this whillalu?" asked a sober-looking, clerical
gentleman who came riding by.

"'Tis the Bogans going to Ameriky, yer reverence," responded Jim Kalehan, the shoemaker, from his low window. "The folks gived them their wake whilst they were here
to enjoy it and them was the keeners that was goin' hippety
with lame legs and fine joy down the convanient alley for
beer, God bless the poor souls!"

Mike Bogan and Biddy his wife looked behind them again
and again. Mike blessed himself fervently as he caught a last
glimpse of the old church on the hill where he was christened and married, where his father and his grandfather had
been christened and married and buried. He remembered
the day when he had first seen his wife, who was there from
Glengariff to stay with her old aunt, and coming to early
mass, had looked to him like a strange sweet flower abloom
on the gray stone pavement where she knelt. The old church
had long stood on the steep height at the head of Bantry
street and watched and waited for her children. He would

never again come in from his little farm in the early morning—he never again would be one of the Bantry men. The golden stories of life in America turned to paltry tinsel, and a love and pride of the old country, never forgotten by her sons and daughters, burned with fierce flame on the inmost altar of his heart. It had all been very easy to dream fine dreams of wealth and landownership, but in that moment the least of the pink daisies that were just opening on the roadside was dearer to the simple-hearted emigrant than all the world beside.

"Lave me down for a bit of sod," he commanded the wondering young driver, who would have liked above all things to sail for the new world. The square of turf from the hedge foot, sparkling with dew and green with shamrock and gay with tiny flowers, was carefully wrapped in Mike's best Sunday handkerchief as they went their way. Biddy had covered her head with her shawl—it was she who had made the plan of going to America, it was she who was eager to join some successful members of her family who had always complained at home of their unjust rent and the difficulties of the crops. Everybody said that the times were going to be harder than ever that summer, and she was quick to catch at the inflammable speeches of some lawless townsfolk who were never satisfied with anything. As for Mike, the times always seemed alike, he did not grudge hard work and he never found fault with the good Irish weather. His nature was not resentful, he only laughed when Biddy assured him that the gorse would soon grow in the thatch of his head as it did on their cabin chimney. It was only when she said that, in America they could make a gentleman of baby Dan, that the father's blue eyes glistened and a look of determination came into his face.

"God grant we'll come back to it some day," said Mike softly. "I didn't know, faix indeed, how sorry I'd be for lavin' the owld place. Awh Biddy girl 'tis many the weary day we'll think of the home we've left," and Biddy removed the shawl one instant from her face only to cover it again and burst into a new shower of tears. The next day but one they were sailing away out of Queenstown harbor to the high seas. Old Ireland was blurring its green and purple coasts moment by moment; Kinsale lay low, and they had lost sight of the white cabins on the hillsides and the pastures golden with furze. Hours before the old women on the wharves had turned away from them shaking their great cap borders. Hours before their own feet had trodden the soil of Ireland for the last time. Mike Bogan and Biddy had left home, they were well on their way to America. Luckily nobody had been with them at last to say good-by—they had taken a more or less active part in the piteous general leave-taking at Queenstown, but those were not the faces of their own mothers or brothers to which they looked back as the ship slid away through the green water.

"Well, sure, we're gone now," said Mike setting his face westward and tramping the steerage deck. "I like the say too, I belave, me own grandfather was a sailor, an' 'tis a fine life for a man. Here's little Dan goin' to Ameriky and niver mistrustin'. We'll be sindin' the gossoon back again, rich and fine, to the owld place by and by, 'tis thrue for us, Biddy."

But Biddy, like many another woman, had set great changes in motion and then longed to escape from their consequences. She was much discomposed by the ship's unsteadiness. She accused patient Mike of having dragged her away from home and friends. She grew very white in the face, and was helped to her hard steerage berth where she had plenty of time for reflection upon the vicissitudes of seafaring. As for Mike, he grew more and more enthusiastic day by day over their prospects as he sat in the shelter of the bulkhead and tended little Dan and talked with his companions as they sailed westward.

Who of us have made enough kindly allowance for the homesick quick-witted ambitious Irish men and women, who have landed every year with such high hopes on our shores. There are some of a worse sort, of whom their native country might think itself well rid—but what thrifty New England housekeeper who takes into her home one of the pleasant-faced little captive maids, from Southern Ireland, has half understood the change of surroundings. That was a life in the open air under falling showers and warm sunshine, a life of wit and humor, of lavishness and lack of provision for more than the passing day—of constant companionship with one's neighbors, and a cheerful serenity and lack of nervous anticipation born of the vicinity of the Gulf Stream. The climate makes the characteristics of Cork and Kerry; the fierce energy of the Celtic race in America is forced and stimulated by our own keen air. The beauty of Ireland is little hinted at by an average orderly New England town—many a young girl and many a blundering sturdy fellow is heartsick with the homesickness and restraint of his first year in this golden country of hard work. To so many of them a house has been but a shelter for the night—a sleeping-place: if you remember that, you do not wonder at fumbling fingers or impatience with our houses full of trinkets. Our needless tangle of furnishing bewilders those who still think the flowers that grow of themselves in the Irish thatch more beautiful than anything under the cover of our prosaic shingled roofs.

"Faix, a fellow on deck was telling me a nate story the day," said Mike to Biddy Bogan, by way of kindly amusement. "Says he to me, 'Mike,' says he, 'did ye ever hear of wan Pathrick O'Brien that heard some bla'guard tell how in Ameriky you picked up money in the streets?' 'No,' says I. 'He wint ashore in a place,' says he, 'and he walked along and he come to a sign on a wall. Silver Street was on it. "I 'ont stap here," says he, "it ain't wort my while at all, at all. I'll go on to Gold Street," says he, but he walked ever since and he ain't got there yet."'

Biddy opened her eyes and laughed feebly. Mike looked so bronzed and ruddy and above all so happy, that she took heart. "We're sound and young, thanks be to God, and we'll earn an honest living," said Mike, proudly. "'Tis the childher I'm thinkin' of all the time, an' how they'll get a chance the best of us niver had at home. God bless old Bantry forever in spite of it. An' there's a smart rid-headed man that has every bother to me why 'ont I go with him and keep a tidy bar. He's been in the same business this four year gone since he come out, and twenty pince in his pocket when he landed, and this year he took a month off and went over to see the ould folks and build 'em a dacint house intirely, and hire a man to farm wid 'em now the old ones is old. He says will I put in my money wid him, an he'll give me a great start I wouldn't have in three years else."

"Did you have the fool's head on you then and let out to him what manes you had?" whispered Biddy, fiercely and lifting herself to look at him.

"I did then; 'twas no harm," answered the unsuspecting Mike.

"'Twas a black-hearted rascal won the truth from you!" and Biddy roused her waning forces and that very afternoon appeared on deck. The red-headed man knew that he had lost the day when he caught her first scornful glance.

"God pity the old folks of him an' their house," muttered the sharp-witted wife to Mike, as she looked at the low-lived scheming fellow whom she suspected of treachery.

"He said thim was old clothes he was wearin' on the sea," apologized Mike for his friend, looking down somewhat consciously at his own comfortable corduroys. He and Biddy had been well to do on their little farm, and on good terms with their landlord the old squire. Poor old gentleman, it had been a sorrow to him to let the young people go. He was a generous, kindly old man, but he suffered from the evil repute of some short-sighted neighbors. "If I gave up all I had in the world and went to the almshouse myself, they would still damn me for a landlord," he said, desperately one day. "But I never thought Mike Bogan would throw up his good chances. I suppose some worthless fellow called him stick-in-the-mud and off he must go."

There was some unhappiness at first for the young people in America. They went about the streets of their chosen town for a day or two, heavy-hearted with disappointment. Their old neighbors were not housed in palaces after all, as the letters home had suggested, and after a few evenings of visiting and giving of messages, and a few days of aimless straying about, Mike and Biddy hired two rooms at a large rent up three flights of stairs, and went to housekeeping. Little Dan rolled down one flight the first day; no more tumbling on the green turf among the daisies for him, poor baby boy. His father got work at the forge of a carriage shop, having served a few months with a smith at home, and so taking rank almost as a skilled laborer. He was a great favorite speedily, his pay was good, at least it would have been good if he had lived on the old place among the fields, but he and Biddy did not know how to make the most of it here, and Dan had a baby sister presently to keep him company, and then another and another, and there they lived up-stairs in the heat, in the cold, in daisy time and snow time, and Dan was put to school and came home with a knowledge of sums in a-rithmetic which set his father's eyes dancing with delight, but with a knowledge besides of foul language and a brutal way of treating his little sisters when nobody was looking on.

Mike Bogan was young and strong when he came to America, and his good red blood lasted well, but it was against his nature to work in a hot half-lighted shop, and in a very few years he began to look pale about the mouth and shaky in the shoulders, and then the enthusiastic promises of the red-headed man on the ship, borne out, we must allow, by Mike's own observation, inclined him and his hard earned capital to the purchase of a tidy looking drinking shop on a side street of the town. The owner had died and his widow wished to go West to live with her son. She knew the Bogans and was a respectable soul in her way. She and her husband had kept a quiet place, everybody acknowledged, and everybody was thankful that since drinking shops must be kept, so decent a man as Mike Bogan was taking up the business.

2

The luck of the Bogans proved to be holding true in this generation. Their proverbial good fortune seemed to come rather from an absence of bad fortune than any special distinction granted the generation or two before Mike's time. The good fellow sometimes reminded himself gratefully of Peggy Muldoon's blessing, and once sent her a pound to keep Christmas upon. If he had only known it, that unworthy woman bestowed curses enough upon him because he did not repeat it the next year, to cancel any favors that might have been anticipated. Good news flew back to Bantry of his prosperity, and his comfortable home above the store was a place of reception and generous assistance to all the westward straying children of Bantry. There was a bit of garden that belonged to the estate, the fences were trig and neat, and neither Mike nor Biddy were persons to let things look shabby while they had plenty of money to keep them clean and whole. It was Mike who walked behind the priest on Sundays when the collection was taken. It was Mike whom good Father Miles trusted more than any other member of his flock, whom he confided in and consulted, whom perhaps his reverence loved best of all the parish because they were both Bantry men, born and bred. And nobody but Father Miles and Biddy and Mike Bogan knew the full extent of the father's and mother's pride and hope in the cleverness and beauty of their only son. Nothing was too great, and no success seemed impossible when they tried to picture the glorious career of little Dan.

Mike was a kind father to his little daughters, but all his hope was for Dan. It was for Dan that he was pleased when people called him Mr. Bogan in respectful tones, and when he was given a minor place of trust at town elections, he thought with humble gladness that Dan would have less cause to be ashamed of him by and by when he took his own place as gentleman and scholar. For there was something different about Dan from the rest of them, plain Irish folk that they were. Dan was his father's idea of a young lord; he would have liked to show the boy to the old squire, and see his look of surprise. Money came in at the shop door in a steady stream, there was plenty of it put away in the bank and Dan must wear well-made clothes and look like the best fellows at the school. He was handsomer than any of them, he was the best and quickest scholar of his class. The president of the great carriage company had said that he was a very promising boy more than once, and had put his hand on Mike's shoulder as he spoke. Mike and Biddy, dressed in their best, went to the school examinations year after year and heard their son do better than the rest, and saw him noticed and admired. For Dan's sake no noisy men were allowed to stay about the shop. Dan himself was forbidden to linger there, and so far the boy had clear honest eyes, and an affectionate way with his father that almost broke that honest heart with joy. They talked together when they went to walk on Sundays, and there was a plan, increasingly interesting to both, of going to old Bantry some summer—just for a treat. Oh happy days! They must end as summer days do, in winter weather.

There was an outside stair to the two upper stories where the Bogans lived above their place of business, and late one evening, when the shop shutters were being clasped together below, Biddy Bogan heard a familiar heavy step and hastened to hold her brightest lamp in the doorway.

"God save you," said his reverence Father Miles, who was coming up slowly, and Biddy dropped a decent courtesy and devout blessing in return. His reverence looked pale and tired, and seated himself wearily in a chair by the window—while Biddy coasted round by a bedroom door to "whist" at two wakeful daughters who were teasing each other and chattering in bed.

"'Tis long since we saw you here, sir," she said respectfully. "'Tis warm weather indade for you to be about the town, and folks sick an' dyin' and needing your help, sir. Mike'll be up now, your reverence. I hear him below."

Biddy had grown into a stout mother of a family, red-faced and bustling; there was little likeness left to the rose of Glengariff with whom Mike had fallen in love at early mass in Bantry church. But the change had been so gradual that Mike himself had never become conscious of any damaging difference. She took a fresh loaf of bread and cut some generous slices and put a piece of cheese and a knife on the table within reach of Father Miles's hand. "I suppose 'tis waste of time to give you more, so it is," she said to him. "Bread an' cheese and no better will you ate I suppose, sir," and she folded her arms across her breast and stood looking at him.

"How is the luck of the Bogans to-day?" asked the kind old man. "The head of the school I make no doubt?" and at this moment Mike came up the stairs and greeted his priest with reverent affection.

"You're looking faint, sir," he urged. "Biddy get a glass now, we're quite by ourselves sir—and I've something for sickness that's very soft and fine entirely."

"Well, well, this once then," answered Father Miles, doubtfully. "I've had a hard day."

He held the glass in his hand for a moment and then pushed it away from him on the table. "Indeed it's not wrong in itself," said the good priest looking up presently, as if he had made something clear to his mind. "The wrong is in ourselves to make beasts of ourselves with taking too much of it. I don't shame me with this glass of the best that you've poured for me. My own sin is in the coffee-pot. It wilds my head when I've got most use for it, and I'm sure of an aching pate—God forgive me for indulgence; but I must have it for my breakfast now and then. Give me a bit of bread and cheese; yes, that's what I want Bridget," and he pushed the glass still farther away.

"I've been at a sorry place this night," he went on a moment later, "the smell of the stuff can't but remind me. 'Tis a comfort to come here and find your house so clean and decent, and both of you looking me in the face. God save all poor sinners!" and Mike and his wife murmured assent.

"I wish to God you were both out of this business and every honest man with you," said the priest, suddenly dropping his fatherly, Bantry good fellowship and making his host conscious of the solemnity of the church altar. "'Tis a decent shop you keep, Mike, my lad, I know. I know no harm of it, but there are weak souls that can't master themselves, and the drink drags them down. There's little use in doing away with the shops though. We've got to make young men strong enough to let drink alone. The drink will always be in the world. Here's your bright young son; what are they teaching him at his school, do ye know? Has his characther grown, do ye think Mike Bogan, and is he going to be a man for good, and to help decent things get a start and bad things to keep their place? I don't care how he does his sums, so I don't, if he has no characther, and they may fight about beer and fight about temperance and carry their Father Matthew flags flying high, so they may, and it's all no good, lessen we can raise the young folks up above the place where drink and shame can touch them. God grant us help," he whispered, dropping his head on his breast. "I'm getting to be an old man myself, and I've never known the temptation that's like a hounding devil to many men. I can let drink alone, God pity those who can't. Keep the young lads out from it Mike. You're a good fellow, you're careful, but poor human souls are weak, God knows!"

"'Tis thrue for you indade sir!" responded Biddy. Her eyes were full of tears at Father Miles's tone and earnestness, but she could not have made clear to herself what he had said.

"Will I put a dhrap more of wather in it, your riverence?" she suggested, but the priest shook his head gently, and, taking a handful of parish papers out of his pocket, proceeded to hold conference with the master of the house. Biddy waited a while and at last ventured to clear away the good priest's frugal supper. She left the glass, but he went away without touching it, and in the very afterglow of his parting blessing she announced that she had the makings of a pain within, and took the cordial with apparent approval.

Mike did not make any comment; he was tired and it was late, and long past their bedtime.

Biddy was wide awake and talkative from her tonic, and soon pursued the subject of conversation.

"What set the father out wid talking I do' know?" she inquired a little ill-humoredly. "'Twas thrue for him that we kape a dacint shop anyhow, an' how will it be in the way of poor Danny when it's finding the manes to put him where he is?"

"'Twa'n't that he mint at all," answered Mike from his pillow. "Didn't ye hear what he said?" after endeavoring fruitlessly to repeat it in his own words—"He's right, sure, about a b'y's getting thim books and having no char’acther. He thinks well of Danny, and he knows no harm of him. Wisha! what'll we do wid that b'y, Biddy, I do' know! 'Fadther,' says he to me today, 'why couldn't ye wait an' bring me into the wurruld on American soil,' says he 'and maybe I'd been president,' says he, and 'twas the thruth for him."

"I'd rather for him to be a priest meself," replied the mother.

"That's what Father Miles said himself the other day," announced Mike wide awake now. "'I wish he'd the makings of a good priest,' said he. 'There'll soon be need of good men and hard picking for 'em too,' said he, and he let a great sigh. "Tis money they want and place they want, most o' them bla'guard b'ys in the siminary. 'Tis the old fashioned min like mesilf that think however will they get souls through this life and through heaven's gate at last, wid clane names and God-fearin', dacint names left after them.' Thim was his own words indade."

"Idication was his cry always," said Bridget, blessing herself in the dark. "'Twas only last confission he took no note of me own sins while he redded himself in the face with why don't I kape Mary Ellen to the school, and myself not an hour in the day to rest my poor bones. 'I have to kape her in, to mind the shmall childer,' says I, an' 'twas thrue for me, so it was." She gave a jerk under the blankets, which represented the courtesy of the occasion. She had a great respect and some awe for Father Miles, but she considered herself to have held her ground in that discussion.

"We'll do our best by them all, sure," answered Mike. "'Tis tribbling me money I am ivery day," he added, gayly. "The lord-liftinant himsilf is no surer of a good buryin' than you an' me. What if we made a priest of Dan intirely?" with a great outburst of proper pride. "A son of your own at the alther saying mass for you, Biddy Flaherty from Glengariff!"

"He's no mind for it, more's the grief," answered the

mother, unexpectedly, shaking her head gloomily on the pillow, "but marruk me wuds now, he'll ride in his carriage when I'm under the sods, give me grace and you too Mike Bogan! Look at the airs of him and the toss of his head. 'Mother,' says he to me, 'I'm goin' to be a big man!' says he, 'whin I grow up. D' ye think anybody'll take me fer an Irishman?'"

"Bad cess to the bla'guard fer that then!" said Mike. "It's spoilin' him you are. 'Tis me own pride of heart to come from old Bantry, an' he lied to me yesterday gone, saying would I take him to see the old place. Wisha! he's got too much tongue, and he's spindin' me money for me."

But Biddy pretended to be falling asleep. This was not the first time that the honest pair had felt anxiety creeping into their pride about Dan. He frightened them sometimes; he was cleverer than they, and the mother had already stormed at the boy for his misdemeanors, in her garrulous fashion, but covered them from his father notwithstanding. She felt an assurance of the merely temporary damage of wild oats; she believed it was just as well for a boy to have his freedom and his fling. She even treated his known lies as if they were truth. An easy-going comfortable soul was Biddy, who with much shrewdness and only a trace of shrewishness got through this evil world as best she might.

The months flew by. Mike Bogan was a middle-aged man, and he and his wife looked somewhat elderly as they went to their pew in the broad aisle on Sunday morning. Danny usually came too, and the girls, but Dan looked contemptuous as he sat next his father and said his prayers perfunctorily. Sometimes he was not there at all, and Mike had a heavy heart under his stiff best coat. He was richer than any other member of Father Miles's parish, and he was known and respected everywhere as a good citizen. Even the most ardent believers in the temperance cause were known to say that little mischief would be done if all the rumsellers were such men as Mr. Bogan. He was generous and in his limited way public spirited. He did his duty to his neighbor as he saw it. Every one used liquor more or less, somebody must sell it, but a low groggery was as much a thing of shame to him as to any man. He never sold to boys, or to men who had had too much already. His shop was clean and whole-some, and in the evening when a dozen or more of his respectable acquaintances gathered after work for a social hour or two and a glass of whiskey to rest and cheer them after exposure, there was not a little good talk about affairs from their point of view, and plenty of honest fun. In their own houses very likely the rooms were close and hot, and the chairs hard and unrestful. The wife had taken her bit of recreation by daylight and visited her friends. This was their comfortable club-room, Mike Bogan's shop, and Mike himself the leader of the assembly. There was a sober-mindedness in the man; his companions were contented though he only looked on tolerantly at their fun, for the most part, without taking any active share himself.

One cool October evening the company was well gathered in, there was even a glow of wood fire in the stove, and two of the old men were sitting close beside it. Corny Sullivan had been a soldier in the British army for many years, he had been wounded at last at Sebastopol, and yet here he was, full of military lore and glory, and propped by a wooden leg. Corny was usually addressed as Timber-toes by his familiars; he was an irascible old fellow to deal with, but as clean as a whistle from long habit and even stately to look at in his arm-chair. He had a nephew with whom he made his home, who would give him an arm presently and get him home to bed. His mate was an old sailor much bent in the back by rheumatism, Jerry Bogan; who, though no relation, was tenderly treated by Mike, being old and poor. His score was never kept, but he seldom wanted for his evening grog. Jerry Bogan was a cheerful soul; the wit of the Celts and their pathetic wistfulness were delightful in him. The priest liked him, the doctor half loved him, this old-fashioned Irishman who had a graceful compliment or a thrust of wit for whoever came in his way. What a treasury of old Irish lore and legend was this old sailor! What broadness and good cheer and charity had been fostered in his sailor heart! The delight of little children with his clever tales and mysterious performances with bits of soft pine and a sharp jackknife, a very Baron Munchausen of adventure, and here he sat, round backed and head pushed forward like an old turtle, by the

fire. The other men sat or stood about the low-walled room. Mike was serving his friends; there was a clink of glass and a stirring and shaking, a pungent odor of tobacco, and much laughter.

"Soombody, whoiver it was, thrun a cat down in Tom Auley's well las' night," announced Corny Sullivan with more than usual gravity.

"They'll have no luck thin," says Jerry. "Anybody that meddles wid wather 'ill have no luck while they live, faix they 'ont thin."

"Tom Auley's been up watchin' this three nights now," confides the other old gossip. "Thim dirty b'y's troublin' his pigs in the sthy, and having every stramash about the place, all for revinge upon him for gettin' the police afther thim when they sthole his hins. 'Twas as well for him too, they're dirty bligards, the whole box and dice of them."

"Whishper now!" and Jerry pokes his great head closer to his friend. "The divil of 'em all is young Dan Bogan, Mike's son. Sorra a bit o' good is all his schoolin', and Mike's heart'll be soon broke from him. I see him goin' about wid his nose in the air. He's a pritty boy, but the divil is in him an' 'tis he ought to have been a praste wid his chances and Father Miles himself tarkin and tarkin wid him tryin' to make him a crown of pride to his people after all they did for him. There was niver a spade in his hand to touch the ground yet. Look at his poor father now! Look at Mike, that's grown old and gray since winther time." And they turned their eyes to the bar to refresh their memories with the sight of the disappointed face behind it.

There was a rattling at the door-latch just then and loud voices outside, and as the old men looked, young Dan Bogan came stumbling into the shop. Behind him were two low fellows, the worst in the town, they had all been drinking more than was good for them, and for the first time Mike Bogan saw his only son's boyish face reddened and stupid with whiskey. It had been an unbroken law that Dan should keep out of the shop with his comrades; now he strode forward with an absurd travesty of manliness, and demanded liquor for himself and his friends at his father's hands.

Mike staggered, his eyes glared with anger. His fatherly pride made him long to uphold the poor boy before so many witnesses. He reached for a glass, then he pushed it away— and with quick step reached Dan's side, caught him by the collar, and held him. One or two of the spectators chuckled with weak excitement, but the rest pitied Mike Bogan as he would have pitied them.

The angry father pointed his son's companions to the door, and after a moment's hesitation they went skulking out, and father and son disappeared up the stairway. Dan was a coward, he was glad to be thrust into his own bedroom upstairs, his head was dizzy, and he muttered only a feeble oath. Several of Mike Bogan's customers had kindly disappeared when he returned trying to look the same as ever, but one after another the great tears rolled down his cheeks. He never had faced despair till now; he turned his back to the men, and fumbled aimlessly among the bottles on the shelf. Some one came in, unconscious of the pitiful scene, and impatiently repeated his order to the shopkeeper.

"God help me, boys, I can't sell more this night!" he said brokenly. "Go home now and lave me to myself."

They were glad to go, though it cut the evening short. Jerry Bogan bundled his way last with his two canes. "Sind the b'y to say," he advised in a gruff whisper. "Sind him out wid a good captain now, Mike, 'twill make a man of him yet."

A man of him yet! alas, alas—for the hopes that had been growing so many years. Alas for the pride of a simple heart, alas for the day Mike Bogan came away from sunshiny old Bantry with his baby son in his arms for the sake of making that son a gentleman.

3

Winter had fairly set in, but the snow had not come, and the street was bleak and cold. The wind was stinging men's faces and piercing the wooden houses. A hard night for sailors coming on the coast—a bitter night for poor people everywhere.

From one house and another the lights went out in the street where the Bogans lived; at last there was no other lamp than theirs, in a window that lighted the outer stairs. Sometimes a woman's shadow passed across the curtain and waited there, drawing it away from the panes a moment as if to listen the better for a footstep that did not come. Poor Biddy had waited many a night before this. Her husband was far from well, the doctor said that his heart was not working right, and that he must be very careful, but the truth was that Mike's heart was almost broken by grief. Dan was going the downhill road, he had been drinking harder and harder, and spending a great deal of money. He had smashed more than one carriage and lamed more than one horse from the livery stables, and he had kept the lowest company in vilest dens. Now he threatened to go to New York, and it had come at last to being the only possible joy that he should come home at any time of night rather than disappear no one knew where. He had laughed in Father Miles's face when the good old man, after pleading with him, had tried to threaten him.

Biddy was in an agony of suspense as the night wore on. She dozed a little only to wake with a start, and listen for some welcome sound out in the cold night. Was her boy freezing to death somewhere? Other mothers only scolded if their sons were wild, but this was killing her and Mike, they had set their hopes so high. Mike was groaning dreadfully in his sleep to-night—the fire was burning low, and she did not dare to stir it. She took her worn rosary again and tried to tell its beads. "Mother of Pity, pray for us!" she said, wearily dropping the beads in her lap.

There was a sound in the street at last, but it was not of one man's stumbling feet, but of many. She was stiff with cold, she had slept long, and it was almost day. She rushed with strange apprehension to the doorway and stood with the flaring lamp in her hand at the top of the stairs. The voices were suddenly hushed. "Go for Father Miles!" said somebody in a hoarse voice, and she heard the words. They were carrying a burden, they brought it up to the mother who waited. In their arms lay her son stone dead; he had been stabbed in a fight, he had struck a man down who had sprung back at him like a tiger. Dan, little Dan, was dead, the luck of the Bogans, the end was here, and a wail that pierced the night, and chilled the hearts that heard it, was the first message of sorrow to the poor father in his uneasy sleep.

The group of men stood by—some of them had been drinking, but they were all awed and shocked. You would have believed every one of them to be on the side of law and order. Mike Bogan knew that the worst had happened. Biddy had rushed to him and fallen across the bed; for one minute her aggravating shrieks had stopped; he began to dress himself, but he was shaking too much; he stepped out to the kitchen and faced the frightened crowd.

"Is my son dead, then?" asked Mike Bogan of Bantry, with a piteous quiver of the lip, and nobody spoke. There was something glistening and awful about his pleasant Irish face. He tottered where he stood, he caught at a chair to steady himself. "The luck o' the Bogans is it?" and he smiled strangely, then a fierce hardness came across his face and changed it utterly. "Come down, come down!" he shouted, and snatching the key of the shop went down the stairs himself with great sure-footed leaps. What was in Mike? was he crazy with grief? They stood out of his way and saw him fling out bottle after bottle and shatter them against the wall. They saw him roll one cask after another to the doorway, and out into the street in the gray light of morning, and break through the staves with a heavy axe. Nobody dared to restrain his fury—there was a devil in him, they were afraid of the man in his blinded rage. The odor of whiskey and gin filled the cold air—some of them would have stolen the wasted liquor if they could, but no man there dared to move or speak, and it was not until the tall figure of Father Miles came along the street, and the patient eyes that seemed always to keep vigil, and the calm voice with its flavor of Bantry brogue, came to Mike Bogan's help, that he let himself be taken out of the wrecked shop and away from the spilt liquors to the shelter of his home.

A week later he was only a shadow of his sturdy self, he was lying on his bed dreaming of Bantry Bay and the road to Glengariff—the hedge roses were in bloom, and he was trudging along the road to see Biddy. He was working on the old farm at home and could not put the seed potatoes in their trench, for little Dan kept falling in and getting in his way. "Dan's not going to be plagued with the bad craps," he muttered to Father Miles who sat beside the bed. "Dan will be a fine squire in Ameriky," but the priest only stroked his hand as it twitched and lifted on the coverlet. What was Biddy doing, crying and putting the candles about him? Then Mike's poor brain grew steady.

"Oh, my God, if we were back in Bantry! I saw the gorse bloomin' in the t'atch d'ye know. Oh wisha wisha the poor ould home an' the green praties that day we come from it—with our luck smilin' us in the face."

"Whist darlin': kape aisy darlin'!" mourned Biddy, with a great sob. Father Miles sat straight and stern in his chair by the pillow—he had said the prayers for the dying, and the holy oil was already shining on Mike Bogan's forehead. The keeners were swaying themselves to and fro, there where they waited in the next room.

A Little
Captive Maid

1

The early winter twilight was falling over the town of Kenmare; a heavy open carriage with some belated travelers bounced and rattled along the smooth highway, hurrying toward the inn and a night's lodging. Two slender young figures drew back together into the leafless hedge by the roadside and stood there, whispering and keeping fast hold of hands after the simple fashion of children and lovers. There was an empty bird's nest close beside them, and they looked at that, and after they had watched the carriage a moment, and even laughed because Dinny Killoren, the driver, had recognized their presence by a loud snap of his whip, they still loitered. The girl turned away from her lover, who only looked at her, and felt the soft lining of the nest with the fingers of her left hand. Johnny Morris's handsome young face looked pinched and sad in the gray dampness of the dusk.

"The poor tidy cr'atures!" said Nora Connelly. "Look now at their little house, Johnny, how nate it is, and they gone from it. I mind the birds singing in the hedge one day last summer, and I walking by in the road."

"Wisha, 'tis our own tidy house I'm thinking of," said Johnny reproachfully; "I've long dramed of it, and now whatever will I do and you gone away to Ameriky? Faix, it's too hard for us, Norry dear; we'll get no luck from your goin'; 'twas the Lord mint us for aich other!"

"I'm safe to come back, darling," said Nora, troubled by her lover's lamentations. "'Tis for the love of you I'm going, sure, Johnny dear! I suppose 'tis yourself won't want me then aither, when I come back; sure they says folks dries all up there, and gets brown and small wit' the heat that's in it. Promise now that you'll say nothing sharp, so long as I'm fine an' rich coming home!"

"Don't break me heart, Nora, wit' your wild talk; who else but yourself would be joking, and our hearts breaking wit' parting, and this our last walk together," mourned the young man. "Come, darling, we must be going on. 'Tis a good way yet through the town, an' your aunt's ready to have my life now for not sinding you back at t'ree o'clock."

"Let her wait!" said Nora scornfully. "I'll be free of her, then, this time to-morrow. 'Tis herself'll be keenin' after me as if 'twas wakin' me she was, and the cold heart of stone that's inside her and no tears to her eyes. They might be glass buttons in her old head, they might then! I'd love you to the last day I lived, John Morris, if 'twas only to have the joke on her;" and Nora's eyes sparkled with fun. "I'd spite her if I could, the old crow! Sorra a bit of lave-takin' have I got from her yet, but to say I must sind home my passage-money inside the first month I'm out. Oh, but, Johnny, I'll be so lonesome there; 'tis a cold home I had since me mother died, but God help me when I'm far from it!" The girl and her lover were both crying now; Johnny kissed her and put his arms tenderly about her, there where they stood alone by the roadside; both knew that the dreaded hour of parting had come.

Presently, as if moved by the stern hand of fate rather than by their own will, they walked away along the road, still weeping. They came into the town, where lights were bright in the houses. There was the usual cheerful racket about the inn. The Lansdowne Arms seemed to be unusually popu-lous and merry for a winter night. Somebody called to Johnny Morris from a doorway, but he did not answer. Close by were the ruins of the old abbey, and he drew Nora with him be-tween the two stones which made a narrow entrance-way

to the grounds. It was dreary enough there among the win-
try shadows, the solemn shapes of the crumbling ruin, and
the rustling trees.

"Tell me now once more that you love me, darling," sobbed
the poor lad; "you're goin' away from me, Nora, an' 'tis you'll
find it aisy to forget. Everything you lave will be speakin' to me
of you. Oh, Nora, Nora! howiver will I lave you go to Ameriky!
I was no man at all, or why didn't I forbid it? 'Tis only I was
too poor to keep you back, God help me! *O Dea! O Dea!*"

"Be quiet now," said Nora. "I'll not forget you. I'll save all
my money till I'll come back to you. We're young, dear lad,
sure; kiss me now an' say good-by, my fine gay lad, and then
walk home quiet wit' me through the town. I call the holy
saints to hear me that I won't forget."

And so they kissed and parted, and walked home quiet
through the town as Nora had desired. She stopped here
and there for a parting word with a friend, and there was
even a sense of dignity and consequence in the poor child's
simple heart because she was going to set forth on her great
journey the next morning, while others would ignobly remain in Kenmare. Thank God, she had no father and mother
to undergo the pain of seeing her disappear forever from
their eyes. The poor heart-broken Irish folk who let their
young sons and daughters go away from them to America,—
which of us has stopped half long enough to think of their
sorrows and to pity them? What must it be to see the little
companies set forth on their way to the sea, knowing that
they will return no more? The fever for emigration is a heart-
rending sort of epidemic, and the boys and girls who dream
of riches and pleasure until they are impatient of their homes
in poor, beautiful Ireland! alas, they sail away on the crowded
ships to find hard work and hard fare, and know their mistakes about finding a fairy-land too late, too late! And Nora
Connelly's aunt had hated Johnny Morris, and laid this
scheme for separating them, under cover of the furtherance
of Nora's welfare. They had been lovers from their child-
hood, and Johnny's mother, from whom Nora had just parted
on that last sad evening, was a sickly woman and poor as
poverty. Johnny was like son and daughter both, he could
never leave her while she lived; they had needed all of Nora's
cheerfulness and love, and now they were going to lose her,

perhaps forever. Everybody knew how few come back from America; no wonder that these Irish hearts were sad with parting.

On the morrow there was little time for leave-takings. Some people tried to make it a day of jokes and festivities when such parties of emigrants left the country-side, but there was always too much sadness underneath the laughter; and the chilly rain fell that day as if Ireland herself wept for her wandering children,—poor Ireland, who gives her best to the great busy countries over seas, and longs for the time when she can be rich and busy herself, and keep the young people at home and happy in field and town. What does the foreign money cost that comes back to the cottage households broken as if by death? What does it cost to the aching hearts of fathers and mothers, to the homesick lads and girls in America, with the cold Atlantic between them and home?

2

The winter day was clear and cold, with a hint of coming spring in the blue sky. As you came up Barry Street, the main thoroughfare of a thriving American town, you could not help noticing the thick elm branches overhead, and the long rows of country horses and sleighs before the stores, and a general look of comfortably mingled country and city life.

The high-storied offices and warehouses came to an end just where the hill began to rise, and on the slope, to the left, was a terraced garden planted thick with fruit-trees and flowering shrubbery. Above this stood a large, old-fashioned white house close to the street. At first sight one was pleased with its look of comfort and provincial elegance, but as you approached, the whole lower story seemed unused. If you glanced up at a window of the second story, you were likely to see an elderly gentleman looking out, pale and unhappy, as if invalidism and its enforced idleness were peculiarly hard for him to bear. Sometimes you might catch sight of the edge of a newspaper, but there was never a book in his hand, there was never a child's face looking out to companion the old man. People always spoke of poor old Captain Balfour nowadays, but only a few months before, he had been the

leading business man of the city, absorbed in a dozen different enterprises. A widower and childless, he felt himself to
be alone indeed in this time of illness and despondency. Early
in life he had followed the sea, from choice, not necessity,
but for many years he had been master of the old house
and garden on Barry Street, his inherited home. People always spoke of him with deference and respect, they pitied
him now in his rich and pitiful old age. In the early autumn
a stroke of paralysis had dulled and disabled him, and its
effect was more and more puzzling, and irritating beside to
the captain's pride.

He more and more insisted upon charging his long cap-
tivity and uncomfortable condition at the doors of his medi-
cal advisers and the household. At first, in dark and gloomy
weather, or in days of unusual depression, a running fire of
comments was kept up toward those who treated him like a
child, and who made an apothecary's shop of his stomach,
and kept him upon such incomprehensible diet. A slice of
salt beef and a captain's biscuit were indignantly demanded
at these times, but it was touching to observe that the person in actual attendance was always treated with extreme
consideration or even humble gratitude, while the offend-
ers were always absent. "They" were guilty of all the wrongs
and kept the captain miserable; they were impersonal foes of
his peace; there never was anything but a kind word for
Mrs. Nash, the housekeeper, or Reilly, the faithful attendant;
there never were any personal rebukes administered to the
cook; and as for the doctor, Captain Balfour treated him as
one gentleman should treat another.

Until early in January, when once in a while even the hith-
erto respected Mrs. Nash was directly accused of a total lack
of judgment, and James Reilly could not do or say anything
to suit, and the lives of these honest persons became nearly
unbearable; the maid under Mrs. Nash's charge (for the
household had always been kept up exactly as in Mrs.
Balfour's day) could not be expected to consider the captain's
condition and her own responsibilities as his older and deeply
attached companions could, and, tired of the dullness and
idleness of the old house, fell to that state where dismissal
was inevitable. Then neither Mrs. Nash nor Reilly knew what
to do next; they were not as young as they had been, and, to

use their own words, minded the stairs. At last Reilly, a sensible man, proposed a change in the order of housekeeping. The captain might never come downstairs any more; they could shut up the dining-room and the parlors, and make their daily work much lighter.

"An' I won't say that I haven't got word for you of a tidy little girl," said Reilly, beseechingly. "She's a relation to my cousins the Donahues, and as busy as a sparrow. She'll work beside you an' the cook like your own shild, she will that, Mrs. Nash, and is a light-hearted shild the day through. She's just over too, the little greenhorn!"

"Perhaps she'll be just what we want, Reilly," agreed the housekeeper, after reflection. "Send her up to see me this very evening, if you're going where she is."

So the very next day, into the desolate old house came young Nora Connelly, a true child of the old country, with a laughing gray eye and a smooth girlish cheek, and a pretty touch of gold at the edge of the fair brown hair about her forehead. It was a serious little face, not beautiful, except in its delightful girlishness. She was a friendly, kindly little creature, fond of her simple pleasures, and willing to work hard the day through. The great house itself was a treasure-house of new experience, and she felt her position in the captain's family to be a valued promotion.

One morning, life looked very dark to the master. Everything had been going wrong since breakfast, and the captain rang for Reilly when he had just gone out, and Mrs. Nash was busy with a messenger.

"Go up, will you, Nora?" she said anxiously, "and say that I'll be there in a minute. Reilly's just left him."

And Nora sped away, nothing loath; she had never taken a satisfactory look at the master, and this was the fourth day since she had come to the house.

She opened the door and saw a handsome, fretful, tired old gentleman, whose newspaper had slipped from his hand and gone out of reach. She hurried to pick it up, without being told.

"Who are you?" inquired the captain, looking at her with considerable interest.

"Nora Connelly, sir," said the girl in a delicious Irish voice.

"I'm your new maid, sir, since Winsday. I feel very sorry for your bein' ill, sir."

"There's nothing the matter with me," growled the captain unexpectedly.

"Wisha, sir, I'm glad of that!" said Nora, with a wag of her head like a bird, and a light in her eye. "Mrs. Nash'll be here at once, sir, for your ordhers. She is daling wit' a boy below in the hall. You are looking fine an' comfortable the day, sir."

"I never was so uncomfortable in my life," said the captain. "You can open that window."

"And it snowing fast, sir? You'll let out all the fine heat; heat's very dear now and cold is cheap, so it is, with poor folks. 'Tis a great pity you've no turfs now to keep your fire in for you. 'Tis very strange there do be no turf in this foine country;" and she looked at the captain with a winning smile. The captain smiled back again in spite of himself.

Nora stood looking out of the window; she seemed to be thinking of herself instead of the invalid.

"What did you say your name was?" asked the old gentleman, a moment later, frowning his eyebrows at her like pieces of artillery.

"Plase, sir, I'm Nora Connelly, from the outside o' Kenmare." She made him the least bit of a courtesy, as if a sudden wind had bent her like a long-stemmed flower.

"How came you here?" His mouth straightened into a smile as he spoke, in spite of a determination to be severe.

"I'm but two weeks over, sir. I come over to me cousins, the Donahues, seeking me fortune. I'd like Ameriky, 'tis a fine place, sir, but I'm very homesick intirely. I'm as fast to be going back as I was to be coming away;" and she gave a soft sigh and turned away to brush the hearth.

"Well, you must be a good girl," said the captain, with great propriety, after a pause.

"'Deed, sir, I am that," responded Nora sincerely. "No one had a word to fling afther me and I coming away, but crying afther me. Nobody'll tell anything to my shame when my name'll be spoke at home. My mother brought me up well, God save her, she did, then!"

This unaffected report of her own good reputation was pleasing to Nora's employer; the sight of Nora's simple, pleasant Irish face and the freshness of her youth was the most delightful thing that had happened in many a dreary day. He felt in his waistcoat pocket with sudden impulse, sure of finding a bit of money there with which Nora Connelly might buy herself a ribbon. He was strongly inclined toward making her feel at home in the old house which had grown to be such a prison to himself. But there was no money in the pocket, as there always used to be when he was well. He had not needed any before in a long time. He began to fret about this, and to wonder what they had done with his pocket-book; it was ignominious to be treated like a school-boy. While he brooded over his wrongs, Nora heard Mrs. Nash's hurrying footsteps in the hall, but as she slipped away it was plain that she had found time enough to bestow her entire sympathy, and even affection, upon the captain in this brief interview.

"He's dull, poor gentleman,—he's very sad all day by himself, and so pleasant spoken, the cr'ature!" she said to herself indignantly, as she went running down the stairs.

It was not long before, to everybody's surprise, Captain Balfour gained strength, and began to feel so much better that Nora was often posted in the room or the hall close by to run his frequent errands and pick up his newspapers as they fell. This gave Mrs. Nash and Reilly a chance to look after their other business affairs, and to take their ease after so long a season of close attendance. The captain had a gruff way of asking, "Where's that little girl?" as if he only wished to see her to scold roundly; and Nora was always ready to come with her sewing or any bit of housework that could be carried, and to entertain her master by the hour. The more irritable his temper, the more unconscious and merry she always seemed.

"I was down last night wit' me cousins, so I was," she informed him one morning, while she brushed up the floor about the fireplace on her hands and knees. "You'd ought to see her little shild, sir; indade she's the darling cr'ature. I never saw any one so crabbed and smart for the size of her. She ain't the heighth of a bee's knee, sir!"

"Who isn't?" inquired the captain absently, attracted for the moment by the pleasing smile.

"Me cousin's little shild, sir," answered Nora appealingly, with a fear that she had failed in her choice of a subject. "'Tis no more than the heighth of a bee's knee she is, the colleen, and has every talk to you like a little grandmother,—the big words of her haves to come sideways out of her mouth. I'd like it well if her mother would dress her up prertty, and I'd go fetch her for you see."

The captain made an expressive sound of disdain, and Nora brushed away at the rug in silence. He looked out of the window and drummed on the arm of his chair. It was a very uncomfortable morning. There was a noise in the street, and Nora pricked up her ears with her head alert like a young hare, stood up on her knees, and listened.

"I'll warrant it's me heart's darling tooting at the fife," she exclaimed.

"Nothing but a parcel of boys," grumbled the captain.

"Faix it's he, then, the dacint lad!" said Nora, by this time close to the other front window. "Look at him now, sir, goin' by! He's alther-b'y in the church, and a lovely voice in him. Me cousins is going to have him learn music. That's 'The girl I left behind me,' he's got in the old fife now."

"Hard to tell what it is," growled the captain. "Anything for a racket, I dare say."

"She was only making an excuse of the brushing to linger with him a little while." Illustrated by Herbert Denman, engraved by W. B. Witte; *Scribner's Magazine*, 1891. Courtesy Dartmouth College Library.

"Faix, sir, I was thinking meself the tune come out of it tail first," agreed Nora with ready sympathy. "He's the big brother to the little sisther I told you of just now. 'Twas Dan Sullivan gave Johnny the old fife; himself used to play it in a company. There's a kay or two gone, I'm misthrusting; anyway there's teeth gone in the tune."

Nora was again brushing the floor industriously. The captain was listless and miserable; the silence vexed him even more than the harmless prattle.

"I used to play the flute pretty well myself when I was a young man," he said pleasantly, after a while.

"I'd like well to hear you, then, sir," said Nora enthusiastically. She was only making an excuse of the brushing to linger with him a little while. "Oh, but your honor would have liked to hear me mother sing. God give her rest, but she had the lovely voice for you! They'd be sinding for her from three towns away to sing with the fiddle for weddings and dances. If you'd hear her sing the 'Pride of Glencoe' 'twould take the heart out of you, it would indade."

"My wife was a most beautiful singer when she was young. I like to hear a pretty voice," said the captain sadly.

"'Twas me dear mother had it, then," answered Nora. "I do be often minding her singing when I'm falling asleep. I hear her voice very plain sometimes. My mother was from the north, sir, and she had tunes that didn't be known to the folks about Kenmare. 'Inniskillen Dragoon' was one of the best liked, and it went lovely with the wheel when she'd be spinning. Everybody'd be calling for her to sing that tune. Strangers would come and ask her for a song that were passing through the town. There was great talk always of me mother's singing; they'd know of her for twinty miles round. Whin I see the fire gone down in red coals like this, like our turf at home, and it does be growing dark, I remember well 'twas such times she'd sing like a bird for us, being through her long day's work, an' all of us round the fire kaping warm if we could, a winter night. Oh, but she'd sing then like a lark in the fields, God rest her!"

Nora brushed away a tear and blessed herself. "You'd like well to hear me mother sing, sir, I'm telling you God's truth," she said simply. And the old captain watched her and smiled, as if he were willing to hear more.

"Folks would pay her well, too. They'd all be afraid she'd stop when she'd once begin. There was nobody but herself could sing with the fiddle. I mind she came home one morning when she'd been sint for to a great wedding,—'twas a man's only daughter that owned his own land. And me mother came home to us wit' a collection of twilve and eight-pince tied up in her best apron corner. We'd as good as a wedding ourselves out of it too; 'twas she had the spinding hand, the cr'ature; and we had a roast goose that same night and asked frinds to it. Folks don't have the good fun here they has in the old counthry, sir, so they don't."

"There used to be good times here," said the poor old captain.

"I'm thinking 'twould be dale the better if you wint and stayed for a while over there," urged the girl affectionately. "It'll soon be comin' green and illigant while it's winther here still; the gorse'll be blooming, sir, and the little daisies thick under your two feet, and you'd be sitting out in the warm rain and sun, and feeling the good of the ground. If you'd go to Glengariff, I think you'd be soon well, I do, then, Captain Balfour, your honor, sir."

"I'm too old, Nora," replied the captain dismally, but not without interest.

"Sure there ain't a boy in the town that has the spark in his eye like yourself, sir," responded Nora, with encouraging heartiness. "I'd break away from these sober old folks and the docthers and all, and take ship, and you'd be soon over the say, and live like a lord in the first cabin; and you'd land aisy on the tinder in the cove o' Cork, and slape that night in the city, and go next day to the Eccles Hotel in Glengariff. Oh, wisha, the fine place it is wit' the say forninst the garden wall. You'd get a swim in the clane salt wather, and be as light as a bird. Sure I wouldn't be tased wit' so much docthoring and advising, and you none the betther wit' it."

"Why couldn't I have a swim in the sea here?" inquired the captain indulgently.

"Sure, it wouldn't be the same at all," responded Nora, with contempt. "'Tis the sayshore of the old country will do you the most good. The say is very salt entirely by Glengariff; the bay runs up to it, and you'd get a strong boatman would row you up and down, and you'd walk in the green lanes, and the folks in the houses would give you good-day; and if you'd be afther givin' old Mother Casey a trippence, she'd down on her two little knees and pray for your honor till you'd be running home like a light-horseman."

The old man laughed heartily for the first time that day. "I used to be the fastest runner of any lad in school," he said, with pride.

"Sure you might thry it again, wit' Mrs. Casey's kind help, sir," insisted the girl. "Now go to Glengariff this next month o' May, sir, do!"

"Perhaps I will," said the captain decidedly. "I'm not going to keep up this sort of thing much longer, I can tell them that! If they can't do me any good, they may say so, and I'll steer my own course. That's a good idea about the salt water."

The old man fell into a pleasant sleep, with a contented smile on his face. The fire flickered and snapped, and Nora sat still looking into it; her thoughts were far away. Perhaps her unkind aunt would find means to stop the letters between Johnny Morris and herself. Oh, if her mother were only alive, if the scattered household were once more together! It would be a long time at this rate, before she could go back to Johnny with a hundred pounds.

The fire settled itself together and sent up a bright blaze. The old man opened his eyes and looked bewildered; she stepped quickly to his side. "You'll be askin' for Mr. Reilly?" she said.

"No, no," responded the captain firmly. "What was the name of that place you were talking about?"

"Whiddy Island, sir, where me father was born?" Nora's thoughts had wandered far and wide; she was thinking that she had heard that land was cheap on Whiddy and the fishing fine. She and Johnny had often thought they might do better than in Kenmare.

"No, no," said the captain again, sternly.

"Oh, Glengariff," she exclaimed. "Yes, sir, we were talking"—

"That's it," responded the captain complacently. "I should like to know something more about the place."

"I was never in it but twice," exclaimed Nora, "but 'twas lovely there intirely. My father got work at fishin', and 'twas one summer we left Kenmare and went to a place, Balti-more was the name, beyond Glengariff itself, toward the illigant town of Bantry, sir. I saw Bantry, sir, when I was young. We were all alive and together then, my father and mother and all of us; the old shebeen we lived in looked like the skull of a house, it was so old, and the roof falling in on us, but thank God, we were happy in it. Oh, Ireland's the lovely counthry, sir."

"No bad people at all there?" asked the captain, looking at her kindly.

"Oh, sir, there are then," said the little maid regretfully. "I have sins upon my own soul, truth I have, sir. The sin of staling was my black shame when I was growing up, then."

"What did you ever steal, child?" asked the captain.

"Mostly eggs, sir," said Nora, humbly.

"I dare say you were hungry," said the old man, taking up his newspaper and pretending to frown at the shipping-list.

"Oh, no, captain, 'twas not that always. I used to follow an old spickled hen of my mother's and wait for the egg. I'd track her within the furze, and when I'd be two days gettin' two eggs I'd run wit' 'em to sell 'em, and 'twas to buy things to sew for me doll I'd spind the money. I'd ought to make confission for it now, too. I'm ashamed, thinkin' of it. And the spickled hen was one that laid very large white eggs intirely, and whiles my poor mother would be missing them and thinking the old hen was no good and had best be killed, the honest cr'ature, and go to market that way when poulthry was dear. I'd like one of her eggs now to boil it myself for you, sir; t'would be fine atin' for you coming right in from some place under the green bushes. I think that hen long's dead, I didn't see her a long while before I was lavin'. A woman called Johanna Spillane bought her from my aunt when my mother was dead. She was a very honest, good hen; a top-knot hen, sir."

"I dare say," said the captain, looking at his newspaper; he did not know why the simple chatter touched and pleased him so. He shrugged his shoulders and moved about in his easy-chair, frowned still more at the shipping-list, and so got the better of his emotion."

"I see that the old brig Miranda has gone ashore on the Florida Keys," he said, as if speaking to a large audience of retired shipmasters. "Stove her bows, rigging cut loose and washed overboard; total wreck. I suppose you never saw a wreck?" He turned and regarded Nora affectionately.

"I did, sir, then," said Nora Connelly, flushing with satisfaction. "We got news of it one morning early, and all trooped to the shore, every grown person and child in the place, laving out Mother Dolan, the ould lady that had no use of her two legs; and all the women, me mother and all, took their babies to her and left them, and she entreatin'—you'd hear the bawls of her a mile away—that some of the folks would take her wit' 'em on their backs to see what would she get wit' the rest; but we left her screechin' wit' all the poor shilder, and I was there with the first, and the sun coming up, and the ship breaking up fine out a little way in the rocks. 'Twas loaded with sweet oranges she was, and they all comin' ashore like yellow ducklings in the high wather. I got me fill for once, I did, indeed."

"Dear, dear," said the captain. "Did the crew get ashore?"

"Well, I belave not, sir, but I couldn't rightly say. I was small, and I took no notice. I mind there were strangers round that day, but sailors or the nixt parish was one to me then. The tide was going out soon, and then we swarmed aboard, and wisha, the old ship tipped up wit' us in it, and I thought I was killed. 'Twas a foine vessel, all gilded round the cabin walls, and I thought in vain 'twould be one like her comin' to Ameriky. There was wines aboard, too, and all the men got their fill. Mesilf was gatherin' me little petticoat full of oranges that bobbed in the wather in the downside of the deck. Wisha, sir, the min were pushin' me and the other shilder into the wather; they were very soon tight, sir, and my own father was wit' 'em, God rest his soul! and his cheeks as red as two roses. Some busybody caught him ashore and took him to the magistrate,—that was the squire of our place, sir, and an illigant gentleman. The bliguards was holdin' my father, and I running along, screechin' for fear he'd be goin' to jail on me. The old squire began to laugh, poor man, when he saw who it was, and says he, 'Is it yoursilf, Davy?' and says my father, 'It's mesilf, God save your honor, very tight intirely, and feelin' as foine as any lord in Ireland. Lave me go, and I'll soon slape it off under the next furze-bush that'll stop still long enough for me by the roadside,' says he. The squire says, 'Lave him go, boys, 'twas from his ating the oranges!' says he, and the folks give a great laugh all round. He was doin' no harrum, the poor man! I run away again to the say, then; I forget was there any more happened that day."

"She must have been a fruiter from the Mediterranean. I can't think what she was doing up there on the west coast, out of her bearings," said the captain.

"Faix, sir, I couldn't tell you where she was from, if it's the ship you mane; but she wint no further than our parish and the Black Rocks. I heard tell of plinty other foine wrecks, but I was to that mesilf."

3

The lengthening days of late winter went slowly by, and at last it was spring, and the windows were left open all day in the captain's room. The household had accepted the fact that nobody pleased the invalid as Nora did, and there was no feeling of jealousy; it was impossible not to be grateful to any one who could invariably spread the oil of sympathy and kindness over such troubled waters. James Reilly and Mrs. Nash often agreed upon the fact that the captain kept all the will he ever had, but little of the good judgment. Yet, in spite of this they took it upon them to argue with him upon every mistaken point. Nora alone had the art of giving a wide berth to dangerous subjects of conversation, and she could twist almost every sort of persistence or aggravation into a clever joke. She had grown very fond of the lonely old man; the instinct toward motherliness in her simple heart was always ready to shelter him from his fancied wrongs, and to quiet him in the darkest hours of fretfulness and pain.

Young Nora Connelly's face had grown thin during the long winter, and she lost the pretty color from her cheeks as spring came on. She was used to the mild air of Ireland, and to an out-of-door life, and she could not feel like herself in the close rooms of Captain Balfour's house on Barry Street. By the time that the first daffodils were in bloom on the south terrace, she longed inexpressibly for the open air, and used to disappear from even the captain's sight into the garden, where at times she took her turn with the gardeners at spading up the rich soil, and worked with a zeal which put to shame their languid efforts. Something troubled the girl, however; she looked older and less happy; sometimes it was very plain to see that she had been crying.

One morning, when she had been delayed unusually with her downstairs work, the captain grew so impatient that he sent Reilly away to find her. Nora quickly set down a silver candlestick, and wiped her powdery hands upon her apron as she ran upstairs. The captain was standing in the middle of the floor, scowling like a pirate in a picture-book, and even when Nora came in, he did not smile. "I'm going out to take a walk," he said angrily.

"Come on, then, sir," said Nora. "I'll run for your coat and hat, if you'll tell me where"—

"Pooh, pooh, child!"—the pacified captain was smiling broadly. "I only want to take a couple of turns here in the hall. You forget how long I've been house-bound. I'm a good deal better; I'll have that meddling Reilly know it, too; and I won't be told what I may do and what I may not."

"'Tis thrue for you, sir," said Nora amiably. "Steady your-self with my arrum, now, and we'll go to the far end of the hall and back again. 'Twas the docther himself said a while ago that ye'd ought to thry walking more, and 'twas your honor was like to have the life of him. You're a very conthrairy gentleman, if I may be so bold!"

The captain laughed, but the business of dragging his poor heavy foot was more serious than he had expected, in spite of all his brave determination. Nora did her best to beguile him from too much consciousness of his feebleness and disappointment.

"Sure if you'd see ould Mother Killahan come hobbling into church, you'd think yourself as good as a greyhound," she said presently, while the master rested in one of the chairs at the hall's end. "She's very old intirely. I saw her myself asleep at her beads this morning, but she do be very steady on her two knees, and whiles she prays and says a bead or two, and whiles she gets a bit of sleep, the poor cr'ature. She does be staying in the church a dale this cold weather, and Father Dunn is very aisy with her. She makes the stations every morning of the year, so she does, and one day she come t'rough the deep snow in a great storm there was, and she fell down with weakness on the church steps; and they told Father Dunn, and said how would they get her home, and he come running himself, scolding all the way, and took her up in his arrums, and wint back with her to his own house. You'd thought she was his own mother, sir. 'She's one of God's poor,' says he, with the tears in his eyes. Oh, captain, sir! I wish it was Father Dunn was praste to you, I do then! I'm thinking he'd know what prayers would be right for you; and himself was born in the country forninst Glengariff, and would tell you how foine it was for your stringth. If you'd get better, sir, and we'd meet him on the street, we'd be afther asking his riverence."

The captain made no answer; he was tired and spent, and sank into his disdained easy-chair, grateful for its comfortable support. The mention of possible help for his feeble frame from any source clung to his erratic memory, and after a few days one of the thoughts that haunted his mind was that Father Dunn, a kind-faced, elderly man, might be of use in this great emergency. To everybody's surprise, his bodily strength seemed to be slowly returning as the spring days went by, but there was oftener and oftener an appealing, childish look in his face,—the firm lines of it were blurred, even while there was a steady renewing of his shattered forces. At last he was able to drive down the busy street one day, with Reilly, in his familiar chaise. The captain's old friends gathered to welcome him, and he responded to their salutations with dignity and evident pleasure; but once or twice, when some one congratulated him upon certain successful matters of business which he had planned before his illness, there was only a troubled look of dullness and almost pain for answer.

One day, Nora Connelly stole out into the garden in the afternoon, and sat there idly under an old peach-tree. The green fruit showed itself thick all along the slender boughs. Nora had been crying already, and now she looked up through the green leaves at the far blue sky, and then began to cry again. She was sadly homesick, poor child! She longed for her lover, whom she feared now never to see. Like a picture she recalled the familiar little group of thatched houses at home, with their white walls and the narrow green lanes between; she saw the pink daisies underfoot, and the golden gorse climbing the hill till it stood against the white clouds.

She remembered the figures of the blue-cloaked women who went and came, the barefooted, merry children, and the dabbling ducks; then she fell to thinking lovingly of her last walk with Johnny Morris, the empty bird's nest, and all their hopes and promises the night before she left home. She had been willful in yielding to her aunt's plans; she knew that Johnny feared her faithlessness, but it was all for love of him that she had left him. She knew how poor they were at home. She had faithfully sent a pound a month to her aunt, and though she had had angry appeals for more, the other pound that she could spare, leaving but little for herself, had been sent in secret to Johnny's mother. She always dreaded the day when her avaricious aunt should find this out and empty all the vials of her wrath of covetousness. Nora, to use her own expression, was as much in dread of this aunt as if the sea were a dry ditch. Alas! she was still the same poor Nora Connelly, though rich and busy America stretched eastward and westward from where she made her new home. It was only by keeping her pounds in her pocket that she could gather enough to be of real and permanent use to those she loved; and yet their every-day woes, real or fictitious, stole the pounds from her one by one.

So she sat crying under the peach-tree until the pale old captain came by, in the box-bordered walk, with scuffling, unsteady steps. He saw Nora and stopped, leaning on his cane.

"Come, come, Nora!" he said anxiously. "What's the matter, my girl?"

Nora looked up at him and smiled instantly. It was as if the warm Irish sunshine had broken out in the middle of a May shower. A long spray of purple foxglove grew at her feet, and the captain glanced down at it. The sight of it was almost more than she could bear, this flower that grew in the hedgerows at home. She felt as if the flower were exiled like herself and trying to grow in a strange country.

"Don't touch it, sir," she faltered, as the captain moved it with his cane; "'tis very bad luck to meddle with that: they say yourself will be meddled with by the fairies. Fairy Fingers is the name of that flower; we were niver left pick it. Oh, but it minds me of home!"

"What's the matter with you to-day?" asked the captain.

"I've been feeling very sad, sir; I can't help it, either, thinkin' o' me home I've left and me dear lad that I'll see no more. I was wrong to lave him, I was indeed."

"What lad?" asked Captain Balfour suspiciously. "I'll have no nonsense nor lads about my place. You're too young"— He looked sharply at the tearful young face. "Mrs. Nash can't spare you, either," he added humbly, in a different tone.

"Faix, sir, it's at home he is, in the old counthry, without me; he'll niver throuble ye, me poor Johnny," Nora explained sadly enough. She had risen with proper courtesy, and was standing by the old man; now she ventured to take hold of his arm. He looked flushed and eager, and she forgot herself in the instinct to take care of him.

"Where do you be going so fast?" she asked with a little laugh. "I'm afther believing 'tis running away you are."

The captain regarded her solemnly; then he laughed, too. "Come with me," he said. "I'm going to make a call."

"Where would it be?" demanded the girl, with less than her usual deference.

"Come, come! I want to be off," insisted the old gentleman. "We'll go out of this little gate in the fence. I've got to see your Father Dunn on a matter of business," he said, as if he had no idea of accepting any remonstrance.

Nora knew that the doctor and all the elder members of the household approved of her master's amusing himself and taking all the exercise he could. She herself approved his present intentions entirely; it was not for her to battle with the head of the house, at any rate, so she dutifully and with great interest and anxiety set forth beside him down the path, on the alert for any falterings or missteps.

They went out at the gate in the high fence; the master remembered where to find the key, and he seemed in excellent spirits. The side street led them down the hill to Father Dunn's house, but when they reached it the poor captain was tired out. Nora began to be frightened, as she stole a look at him. She had forgotten, in the pride of her own youthful strength, that it would be such a long walk for him. She was anxious about the interview with Father Dunn; she had no idea how to account for their presence, but she had small opinion of the merits and ability of the captain's own parish minister, and felt confident of the good result, in some way, of the visit. Presently the priest's quick step was heard in the passage; Nora rose dutifully as he came in, but was only noticed by a kindly glance. The old captain tried to rise, too, but could not, and Father Dunn and he greeted each other with evident regard and respect. Father Dunn sat down with a questioning look; he was a busy man with a great parish, and almost every one of his visitors came to him with an important errand.

The room was stiff-looking and a little bare; everything in it was well worn. There was a fine portrait of Father Dunn's predecessor, or, it should rather be said, a poor portrait of a fine man, whose personal goodness and power of doing Christian service shone in his face. Father Miles had been the first priest in that fast-growing inland town, and the captain had known and respected him. He did not say anything now, but sat looking up, much pleased, at the picture. This parlor of the priest's house had a strangely public and impersonal look; it had been the scene of many parish weddings and christenings, and sober givings of rebuke and kindly counsel. Nora gazed about her with awe; she had been brought up in great reverence of holy things and of her spiritual pastors and masters; but she could not help noticing that the captain was a little astray in these first few moments. There stole in upon his pleased contemplation of the portrait a fretful sense of doing an unaccustomed thing, and he could not regain his familiar dignity and self-possession; that conscious right to authority which through long years had stood him in such good stead. He was only a poor broken-down, sick old man; he had never quite understood the truth about himself before, and the thought choked him; he could not speak.

"The masther was coveting to spake with your riverence about Glengariff," ventured Nora timidly, feeling at last that the success of the visit depended wholly upon herself.

"Oh, Glengariff, indeed!" exclaimed the good priest, much relieved. He had discovered the pathetic situation at last, and his face grew compassionate.

"This little girl seems to believe that it would set me up to have a change of air. I haven't been very well, Father Dunn." The captain was quite himself again for the moment, as he spoke. "You may not have heard that the doctors have had hold of me lately? Nora, here, has been looking after me very well, and she speaks of some sea-bathing on your Irish coast. I may not be able to leave my business long enough to do any good. It's going to the dogs, at any rate, but I've got enough to carry me through."

Nora was flushing with eagerness, but the priest saw how white the old captain's fingers were, where they clasped his walking-stick, how blurred and feeble his face had grown. The thought of the green hills and hollows along the old familiar shore, the lovely reaches of the bay, the soft air, the flowery hedgerows, came to his mind as if he had been among them but yesterday.

"I wish that you were there, sir, I do indeed," said Father Dunn. "It is nearer like heaven than any spot in the world to me, is old Glengariff. You would be pleased there, I'm certain. But you're not strong enough for the voyage, I fear, Captain Balfour. You'd best wait a bit and regain your strength a little more. A man's home is best, I think, when he's not well."

The captain and Nora both looked defeated. Father Dunn saw their sadness, and was sure that his kindest duty was to interest this poor guest, and to make a pleasure for him, if possible.

"I can tell you all about it, sir, and how you might get there," he went on hastily, shaking his head to some one who had come to summon him. "Land at Queenstown, go right up to Cork and pass the night, and then by rail and coach next day, — 'tis but a brief journey and you're there. 'Tis a grand little hotel you'll find close to the bay, — 'twas like a palace to me in my boyhood, with the fine tourists coming and going; well, I wish we were there this day, and I showing you up and down the length of the green country."

"Just what I want. I've been a busy man, but when I take a holiday, give me none of your noisy towns," said the captain, eager and cheerful again.

"You'd be so still there that a bird lighting in the thatch would wake you," said Father Dunn. "Ah, 'tis many a long year since I saw the place. I dream of it by night sometimes, Captain Balfour, God bless it!"

Nora could not keep back the ready tears. The very thought that his reverence had grown to manhood in her own dear country-side was too much for her.

"You're not thinking of going over this summer?" asked the captain wistfully. "I should be gratified if you would bear me company, sir; I'd try to do my part to make it pleasant." But the good father shook his head and rose hastily, to stand by the window that looked out into his little garden.

"We'd make a good company," said he presently, turning toward them and smiling, "with young Nora here to show us our way. You can't have had time yet, my child, to forget the old roads across country!" and Nora fairly sobbed.

"Pray for the likes of me, sir!" she faltered, and covered her face with her hands. "Oh, pray for the masther too, your riverence Father Dunn, sir; 'tis very wake he is, and 'tis mesilf that's very lonesome in Ameriky, an' I'm afther laving the one I love!"

"Be quiet, now!" said the priest gravely, checking her with a kindly touch of his hand, and glancing at Captain Balfour. The poor old man looked in a worried way from one to the other, and Father Dunn went away to fetch him a glass of wine. Then he was ready to go home, and Father Dunn got his hat and big cane, pleading that an errand was taking him in the same direction.

"If I thought it would do me any good, I would start for that place we were speaking of to-morrow," said the captain as they set forth. "You know to what I refer, the sea-bathing and all." The priest walked slowly; the captain's steps grew more and more faltering and unsteady. Nora Connelly followed anxiously. There flitted through Father Dunn's mind phrases out of the old Bible story,—"a great man and honorable;" "a valiant man and rich," "but a leper;" the little captive maid that brought him to the man of God. Alas, Father Dunn could tell the captain of no waters of Jordan that would make him a sound man; he could only say to him, "Go in peace," like the prophet of old.

When they reached home the household already sought the captain in despair, but it happened that nobody was in the wide, cool hall as they entered.

"I hope that you will come in and take a glass of wine with me. You have treated me with brotherly kindness, sir," said the master of the house; but Father Dunn shook his head and smiled as he made the old man comfortable in a corner of the broad sofa, taking his hat and stick from him and giving them to Nora. "Not to-day, Captain Balfour, if you will excuse me."

The captain looked disappointed and childish. "I am going to send you a bottle of my father's best old madeira," he said. "Sometimes, when a man is tired out or has a friend come in to dine"— But he was too weary himself to finish the sentence. The old house was very still; there were distant voices in the garden; a door at the end of the hall opened into an arbor where flickers of light were shining through the green vine leaves. Everything was stately and handsome; there was a touch everywhere of that colonial elegance of the captain's grandfather's time which had never been sacrificed to the demon of change, that restless American spirit which has spoiled the beauty of so many fine and simple old houses.

The priest was used to seeing a different sort of household interior, his work was among the poor. Then he looked again at the house's owner, an old man, sick, sorry, and alone. "God bless you, sir," he said. "I must be going now."

"Come and see me again," said the captain, opening his eyes. "You are a good man; I am glad to have your blessing." The words were spoken with a manly simplicity and directness that had always been liked by Captain Balfour's friends. "Nora," he whispered, when Father Dunn had gone, "we'll say nothing to Mrs. Nash. I must rest a little while here before we get up the stairs."

4

Toward the end of the summer, things had grown steadily worse, and Captain Balfour was known to be failing fast. The clerks had ceased to come for his signature long before; he had forgotten all about business and pleasure too, and slept a good deal, and sometimes was glad to see his friends and sometimes indifferent to their presence. But one day, when he felt well enough to sit in his great chair by the window, he told Mr. Barton, his good friend and lawyer, that he wished to attend to a small matter of business. "I've arranged everything long ago, as an aging man should," he said. "I don't know that there's any hurry, but I'll mention this item while I think of it. Nora, you may go downstairs," he said sharply to the girl, who had just entered upon an errand of luncheon or medicine, and Nora disappeared; she remembered afterward that it was the only time when, of his own accord and seeming impatience, he had sent her away.

Reilly and Mrs. Nash bore no ill-will toward their young housemate; they were reasonable enough to regard Captain Balfour's fondness for her with approval. There was something so devoted and single-hearted about the young Irish girl that they had become fond of her themselves. They had their own plans for the future, and looked forward to being married when the captain should have no more need of them. It really hurt Mrs. Nash's feelings when she often found Nora in tears, for the desperate longing for home and for Johnny Morris grew worse in the child's affectionate heart instead of better.

One day Reilly had gone down town, leaving the captain asleep. Nora was on guard; Mrs. Nash was at hand in the next room with her sewing, and Nora sat still by the window; the captain was apt to sleep long and heavily at this time of the day. She was busy with some crocheting; it was some edging of a pattern that the sisters of Kenmare had taught Johnny Morris's mother. She gave a little sigh at last and folded her hands in her lap; her gray Irish eyes were blinded with tears.

"What's the matter, child?" asked the captain unexpectedly; his voice sounded very feeble.

Nora started; she had forgotten him and his house.

"Will you have anything, sir?" she asked anxiously.

"No, no; what's the matter child?" asked the old man kindly.

"'Tis me old story; I'm longing for me home, and I can't help it if I died too. I'm like a thing torn up by the roots and left in the road. You're very good, sir, and I would never lave the house and you in it, but 'tis home I think of by night and by day; how ever will I get home?"

Captain Balfour looked at her compassionately. "You're a good girl, Nora; perhaps you'll go home before long," he said.

"'Tis sorra a few goes back; Ameriky's the same as heaven

for the like o' that," answered Nora, trying to smile, and dry-
ing her eyes. "There's many'd go back too but for the presents every one looks to have; 'twould take a dale of money
to plase the whole road as you pass by. 'Tis a kind of fever
the young ones has to be laving home. Some laves good
steady work and home and friends, that might do well.
There's getting to be fine chances for smart ones there with
so many laving."

"Yes, yes," said the captain; "we'll talk that over another
time, I want to go to sleep now;" and Nora flushed with shame
and took up her crocheting again. "'Twas me hope of growing rich, and me aunt's tongue shaming me that gets the
blame," she murmured to herself. The sick man's hands
looked very white and thin on the sides of his chair; she
looked at them and at his face, and her heart smote her for
selfishness. She was glad to be in America, after all.

They never said anything to each other now about going
to Glengariff; a good many days slipped by when the captain
hardly spoke except to answer questions; but in restless evenings, when he could not sleep, people who passed by in
the street could hear Nora singing her old familiar songs of
love and war, sometimes in monotonous, plaintive cadences
that repeated and repeated a refrain, sometimes in livelier
measure, with strange thrilling catches and prolonged high
notes, as a bird might sing to its mate in the early dawn out
in the wild green pastures. The lovely weird songs of the
ancient Irish folk, how old they are, how sweet they are,
who can tell? but now and then a listener of the new world
of the western seas hears them with deep delight, hears them
with a strange, golden sense of dim remembrance, a true,
far-descended birthright of remembrance that can only come
from inheritance of Celtic blood.

When the frost had fallen on the old garden, Captain Balfour
died, and his year of trouble was ended. Reilly and Mrs. Nash,
the cook and Nora, cried bitterly in the kitchen, where the
sudden news found them. Nobody could wish him to come
back, but they cried the more when they thought of that.
There was a great deal said about him in the newspapers;
about his usefulness in town and State, his wealth, his character, and his history; but nobody knew so well as this faith-

ful household how comfortable he had made his lonely home for other people; and those who knew him best thought most of his kindness, his simple manliness, and sincerity of word and deed.

The evening after the funeral, Nora was all alone in her little room under the high roof. She sat on the broad seat of a dormer window, where she could look far out over the city roofs to a glimpse of the country beyond. There was a new moon in the sky, the sunset was clear, the early autumn weather was growing warm again.

The old house was to belong to a nephew of the captain, his only near relative, who had spent a great many years abroad with an invalid wife; it was to be closed for the present, and Mrs. Nash and Mr. Reilly were to be married and live there all winter, and then go up country to live in the spring, where Mrs. Nash owned a little farm. She was of north of Ireland birth, was Mrs. Nash; her first husband had been an American. She told Nora again and again that she might always have a home with her, but the fact remained that Nora must find herself a new place, and she sat in the window wondering with a heavy heart what was going to happen to her. All the way to the burying-ground and back again in the carriage, with the rest of the household, she had sobbed and mourned, but she cried for herself as much as for the captain. Poor little Irish Nora, with her warm heart and her quick instincts and sympathies! how sadly she thought now of the old talk about going to Glengariff; she had clung long to her vain hope that the dream would come true, and that the old captain and his household were all going over seas together, and so she should get home. Would anybody in America ever be so kind again and need her so much as the captain?

Some one had come to the foot of the stairs and was calling Nora loudly again and again. It was dark in the upper entryway, however bright the west had looked just now from her window. She left her little room in confusion; she had begun already to look over her bits of things, her few clothes and treasures, before she packed them to go away. Mrs. Nash seemed to be in a most important hurry, and said that they were both wanted in the dining-room, and it was very pleasant somehow to be wanted and made of consequence again. She had begun to feel like such an unnecessary, stray little person in the house.

The lamps were lighted in the handsome old dining-room, it was orderly and sedate; one who knew the room half expected to see Captain Balfour's fine figure appear in the doorway to join the waiting group. There were some dark portraits on the wall, and the old Balfour silver stood on the long sideboard. Mrs. Nash had set out all the best furnishings, for this day when the master of the house left it forever.

There were not many persons present, and Nora sat down, as some one bade her, feeling very disrespectful as she did it. Mr. Barton, the lawyer, began to read slowly from a large folded paper; it dawned presently upon Nora that this was the poor captain's will. There was a long bequest to the next of kin, there were public gifts, and gifts to different friends, and handsome legacies to faithful Mrs. Nash and James Reilly, and presently the reading was over. There was something quite grand in listening to this talk of thousands and estates, but little Nora, who had no call, as she told herself, to look for anything, felt the more lonely and friendless as she listened. There was a murmur of respectful comment as the reading ended, but Mr. Barton was opening another paper, a small sheet, and looked about him, expecting further attention.

"I am sure that no one will object to the carrying out of our deceased friend's wishes as affirmed in this more recent memorandum. Captain Balfour was already infirm at the time when he gave me the directions, but, as far as I could judge, entirely clear in his mind. He dictated to me the following bequest and signed it. The signature is, I own, nearly illegible, but I am sure that, under the somewhat affecting circumstances, there will be no opposition."

"I desire" (read Mr. Barton slowly), — "I desire the executors of my will to pay five hundred dollars within one month after my death to Nora Connelly; also, to secure her comfortable second-class passage to the port of Queenstown, in Ireland. I mean that, if she still desires, she may return to her home. I am sensible of her patience and kindness, and I

"Dinny Killoren laughed aloud on the side-car." Illustrated by Herbert Denman; *Scribner's Magazine*, 1891. Courtesy Dartmouth College Library.

attempt in this poor way to express my gratitude to a good girl. I wish her a safe return, and that every happiness may attend her future life.

"JOHN BALFOUR"

"'Tis a hundred pounds for ye an' yer passage, me darlin'," whispered the cook excitedly. "'Tis mesilf knew you wouldn't be forgotten an' the rist of us so well remimbered. 'Tis foine luck for ye; Heaven rist his soul, the poor captain!"

Nora was sitting pale and silent. She did not cry now; her heart was deeply touched, her thoughts flew homeward. She seemed to hear the white waves breaking about the ship, and to see the far deep colors of the Irish shore. For Johnny had said again and again that if they had a hundred pounds and their two pairs of hands, he could do as well with his little farm as any man in Ireland.

"Sind for your lad to come over," urged Cousin Donahue, a day later, when the news had been told; but Nora proudly shook her head. She had asked for her passage the very next week. It was a fine country, America, for those with the courage for it, but not for Nora Connelly, that had left her heart behind her. Cousin Donahue laughed and shook his head at such folly, and offered a week's free lodging to herself and Johnny the next spring, when she'd be the second time a greenhorn coming over. But Nora laughed too, and sailed away one Saturday morning in late October, across the windy sea to Ireland.

5

Again it was gray twilight after a short autumn day in the old country, and a tall Irish lad was walking along the high-road that led into Kenmare. He was strong and eager for work, but his young heart was heavy within him. The piece of land which he held needed two men's labor, and work as he might, he must fall behind with his rent.

It was three years since that had happened before, and he had tried so hard to do well with his crops, and had even painfully read a book that was wise about crops which the agent had lent him, and talked much besides with all the good farmers. It was no use, he could not hold his own; times were bad and sorrowful, and Nora was away. He had believed that, whatever happened to her fortunes, he should be able in time to send for her himself and be a well-off man. Oh, for a hundred pounds in his pocket to renew his wornout land! to pay a man to help him with the new ditching. Oh, for courage to fight his way to independence on Irish ground! "I've only got my heart and my two hands, God forgive me!" said Johnny Morris aloud. "God be good to me and Norry, and me poor mother! May be I'll be after getting a letter from me darling the night; 'tis long since she wrote."

He stepped back among the bushes to let a side-car pass that had come up suddenly behind him. He recognized the step of Dinny Killoren's fast pacer, and looked to see if there were room on the car for another passenger, or if perhaps Dinny might be alone and glad to have company. There was only Dinny himself and a woman, who gave a strange cry. The pacer stopped, and Johnny's heart beat within him as if it would come out of his breast. "My God, who's this?" he said.

"Lift me down, lift me down!" said the girl. "Oh, God be thanked, I'm here!" And Johnny leaped forward and caught Nora Connelly in his arms.

"Is it yoursilf?" he faltered, and Nora said, "It's mesilf indeed, then." Dinny Killoren laughed aloud on the side-car, with his pacer backing and jumping and threatening to upset all Nora's goods in the road. There was a house near by; a whiff of turf smoke, drifting low in the damp air, blew into Nora's face; she heard the bells begin to ring in Kenmare. It was the evening of a saint's day, and they rang and rang, and Nora had come home.

So she married the lad she loved, and was a kind daughter to his mother. They spent a good bit of the captain's money on their farm, and gave it a fine start, and were able to flaunt their prosperity in the face of that unkind aunt who had wished to make them spend their lives apart. They were seen early on market days in Kenmare, and Nora only laughed when foolish young people said that the only decent country in the world was America. Sometimes she sat in her doorway in the long summer evening and thought affectionately of Captain Balfour, the poor, kind gentleman, and blessed herself devoutly. Often she said a prayer for him on Sunday morning as she knelt in the parish church, with flocks of blackbirds singing outside among the green hedges, under the lovely Irish sky.

Between Mass and Vespers

Mass was over; the noonday sun was so bright at the church door that, instead of waiting there in a sober expectant group, three middle-aged men of the parish went a few steps westward to stand in the shade of a great maple-tree. There they stood watching the people go by—the small boys and the chattering girls. Now and then one of the older men or women said a few words in Irish to Dennis Call or John Mulligan by way of friendly salutation. They were a contented, pleasant-looking flock, these parishioners of St. Anne's; they might have lost the gayety that they would have kept in the old country, but a look of good cheer had not forsaken them, though many a figure showed the thinness that comes from steady, hard work, and almost every face had the deep lines that are worn only by anxiety. The pretty girls looked as their mothers had looked before them, only they were not so fair and fresh-colored, having been brought up less wholesomely and too much indoors.

"That's a nice gerrl o' Mary Finnerty's," said Dennis Call, gravely, to his mates, following the charming young creature with approving eyes.

"'Deed, then, you're right, Dinny," agreed little Pat Finn, a queer old figure of a shoemaker, who was bent nearly double between the effects of his stooping trade and a natural warp in his bones. "There don't be so pritty a little gerrl as Katy Finnerty walk into church, so there don't! I like her meself; she's got the cut o' the gerrls in Tralee—the prittiest gerrls is in it that's in the whole of Ireland."

"Coom now, then! you do always be bragging for Tralee; there's enough other places as good as it," scoffed Dennis. "Anybody that ain't a Bantry man can tark as they like, they'll have to put up wid second-best whin all's said an' done."

"Whisht now!" said John Mulligan, putting his hand to his forehead and bobbing his head respectfully at Father Ryan, the old priest, who had just come hurrying from the vestry door along a precarious footway of single boards left there since the days of spring mud.

"I hope you're feeling fine the day, sir?" said little Pat Finn, looking up with friendliness and pride at the tall old man. "We're getting good weather now, thank God, sir."

"We are that, Patrick Finn. God bless you, boys!" And Father Ryan went past them down the street to his house, while they all watched him without speaking until he had turned in at the gate with a flutter of his long coat-tails in the spring wind.

"Faix, I wisht we all had the sharp teeth for our dinners that his riverence has now," laughed Dennis. "I'll be bound he's keen for it, honest man. 'Twas to early mass over to White Mills he was, lavin' by break o' day, an' just comin' back an' they sent to him for poor Mary Sullivan that's to be waked this night, God rest her; and he not home from the corp' house an' Mary just dead, but two women come screechin' for him to hurry, there was a shild to be chris- tened waitin' in the church; 'twas one o' Jerry Hannan's wife's, that wint into black fits an' it being two hours born. Then it was high mass he had. I saw him myself puttin' a hand to his head an' humpin' wit' his shoulders, an' he before the alther. 'Tis a great dale o' worruk, so it is, for a man the age o' Father Ryan, may God help him!"

"I'd think the Bishop 'ould give him some aid now. They could sind some young missioner for a while to White Mills. 'Tis out of our own rights we do be, an' he to White Mills, day an' night wit' them French, an' one of us took hurt or dyin'. 'Tis too far to White Mills intirely," protested John Mulligan.

"Well, b'ys, the road's clear for us now, an' I'll say that I've got the match to Father Ryan's hunger in me own inside, 'tis thrue for me. Coom, Pat, now, there's no more gerrls! Get a move on you now, John, the fince is tired from ye!" And being thus suitably urged Dennis's companions started on their way. Dennis himself was a sturdy, middle-aged man, a teamster for the manufacturing company that had long ago gathered these Irish people into the staid and prosperous New England village. They had made a neighborhood by themselves, and were just now alarmed in their turn and disturbed by the presence of a few French Canadians, so thoroughly did they feel at home and believe in their rights to an adopted country. They meant to stay, at any rate, and jealously suspected their lively neighbors of only a temporary appropriation of citizenship that would take more than it gave. Dennis Call would have been a prosperous man and good citizen anywhere, with his soberness and thrift and decent notions; he was much respected by his fellow-townsfolk.

"Coom, now!" exclaimed Pat Finn, trying to keep step with his tall companions, "'Leg over leg, as the dog wint to Dover,'" he added cheerfully. "I might have been coaxing a ride home wit' Braley's folks, they had the one sate saved in the wagon, but I was idlin' me time away wit' the likes of you; a taste of tark is always the ruin of me."

"Good-day to ye, Pat," the others called after him as he crossed over to go down a side-street; but the droll, stooping figure did not turn again, and Mulligan and Dennis went on in the peaceful company. Dennis was a step ahead of his friend. You rarely see the old-fashioned Irish folk walk side by side; perhaps they keep a dim remembrance of footpaths over the open fields and moors. There is less of the formal, military sense than belongs to most Europeans, and a constant suggestion of the flock rather than the platoon.

At this moment two women who had lingered in the church overtook our friends and gave them a cordial greeting. One was the niece of Dennis Call, and almost as old as he. They lived at opposite ends of the town, and she stopped to ask him some questions about his family, while the other two, after hesitating a moment, went their way together. Sunday is the great social occasion for women who are hardly out of their houses all the rest of the week, and Dennis eagerly besought the favor of a visit. "Run home wit' me now for a bite of dinner," he urged. "'Twill be pot-luck, but the folks'll give you a grand welcome, and some of the children will be coming to vespers."

"Yirra now, I can't then, Dinny," the niece insisted, but her face shone with gratification, and they both knew that she was ready to accept.

"Oh, be friendly now an' come an' see the folks," Dennis continued. "The poor woman was in all the week wit' a bad wakeness that troubles her very bad, 'tis the stomach-bone falls down, they all says, but the docther has it that she's only wantin' a bit of strength wit' the spring weather an' all. 'Tis a dale o' work she has all the time, but the little gerrls begins to help iligant now, an' 'twill soon be aisy; they grow very fast. Little Mag is getting a foine dinner the day. Coom, Mary!"

Mary gave a sigh of compassion for the hard-worked mother, whose tiredness she well comprehended. "You're lucky then, Dinnis, and herself is lucky, the two of you bein' together and you gettin' steady work the year through. I know well herself gets a bit of the pain in her, we all gets it, faix! I knows well what it is. 'Tis our folks has hard times, wid my man dead this sivin years gone an' the old 'oman always in her bed, an' I havin' to tind poor Johnny an' herself like two babies. Wisha, wisha! I wasn't to mass—today is four Sundays gone since I heard mass before. Well now, see! I'm goin' wid you like a little lost dog. I'm glad of a treat—but I'll help little Mag wid the dinner, so I will, 'tis a task for the shild."

A lovely readiness to help shone in Mary O'Donnell's homely face. She looked poor and anxious; her bonnet, with its brown and white plaided ribbon and ancient shape, looked as if it might have been ten years in wear. She had worn her poor mourning threadbare and returned to this headgear of an earlier and more prosperous time. She had been full of hope and cheerfulness when she bought the queer old brown bonnet, but a blessed light of hope and kindliness still shone in her eyes.

As they went along, busy with their homely talk, some one lifted a window near them and called "Dennis, Dennis!" in a tone of mild authority.

"'Tis his riverence wants you!" exclaimed Mrs. O'Donnell,

flushing with excitement and pleasure. "I'll be going on slow; do you take your time. Run now, Dinny!"

"I'll be there, sir," said Dennis, already inside the gate, and by the time he reached the steps, Father Ryan opened the door. "Step in," he said; "I must have a word with you. Who's that with you?"

"Mary O'Donnell, she that's brother's-daughter to me, sir; 'tain't often we gets the bit of tark. She's goin' home to dinner with the folks,—herself's at home the day, sir, she's not well."

"I'll stop an' see her one day soon. I missed her at mass. Your wife's a good woman, Dennis."

"An' Mary O'Donnell, too, has done fine—she was afther bein' left very poor, 'tis yourself knows it well, an' has been very kind, sir. She had but the two hands of her for depindence, but we all did what we could." Dennis had blushed at the priest's good words about his wife as if he himself had been praised. "I thank God I'm prospered wit' good health, sir."

The old priest stood still in the narrow entry looking at Dennis Call as if he were not listening and were lost in his own thoughts. Dennis stood with hat in hand; the moment was strangely embarrassing. Father Ryan's strong-featured, good-humored face looked drawn and bluish as if he were really suffering from hunger and fatigue and some unforeseen perplexity beside. There was a cheerful insistent clatter of plates in the little dining-room beyond, and a comforting odor of roast-beef. Dennis felt more puzzled every moment, but he unconsciously smacked his lips in spite of uncertainties as to what the priest wanted.

"My heart's sick, Dennis," said his reverence, and a sudden flicker of light shone in his eyes.

Dennis shifted his weight to the other foot and passed his hat from right hand to left. "What's the matter, then, sir?" he asked anxiously. "Did anybody break the church window again I do' know?" He felt a little impatient; Mary O'Donnell would be far down the street, and the priest's good dinner made a man unbearably hungry. Still Father Ryan was frowning and planning without saying a word, and it made an honest man feel like a thief.

"Dennis, will you take a bit of dinner with me now and run afterward to Fletcher's place and get the best horse that's in, all in fifteen minutes' time? And say we're going on an errand of mercy if anybody puts a question. They'll think it's for the sick while it's for the well, God save us," said the old man.

"I'll do that, sir," said Dennis.

"Let's to dinner then," said Father Ryan. "I suppose good Mary O'Donnell's out of sound of your voice."

Dennis opened the door hastily; it was a relief to do something, and gave a loud call to Mary, who was still loitering not so very far away. "I'll not be home to my dinner," said he. "Do you go on then and tell the folks." So Mary, in happy amaze, went her ways to carry the pleasing news that Dennis was kept to his dinner with the priest.

Father Ryan was already in the dining-room; the roast-beef was smoking on the table, there were onions and potatoes, and even cranberry-sauce from some secret repository of the housekeeper, who was not unmindful of the priest's long morning of hard service. Mrs. Dillon was setting another plate opposite Father Ryan's own. Dennis forgot that he was clinging to his Sunday hat, but when they had blessed themselves, and dinner was fairly begun, and the hat pushed under the table, the guest felt that he could hold his own again, and ventured a sociable remark. Dennis was as quick as he could be, but the priest finished his beef first, and impatiently waved back a noble Sunday pudding which Mrs. Dillon was proudly bringing in at the door. "Run for the mare now, if you've had enough," said he, and Dennis gave a lingering glance at the pudding and departed.

"Lord be good to us, but he's in the hurry!" he grumbled, as he went at a jog trot down the street. It was not yet one o'clock and a lovely May afternoon. The season was early, and the maples in full leaf; the prospect of a drive out into the country, with a light buggy, and possibly Fletcher's best mare, delighted Dennis Call as if he were a schoolboy. He marched into the stable yard with most important manners, and said, in the hearing of a group of stay-at-home loungers, that Father Ryan called for the best team and was in great haste.

"What's up, Dennis, a christening?" inquired an amiable idler; but Dennis plunged his hands deep into his pockets and calmly turned away, and looked up at the blue sky with an air of assurance, exactly as if he were not wishing that he knew, himself. Presently he stepped into the light carriage with the air of a lord, and whirled out of the yard.

"Which way now, sir?" he asked the priest, who was already waiting at his gate, but Father Ryan took the reins himself. "I'm afraid you might go too slow for me," he said, trying to give Dennis a droll, reassuring look, but he could not hide the provocation, and even grief, that he evidently felt. "I don't forget that you are used to heavy teaming," he added, and they both laughed and felt much more at ease. "I must be back in time for vespers," said his reverence, as they passed the church.

The sorrel mare sped along the road; her master had kept her in for his own use later that afternoon, and she was only too fresh and ready. For a while they followed the main road toward the next large town, and passed many of their acquaintances, driving or on foot, and Dennis was not without pride at being seen in the priest's company; but suddenly they turned into a rough, seldom-traveled by-way, that led up among the hills. It seemed as if the errand were to some person in trouble, but presently they had left behind what appeared to be the last house. This was a strange path to follow, and for what reason had Father Ryan desired a companion, unless it were necessary in such a steep and almost dangerous ascent? Once, years before, Dennis had climbed by this deserted road, up to the woodlands of the higher hills; he had been gunning with some young men, and he remembered the small, lonely farms that they had just passed, and how poor and inhospitable they looked in the winter weather; in fact, his remembrance of the holiday was not bright in any way, because he had gained but a poor day's sport. None of the priest's flock lived in this direction, that was one sure thing.

The road seemed to grow steeper and steeper; the sorrel mare stopped once or twice, discouraged, and looked ahead at the hard climb. There were dark hemlocks and pines on either side, illuminated here and there by the vivid green of young birch saplings that stood where they caught the sunlight. The air was fresh and sweet, there were busy birds fluttering and calling; the light tread of the mare seemed to disturb the secluded region, as if nothing had passed that way since the coming of the year.

Father Ryan had not spoken for a long time; all the cheerfulness had faded from his face. "Dennis!" said he suddenly, so that the man at his side turned, startled and open-eyed, to look at him. "Dennis, you remember that smart young Dan Nolan, Tom Nolan's boy, the one that went to the seminary for a while, but left and went West to be a railroad man?"

"I does mind Danny Nolan, sir; they say he's got rich. Him an' John Finnerty's gerrl is courtin' this long time, the pritty gerrl Katy; I saw her coming out from mass the day. John Finnerty do be thinking she's got a great match, the b'y always says in his letters that he's doing fine."

"May God forgive him!" said the priest, under his breath.

"Why, in course I'd know him well, sir," Dennis continued eagerly, in his most communicative manner. "Wasn't he brought up next house to my own by the mill yard, until I moved to the better one I'm in now, thanks be to God, the other one being dacint to look at, but very damp an' the cause of much sickness to every one. Oh, but the fine letters the b'y does be writing home, they brings them and reads them to herself an' me; truth is Tom Nolan's put his money into a mine that Danny's knowing to, out where he is, and they've been at me wouldn't I come wid 'em. Every one says there do be a power o' money in it. The tark is all right, but for Tom not having got any papers; I'd like to see the papers they gives, first; an' I think meself, sir, it's the same with Tom, but he won't let on."

"My God!" said the old priest again.

"An' John Finnerty, the little gerrl's fadther, he sint t'ree hundred—'twas all he had laid by—you know the wife's a great spinder—an' Danny Nolan wrote back he'd find it t'ree thousand this time next year, an' herself has been in the street goin' to the shops ivery night since then, as rich-feeling as a conthractor! Katy, the young thing, sint him out her small savings she got in the mill that she was keeping to buy her wedding with. I was against that when they tould me, but she'd sint to Dan and he wrote a great letter to sind it along, an' he'd put it where it would grow. 'Too many eggs in the one basket,' says I. She's awful proud of Dan, and he do be always writin' the beautiful letters, sir; but he does be knowing his fadther works hard all the time, and at Christmas last year divil a cint came home to any one of them.

They all says it was too far entirely to be gettin' prisents, but they'd like to be showing anything they got the lingth of the town. Tell me now, sir, do ye know of anything wrong? I do be thinkin' you've heard bad news. I couldn't tell why"—

Father Ryan touched the horse and gave a queer groan before he spoke.

"The truth is that Dan Nolan's a swindler," said he. "Those poor souls'll never see their money again."

"Well, something held me back from him, thanks be to God!" protested Dennis with pride, though he looked shocked and anxious. "I come very near givin' him all I had too. Whin a craze gets amongst folks, one must be doing like all the rest; ain't it so, sir? And that Dan was the best scholar in the schools here; don't you mind the praise he'd get from every one, an' his fadther was proud as a paycock. I does be thinkin' them schools has their faults. If a man dies now an' laves a houseful of childher they don't be half so fit to earn their bread as they were in the old times. I'm thinkin' the old folks was wiser wit' the childher, Father Ryan, sir!"

"There never was a boy in any parish I had these forty-five years that I took the pains with that I took with him," said Father Ryan slowly. "I paid the most of his bills myself when he went to the seminary. Poor Tom Nolan couldn't do it, with his small wages and the sickness and the trouble he used to have. Danny was my altar-boy,—a pretty face there was on him, and a laughing eye. He always stood to me for a little brother of mine, and looked the very marrow of him when I first saw him, and Tom came to the mills. My little brother was my playmate, we were always together like twin lambs. I can mind myself now, and I running home alone, crying, to tell my poor mother that we'd run away to the rocks, and a great wave came in and licked him off before my very eyes, and I a bit higher up on the shore. I wake up dreaming of him, stiff with the horror and a cold sweat all over me, after a lifetime that's gone between me and that day. I'm an old man now, Dennis Call, and my mind's always been in a priest's holy business. But I've a warm Irish heart in me, and there are times when I'd like a brother's young child, or one of my sister's that I left long ago in Kerry, or to see my old mother shake her head and have the laugh at me, and I sitting there in the long winter evening in my still house. And when that young Danny Nolan gave a smile at me, like the little lad that went under the sea, and never was afraid, or trying to get away from me because I was the priest, I liked him more than I knew. I couldn't see then why he shouldn't make a good man, and I helped him the best I could. I know plenty of harm of him now, God forgive him and bring him to repentance."

The old man scowled and looked away. His heart was filled with sorrow. Dennis's ready tongue was checked, but he was grumbling to himself about the black heart of Danny Nolan. "I begin to think that sharp wits are the least of all the means by which a man wins true success," said Father Ryan.

"Everybody thought well of Dan Nolan then, sir." Dennis tried to comfort him; he had seen Father Ryan angry and stern, but never cast down like this.

They came to an open, grassy space on a shelf of the great hill. At one side was the cellar where a house had stood long ago; some roses still grew about it, and there was much of the solemn little cypress plant, so often seen in country burying-grounds, growing about the crumbling foundations and straying off into the grass. There was a smooth, broad doorstep partly overgrown, and a hop-vine was sending up its determined shoots near by, where it could find nothing to twine upon. The old doorstep had evidently served as a seat for stray wanderers; there was a place before it that had been worn by feet, like the beginning of a path. The house had been gone many years, but one might have thought that its ghost was there, and the doorstep was still trodden by those unseen inhabitants who went and came. The priest may have thought this, but Dennis saw a gun wad lying by the step, and a little bird fluttered away, as if it had been finding a few stray crumbs.

There was a magnificent view of the widespread lower country—woods and clearings and bushy pasture-lands stretching miles upon miles, with a river dividing them like a shining ribbon; and white villages, with their tiny spires and sprinkled houses and heavy dark mills. As you turned the other way you looked up the dark hill-slope. The road appeared to end here by the deserted farmstead, but some winter wood-roads led off in different directions.

Father Ryan stopped the breathless mare and got down

clumsily. "We'll walk from here, Dennis," he said, and Dennis also alighted. His face was befogged with perplexity. They plunged deep into the woods along one of the half overgrown winter tracks which led up and over a high shoulder of the great hill.

"'Tis like the way to the cave of the foxy 'oman," said Dennis, half aloud, as a dry twig whipped him in the face, and Father Ryan heard him and laughed.

"Well, it's wonderful how those old tales do stay in the mind," he said cheerfully. "I was working away with a book yesterday, a fine hard knot of Latin it was, too, and I got sleepy, and not a bit could I think of but how did the story of the Little Cakeen go that my old granny used to tell me before she'd give me a little cakeen herself that she'd have hidden in her blue cloak. I'd be afraid to eat it, too, after the tale. Well, I think it might be twenty years since I thought of it, but I could not rid my mind of the trick of that foolish story, and it kept twirling itself round and round in my mind. It may be the way with old folks. I begin to feel old."

"'Twas a great story of the Little Cakeen," agreed Dennis solemnly. "I do be telling it to the childher; there's nothing anybody tells that they'd like so well, wit' their little screeches always in the same place. 'Twas the same way wit' my brothers and meself at home. We'd better mind, sir, lest ourselves gets on the fox's back an' into his big mout'. Do you know where you do be going?" Dennis looked about him anxiously.

The priest only laughed; a queer laugh it was that might mean one thing or another.

"Come on!" he said. "You make me think of another old tale they used to be telling at home about one Mrs. O'Flaherty's donkey, that could neither go nor stand still."

At this moment, when the conversation had taken a most sociable and even merry tone, the two men found themselves on the edge of the thick woods, with an open, partly overgrown acre of land before them. The seedling pines had covered a piece of land cleared and deserted again many years before; they had grown close to the tumble-down old house, which had sometimes been used as a shelter by lumbermen who were at work among the hills, or sportsmen who might have taken refuge there in wet weather. Dennis was astonished to find himself there; he remembered the

"Take that, will you now, Danny Nolan.'" Illustrated by C. D. Gibson; *Scribner's Magazine*, 1893. Courtesy Dartmouth College Library.

place well, but they had reached it by so short a path that the priest seemed to have brought him by the aid of magic. Dennis had taken heart at a change for the better in Father Ryan's manner, and was already preparing to laugh at the expected story about a donkey; but Father Ryan looked stern and priestly again and began to stride forward, telling Dennis by a gesture to wait outside the house. "'Tis a den of thieves I'm sure, now," muttered Dennis, but he followed his companion to the door, and stood there, strong and sturdy and not displeased, looking about him suspiciously like a wary sentinel.

The priest stepped softly on the pasture turf among the little pine-trees, and entered the door as if he did not mean to be heard. Immediately there was a scuffle and crash inside and the jar of a heavy fall, at which Dennis Call rushed in with his eyes dancing and his fists clenched.

There, in the middle of the dismal rain-stained room, by an overturned table and broken chair, Father Ryan was fighting with a younger man and getting the worst of it. Dennis pounced down and caught the fellow off by the shoulders. His great thumbs held down the cords like iron bolts; he stood the rascal back on his knees and gave him a terrible shaking. Dennis had been a tidy man at a fight when he was younger, and his rage revived the best of his experience. "Get up, sir; get up, your riverence!" he commanded, in a bold voice. "Lave the beggar to me!" and he kept his clutch with one hand while he administered a succession of sound blows with the other. "Take that, will you now, Danny Nolan, an' that wit' it!" he said scornfully. "Is it full of drink you are, I do' know, to strike down an old an' rispicted man that's been a fadther to you, and he God's priest beside! I'll bate the life out of you and lave you here to the crows an' I get a saucy word out o' your head, so there now!" and Dennis proceeded to cuff and shake his captive unmercifully.

The old priest looked shocked and shaken; he got upon his feet and tried to brush the dust from his black clothes. There was no place to sit, it was a dirty, stifling place, and he turned and went swaying with faltering steps to the door, and Dennis, holding the young man's arm in an unflinching grip, went after him.

"Sit down on the step, sir," he said, anxiously, to the old man. "I hope it isn't faint you are, sir?"

Father Ryan seated himself upon the crumbling door-sill, and Dennis backed himself and his captive against a bowlder that stood in front of the old house, close by. As he turned to take a good look at Dan Nolan, a feeling of contempt stole into his honest face. In the clear light the young man looked so colorless and disreputable, wrecked and ruined by an only too evident life of vice and ignorance of every sort of decent behavior, that he seemed but a poor antago- nist for a man like Dennis Call. There was little left of his boyish good looks and fine spirit. He must have thrown Fa- ther Ryan by some trick that caught him unprepared, for in spite of his age the priest looked much the stronger of the two. Dennis felt a strange anxiety as he saw how badly out of breath Father Ryan was still, and what bad color had come to his lips.

"Will I get you a sup of water, sir?" he asked eagerly. "This thing 'ont run away; or I'll just stun the poor cr'ature a bit wit' me fist so he can't step foot an' he tries. I'm afraid you're bad off, sir, so I am."

"No, no," said Father Ryan. "Let go his arm now."

"I don't dare lave him go, sir," protested Dennis.

"Let go his arm. Stand out, Dan!" and a strange light blazed in the old man's eyes. Danny Nolan, in his smart, dirty, city-made clothes, stood out a step in front of Dennis, a poor wretched image of a young man as ever startled the squirrels and jays of that wild, deserted bit of country. He cast a furtive glance to the right and left, but the old priest raised a warning hand.

"No, you won't run, Dan, my boy," he said. "My old heart is ready to break at the sorry sight of you. Those poor legs of yours would throw you before you could run a rod. Take out the money that's in your pockets. Dennis, keep your eye on him now. Take it out, I say!"

Father Ryan rose to his great height with a black and angry look; his years seemed to fall off his shoulders like a cloak, and Dennis stepped forward eager for the fray. The fellow was at bay. He looked for a moment as sharp and ugly as a weasel, then the cowardice in him showed itself; he began to whimper and weaken, and so fell upon his knees.

"It is in the state's prison that you ought to be. I know it well," said Father Ryan sternly.

"Will I give him a nate kick or two, your riverence?" inquired Dennis suggestively. "May be 'twill help him to mind what you do be saying, the dirty bla'guard."

Danny Nolan, still whimpering, took something from his pocket and dropped it before him on the turf. "There, now," he said, trying to be bold, "let me go."

"Go through his pockets yourself, Dennis," said the priest, and he stood watching while this business was carefully accomplished, and a little heap of counterfeit bills was gathered at their feet, which Dennis had sought for with little tenderness. "What have you hidden in the house beside?" he demanded, looking up in black rage, as Danny Nolan stood there, surly and flushed.

"If 'twas my last word, I'd tell you the same," he answered. "There's no more but this. I was only waiting till evening, so I'd get away. There's two dollars there that's good," he sulkily added, touching the money with his foot.

"Ye'd best give it to his riverence for a collection, then,"
Dennis advised. "Ain't you the dirthy divil!"

"I've had awful hard luck," said Danny, in a grieved tone.
"'Twas a man on the cars give me this"—

"Why didn't you come straight to those who were your
friends?" said Father Ryan sadly. "You have been robbing those
that loved you and taking their little earnings—you are a liar
and a thief. How will you face them now and go to them for
food and shelter? Who'll want to give you a day's work? You
have been living with cheats and liars; see what they have
done for you, and how rich and fine you come home to
those that have praised you the length of the town. What do
you mean to do?"

"They're out after me; the officers are out after me, sir."
The poor rascal instantly turned to his old friend for help. "I
can't stop here; 'twas the man that gave me this stuff to get
rid of it himself, and then went and told."

"You sent down to the mills to some fellows you thought
bad enough to buy this trash. Don't lie to me, Dan! You have
fallen into this sort of thing by your own choice. Come now,
if Dennis and I will stand by you, will you try to be decent
and live honest? You'll be dead this time next year if you
don't, and there's God's truth for you. I'll try you this once
more, God helping me. I'll not send you home to those that
aren't able to keep you. I've a little money put by, and I'll
lend you something for those you have robbed and cheated
with your stories about the mine."

"I was cheated myself in the first place, Father Ryan," said
Nolan. Then he fell to sobbing and covered his face with
both his hands. "I've been bad, you're right, sir, but oh, try
me again. I don't know what'll I do. I'm starved here, and
every bush that rustles turns me cold these three nights. I'll
do the best I can, sir. I wouldn't have said it so easy yesterday, but I'm beat to the ground now. Everybody's turned
against me. I thought some friends of mine would be here
last night"—

"Come, stand up an' behave like a man!" Dennis gave him
a vigorous jerk by way of stimulant. "We mane no harm by
the likes of you. Do now as Father Ryan says, since he's so
willing to try you." There was kindliness in his tone, though

the shake was contradictory. "I'll stand by you meself for Father Ryan's pleasure, but it goes hard wit' me to say the word."

"You'll come to me this evening at eight o'clock," said the priest. "I'll be thinking what's best to do. I can't stand between you and the laws you've broken. You'll stay at my house the night. Mrs. Dillon'll be washing in the morning; the first thing is to make you look decent. Then I'll find a way to talk with your father, poor honest man!"

"I'd as soon go chop at Tom Nolan wit' me ax," muttered Dennis.

The priest stooped and struck a match on the gray rock and touched it to the counterfeit bills, stirring them now and then with his foot as they smouldered. When the few ashes began to blow in the light spring wind, and there was little left but an ugly small scar in the green turf, Father Ryan held out his hand and Danny Nolan tried not to see it and turned away. The old priest could not help a sigh. Then the young man, who had known every sin, threw himself upon the mercy of this merciful old friend. No matter if Dennis stood by with his aggravating sense of honesty, his narrow experience of a stupid mill town, Dan Nolan caught hold of Father Ryan's hand and clung to it as if his whole heart were spent in love and gratitude. "O God, help me; I'll not fail you this night, sir. 'Tis the Lord sent you to me, sir. 'Tis you were always good to me when I was a little boy minding the altar, sir."

"You were always great wit' your fine words and your smart letters," grumbled Dennis, who in spite of himself was much affected. If his own sons should ever go wrong, God send them such a friend. "See now that you give his riverence satisfaction for all the trouble he's taking, and pay him back his money too. There's work enough if you'd only be dacint, but if I'd hear from any of your tricks, or you'd be doing harm among the young folks, Lord be good to me but I'd be the one to break your neck, so I would. When I think of that pritty gerrl you've fooled!" —

"Don't shame the man any more. We'll give him his chance to do better. 'Tis God does the same every day for you and me," said Father Ryan.

The May wind in the pine woods was like the sound of the sea as the two elder men turned away to go down the hill, not once looking back. The old priest left Dan Nolan behind as if he had forgotten him, and Dennis was awed into speechlessness as he walked alongside.

The sorrel mare was restless. She had unwisely browsed the sharp-thorned sprouting rosebushes, and had got the reins tangled about her feet. Father Ryan climbed into the carriage; he began to feel lame and tired, and Dennis, still silent, took the mare by the head and led her carefully down the steepest part of the road. When they came to the lowest slope of the hill he got in and took the reins, and they went quickly home. The church-bells began to ring for vespers as they neared the town.

"I'll be a trifle late, I'm sorry," said the priest. "Leave me at the church and you go on with the mare, Denny. Oh, I'm all right, 'twas fine and pleasant in the green woods. It seems long to me since mass was over."

"My saints in heaven, but ain't he the father to us!" exclaimed Dennis, a moment later. He still felt a delightful sense of excitement and adventure, but after they had parted at the church something choked him, as he thought of Father Ryan's figure as he had seen him go along the little path to the vestry, with that dust on the back of his coat. As he came back to the church himself he overtook Mary O'Donnell, who greeted him with pleasure and even curiosity, and some other friends made mention of the fact that he had been away with the priest. The parishioners were used to being ignorant about most of Father Ryan's affairs; a priest could never make talk about his errands of business and mercy as another man could.

The warm May Sunday indeed seemed long. The vesper service did not often attract Dennis Call. He was always in his place at mass, but he took his Sunday sleep and stroll in the afternoon. He made himself easy in the corner of the pew, he picked some pine-needles out of the cuff of his coat, and he said, a little grudgingly, a prayer for Danny Nolan. He noticed that there was a bruise beginning to show itself on the old priest's forehead, and how the hands trembled that were lifted at the altar. The doctor had been known to say that Father Ryan was not a sound man, that he had better not take long walks alone any more, or overtax himself as he often did, and Dennis wondered vaguely if this were not the reason he had been called upon that day for company.

"I'd like to clout the saucy bla'guard a couple o' times more," he grumbled to himself; but his heart was not without compassion. His own boys were just beginning to put on the airs and to share the ambitions of men, and poor Tom Nolan, his old friend and neighbor, must hear sad news of Danny, and that soon. Dennis blinked his sleepy eyes and looked reverently at Father Ryan's tall figure at the altar. The setting sun brought out the color and tarnished gold thread of the worn vestments. The paper flowers that a French woman had made new at Easter looked gay and almost real in the pleasant light.

"'Tis in many strange places that a priest does be having to serve God," said Dennis to himself. "I'm thinking Danny Nolan'll light out this night wit' the two dollars, an' we'll see no more of him. Faix, 'twould be best for him, the young fool; the likes of him will break every heart, stay or go!"

That night, however, just at dark, Dan Nolan came across the fields, and presently stole out from a thicket at the foot of the priest's little garden, and went into the house. The lights were bright; there was a good supper on the table. As the hungry, crestfallen offender sat there, abashed by all the light and good cheer, the old man's tired face shone with golden hopefulness. Father Ryan even persuaded himself that the look of his own young brother had come back again into Danny Nolan's eyes.

The Gray Mills
of Farley

1

The mills of Farley were close together by the river, and the gray houses that belonged to them stood, tall and bare, alongside. They had no room for gardens or even for little green side-yards where one might spend a summer evening. The Corporation, as this compact village was called by those who lived in it, was small but solid; you fancied yourself in the heart of a large town when you stood midway of one of its short streets, but from the street's end you faced a wide green farming country. On spring and summer Sundays, groups of the young folks of the Corporation would stray out along the country roads, but it was very seldom that any of the older people went. On the whole, it seemed as if the closer you lived to the mill-yard gate, the better. You had more time to loiter on a summer morning, and there was less distance to plod through the winter snows and rains. The last stroke of the bell saw almost everybody within the mill doors.

There were always fluffs of cotton in the air like great white bees drifting down out of the picker chimney. They lodged in the cramped and dingy elms and horse-chestnuts which a former agent had planted along the streets, and the English sparrows squabbled over them in eaves-corners and made warm, untidy great nests that would have contented an Arctic explorer. Somehow the Corporation homes looked like make-believe houses or huge stage-properties, they had so little individuality or likeness to the old-fashioned buildings that made homes for people out on the farms. There was more homelikeness in the sparrows' nests, or even the toylike railroad station at the end of the main street, for that was warmed by steam, and the station-master's wife, thriftily taking advantage of the steady heat, brought her houseplants there and kept them all winter on the broad window-sills.

The Corporation had followed the usual fortunes of New England manufacturing villages. Its operatives were at first eager young men and women from the farms near by, these being joined quickly by pale English weavers and spinners, with their hearty-looking wives and rosy children; then came the flock of Irish families, poorer and simpler than the others but learning the work sooner, and gayer-hearted; now the Canadian-French contingent furnished all the new help, and stood in long rows before the noisy looms and chattered in their odd, excited fashion. They were quicker-fingered, and were willing to work cheaper than any other workpeople yet.

There were remnants of each of these human tides to be found as one looked about the mills. Old Henry Dow, the overseer of the cloth-hall, was a Lancashire man and some of his grandchildren had risen to wealth and prominence in another part of the country, while he kept steadily on with his familiar work and authority. A good many elderly Irishmen and women still kept their places; everybody knew the two old sweepers, Mary Cassidy and Mrs. Kilpatrick, who were looked upon as pillars of the Corporation. They and their compatriots always held loyally together and openly resented the incoming of so many French.

You would never have thought that the French were for a moment conscious of being in the least unwelcome. They came gayly into church and crowded the old parishioners of St. Michael's out of their pews, as on week-days they took their places at the looms. Hardly one of the old parishioners had not taken occasion to speak of such aggressions to Father Daley, the priest, but Father Daley continued to look upon them all as souls to be saved and took continual pains to rub up the rusty French which he had nearly forgotten, in order to preach a special sermon every other Sunday. This caused old Mary Cassidy to shake her head gravely.

"Mis' Kilpatrick, ma'am," she said one morning. "Faix, they ain't folks at all, 'tis but a pack of images they do be, with all their chatter like birds in a hedge."

"Sure then, the holy Saint Francis himself was after saying that the little birrds was his sisters," answered Mrs. Kilpatrick, a godly old woman who made the stations every morning, and was often seen reading a much-handled book of devotion. She was moreover always ready with a friendly joke.

"They ain't the same at all was in them innocent times, when there was plinty saints living in the world," insisted Mary Cassidy. "Look at them thrash, now!"

The old sweeping-women were going downstairs with their brooms. It was almost twelve o'clock, and like the old drayhorses in the mill yard they slackened work in good season for the noonday bell. Three gay young French girls ran downstairs past them; they were let out for the afternoon and were hurrying home to dress and catch the 12:40 train to the next large town.

"That little one is Meshell's daughter; she's a nice child too, very quiet, and has got more Christian tark than most," said Mrs. Kilpatrick. "They live overhead o' me. There's nine o' themselves in the two rooms; two does be boarders."

"Those upper rooms bees very large entirely at Fitzgibbon's," said Mary Cassidy with unusual indulgence.

"'Tis all the company cares about is to get a good rent out of the pay. They're asked every little while by honest folks 'on't they build a trifle o' small houses beyond the church up there, but no, they'd rather the money and kape us like bees in them old hives. Sure in winter we're better for having the more fires, but summer is the pinance!"

"They all says 'why don't folks build their own houses'; they does always be talking about Mike Callahan and how well he saved up and owns a pritty place for himself convanient to his work. You might tell them he'd money left him by a brother in California till you'd be black in the face, they'd stick to it 'twas in the picker he earnt it from themselves," grumbled Mary Cassidy.

"Them French spinds all their money on their backs, don't they?" suggested Mrs. Kilpatrick, as if to divert the conversation from dangerous channels. "Look at them three girls now, off to Spincer with their fortnight's pay in their pocket!"

"A couple o' onions and a bag o' crackers is all they want and a pinch o' lard to their butter," pronounced Mary Cassidy with scorn. "The whole town of 'em 'on't be the worse of a dollar for steak the week round. They all go back and buy land in Canada, they spend no money here. See how well they forget their pocketbooks every Sunday for the collection. They do be very light too, they've more laugh than ourselves. 'Tis myself's getting old anyway, I don't laugh much now."

"I like to see a pritty girl look fine," said Mrs. Kilpatrick. "No, they don't be young but once—"

The mill bell rang, and there was a moment's hush of the jarring, racketing machinery and a sudden noise of many feet trampling across the dry, hard pine floors. First came an early flight of boys bursting out of the different doors, and chasing one another down the winding stairs two steps at a time. The old sweepers, who had not quite reached the bottom, stood back against the wall for safety's sake until all these had passed, then they kept on their careful way, the crowd passing them by as if they were caught in an eddy of the stream. Last of all they kept sober company with two or three lame persons and a cheerful delayed little group of new doffers, the children who minded bobbins in the weave-room and who were young enough to be tired and even timid. One of these doffers, a pale, pleasant-looking child, was all fluffy with cotton that had clung to her little dark plaid dress. When Mrs. Kilpatrick spoke to her she answered in a hoarse voice that appealed to one's sympathy. You felt that the hot room and dry cotton were to blame for such hoarseness; it had nothing to do with the weather.

"Where are you living now, Maggie, dear?" the old woman asked.

"I'm in Callahan's yet, but they won't keep me after to-day," said the child. "There's a man wants to get board there, they're changing round in the rooms and they've no place for me. Mis' Callahan couldn't keep me 'less I'd get my pay raised."

Mrs. Kilpatrick gave a quick glance at Mary Cassidy. "Come home with me then, till yez get a bite o' dinner, and we'll talk about it," she said kindly to the child. "I'd a wish for company the day."

The two old companions had locked their brooms into a three-cornered closet at the stair-foot and were crossing the mill yard together. They were so much slower than the rest that they could only see the very last of the crowd of mill people disappearing along the streets and into the boarding-house doors. It was late autumn, the elms were bare, one could see the whole village of Farley, all its poverty and lack of beauty, at one glance. The large houses looked as if they belonged to a toy village, and had been carefully put in rows by a childish hand; it was easy to lose all sense of size in looking at them. A cold wind was blowing bits of waste and paper high into the air; now and then a snowflake went

"I'm in Callahan's yet, but they won't keep me after to-day,' said the child." Illustrated by Frank O. Small; *The Cosmopolitan*, 1898. Courtesy Dartmouth College Library.

swiftly by like a courier of winter. Mary Cassidy and Mrs. Kilpatrick hugged their old woolen shawls closer about their round shoulders, and the little girl followed with short steps alongside.

2

The agent of the mills was a single man, keen and business-like, but quietly kind to the people under his charge. Some-times, in times of peace, when one looks among one's neighbors wondering who would make the great soldiers and leaders if there came a sudden call to war, one knows with a flash of recognition the presence of military genius in such a man as he. The agent spent his days in following what seemed to many observers to be only a dull routine, but all his steadiness of purpose, all his simple intentness, all his gifts of strategy and powers of foresight, and of turning an interruption into an opportunity, were brought to bear upon this dull routine with a keen pleasure. A man in his place must know not only how to lead men, but how to make the combination of their force with the machinery take its place as a factor in the business of manufacturing. To master work-men and keep the mills in running order and to sell the goods successfully in open market is as easy to do badly as it is difficult to do well.

The agent's father and mother, young people who lived for a short time in the village, had both died when he was only three years old, and between that time and his ninth year he had learned almost everything that poverty could teach, being left like little Maggie to the mercy of his neigh-bors. He remembered with a grateful heart those who were good to him, and told him of his mother, who had married for love but unwisely. Mrs. Kilpatrick was one of these old friends, who said that his mother was a lady, but even Mrs. Kilpatrick, who was a walking history of the Corporation, had never known his mother's maiden name, much less the place of her birth. The first great revelation of life had come when the nine-years-old boy had money in his hand to pay his board. He was conscious of being looked at with a differ-ence; the very woman who had been hardest to him and let him mind her babies all the morning when he, careful little

soul, was hardly more than a baby himself, and then pushed
him out into the hungry street at dinner time, was the first
one who beckoned him now, willing to make the most of
his dollar and a quarter a week. It seemed easy enough to
rise from uttermost poverty and dependence to where one
could set his mind upon the highest honor in sight, that of
being agent of the mills, or to work one's way steadily to
where such an honor was grasped at thirty-two. Every year
the horizon had set its bounds wider and wider, until the
mills of Farley held but a small place in the manufacturing
world. There were offers enough of more salary and higher
position from those who came to know the agent, but he
was part of Farley itself, and had come to care deeply about
his neighbors, while a larger mill and salary were not exactly
the things that could tempt his ambition. It was but a lonely
life for a man in the old agent's quarters where one of the
widows of the Corporation, a woman who had been brought
up in a gentleman's house in the old country, kept house for
him with a certain show of propriety. Ever since he was a
boy his room was never without its late evening light, and
books and hard study made his chief companionship.

As Mrs. Kilpatrick went home holding little Maggie by the
hand that windy noon, the agent was sitting in the company's
counting-room with one of the directors and largest stockholders, and they were just ending a long talk about the mill
affairs. The agent was about forty years old now and looked
fifty. He had a pleasant smile, but one saw it rarely enough,
and just now he looked more serious than usual.

"I am very glad to have had this long talk with you," said
the old director. "You do not think of any other recommen-
dations to be made at the meeting next week?"

The agent grew a trifle paler and glanced behind him to
be sure that the clerks had gone to dinner.

"Not in regard to details," he answered gravely. "There is
one thing which I see to be very important. You have seen
the books, and are clear that nine per cent. dividend can
easily be declared?"

"Very creditable, very creditable," agreed the director; he
had recognized the agent's ability from the first and always
upheld him generously. "I mean to propose a special vote of

thanks for your management. There isn't a minor corporation in New England that stands so well to-day."

The agent listened. "We had some advantages, partly by
accident and partly by lucky foresight," he acknowledged. "I
am going to ask your backing in something that seems to
me not only just but important. I hope that you will not
declare above a six per cent. dividend at that directors' meeting; at the most, seven per cent.," he said.

"What, what!" exclaimed the listener. "No, sir!"

The agent left his desk-chair and stood before the old
director as if he were pleading for himself. A look of protest
and disappointment changed the elder man's face and hard-
ened it a little, and the agent saw it.

"You know the general condition of the people here," he
explained humbly. "I have taken great pains to keep hold of
the best that have come here; we can depend upon them
now and upon the quality of their work. They made no re-
sistance when we had to cut down wages two years ago; on
the contrary, they were surprisingly reasonable, and you know
that we shut down for several weeks at the time of the alter-
ations. We have never put their wages back as we might easily have done, and I happen to know that a good many
families have been able to save little or nothing. Some of
them have been working here for three generations. They
know as well as you and I and the books do when the mills
are making money. Now I wish that we could give them the
ten per cent. back again, but in view of the general depression perhaps we can't do that except in the way I mean. I
think that next year we're going to have a very hard pull to
get along, but if we can keep back three per cent., or even
two, of this dividend we can not only manage to get on without a shut-down or touching our surplus, which is quite small
enough, but I can have some painting and repairing done in
the tenements. They've needed it for a long time—"

The old director sprang to his feet. "Aren't the stockholders going to have any rights then?" he demanded. "Within
fifteen years we have had three years when we have passed
our dividends, but the operatives never can lose a single day's
pay!"

"That was before my time," said the agent, quietly. "We
have averaged nearly six and a half per cent. a year taking

the last twenty years together, and if you go back farther the average is even larger. This has always been a paying property; we've got our new machinery now, and everything in the mills themselves is just where we want it. I look for far better times after this next year, but the market is glutted with goods of our kind, and nothing is going to be gained by cut-downs and forcing lower-cost goods into it. Still, I can keep things going one way and another, making yarn and so on," he said pleadingly. "I should like to feel that we had this extra surplus. I believe that we owe it to our operatives."

The director had walked heavily to the window and put his hands deep into his side-pockets. He had an angry sense that the agent's hands were in his pockets too.

"I've got some pride about that nine per cent., sir," he said loftily to the agent.

"So have I," said the agent, and the two men looked each other in the face.

"I acknowledge my duty to the stockholders," said the younger man presently. "I have tried to remember that duty ever since I took the mills eight years ago, but we've got an excellent body of operatives, and we ought to keep them. I want to show them this next year that we value their help. If times aren't as bad as we fear we shall still have the money—"

"Nonsense. They think they own the mills now," said the director, but he was uncomfortable, in spite of believing he was right. "Where's my hat? I must have my luncheon now, and afterward there'll hardly be time to go down and look at the new power-house with you—I must be off on the quarter-to-two train."

The agent sighed and led the way. There was no use in saying anything more and he knew it. As they walked along they met old Mrs. Kilpatrick returning from her brief noonday meal with little Maggie, whose childish face was radiant. The old woman recognized one of the directors and dropped him a decent curtsey as she had been taught to salute the gentry sixty years before.

The director returned the salutation with much politeness. This was really a pleasant incident, and he took a silver half dollar from his pocket and gave it to the little girl before he went on.

"Kape it safe, darlin'," said the old woman; "you'll need it yet. Don't be spending all your money in sweeties; 'tis a very cold world to them that haves no pince in their pocket."

The child looked up at Mrs. Kilpatrick apprehensively; then the sunshine of hope broke out again through the cloud.

"I am going to save fine till I buy a house, and you and me'll live there together, Mrs. Kilpatrick, and have a lovely coal fire all the time."

"Faix, Maggie. I have always thought some day I'd kape a pig and live pritty in me own house," said Mrs. Kilpatrick. "But I'm the old sweeper yet in Number Two. 'Tis a worrld where some has and more wants," she added with a sigh. "I got the manes for a good buryin', the Lord be praised, and a bitteen more beside. I wouldn't have that if Father Daley was as croping as some."

"Mis' Mullin does always be scolding 'bout Father Daley having all the collections," ventured Maggie, somewhat adrift in so great a subject.

"She's no right then!" exclaimed the old woman angrily; "she'll get no luck to be grudging her pince that way. 'Tis hard work anny priest would have to kape the likes of hersilf from being haythens altogether."

There was a nine per cent. annual dividend declared at the directors' meeting the next week, with considerable applause from the board and sincere congratulations to the agent. He looked thinner and more sober than usual, and several persons present, whose aid he had asked in private, knew very well the reason. After the meeting was over the senior director, and largest stockholder, shook hands with him warmly.

"About that matter you suggested to me the other day," he said, and the agent looked up eagerly. "I consulted several of our board in regard to the propriety of it before we came down, but they all agreed with me that it was no use to cross a bridge until you come to it. Times look a little better, and the operatives will share in the accession of credit to a mill that declares nine per cent. this year. I hope that we shall be able to run the mills with at worst only a moderate cut-down, and they may think themselves very fortunate when so many hands are being turned off everywhere."

The agent's face grew dark. "I hope that times will take a better turn," he managed to say.

"Yes, yes," answered the director. "Good-bye to you, Mr.
Agent! I am not sure of seeing you again for some time," he
added with unusual kindliness. "I am an old man now to be
hurrying round to board meetings and having anything to
do with responsibilities like these. My sons must take their
turn."

There was an eager protest from the listeners, and presently the busy group of men disappeared on their way to
the train. A nine per cent. dividend naturally made the Farley
Manufacturing Company's stock go up a good many points,
and word came presently that the largest stockholder and
one or two other men had sold out. Then the stock ceased
to rise, and winter came on apace, and the hard times which
the agent had foreseen came also.

3

One noon in early March there were groups of men and
women gathering in the Farley streets. For a wonder, nobody was hurrying toward home and dinner was growing
cold on some of the long boarding-house tables.

"They might have carried us through the cold weather;
there's but a month more of it," said one middle-aged man
sorrowfully.

"They'll be talking to us about economy now, some o'
them big thinkers; they'll say we ought to learn how to save;
they always begin about that quick as the work stops," said a
youngish woman angrily. She was better dressed than most
of the group about her and had the keen, impatient look of
a leader. "They'll say that manufacturing is going to the dogs,
and capital's in worse distress than labor—"

"How is it those big railroads get along? They can't shut
down, there's none o' them stops: they cut down sometimes when they have to, but they don't turn off their help
this way," complained somebody else.

"Faith then! they don't know what justice is. They talk
about their justice all so fine," said a pale-faced young
Irishman—"justice is nine per cent. last year for the men that
had the money and no rise at all for the men that did the
work."

"They say the shut-down's going to last all summer anyway. I'm going to pack my kit to-night," said a young fellow who had just married and undertaken with unusual pride and ambition to keep house. "The likes of me can't be idle. But where to look for any work for a mule spinner, the Lord only knows!"

Even the French were sobered for once and talked eagerly among themselves. Halfway down the street, in front of the French grocery, a man was haranguing his compatriots from the top of a packing-box. Everybody was anxious and excited by the sudden news. No work after a week from to-morrow until times were better. There had already been a cut-down, the mills had not been earning anything all winter. The agent had hoped to keep on for at least two months longer, and then to make some scheme about running at half time in the summer, setting aside the present work for simple yarn-making. He knew well enough that the large families were scattered through the mill rooms and that any pay would be a help. Some of the young men could be put to other work for the company; there was a huge tract of woodland farther back among the hills where some timber could be got ready for shipping. His mind was full of plans and anxieties and the telegram that morning struck him like a blow. He had asked that he might keep the card-room prices up to where the best men could make at least six dollars and a half a week and was hoping for a straight answer, but the words on the yellow paper seemed to dance about and make him dizzy. "Shut down Saturday 9th until times are better!" he repeated to himself. "Shut down until times are worse here in Farley!"

The agent stood at the counting-room window looking out at the piteous, defenseless groups that passed by. He wished bitterly that his own pay stopped with the rest; it did not seem fair that he was not thrown out upon the world too.

"I don't know what they're going to do. They shall have the last cent I've saved before anybody suffers," he said in his heart. But there were tears in his eyes when he saw Mrs. Kilpatrick go limping out of the gate. She waited a moment for her constant companion, poor little Maggie the doffer, and they went away up the street toward their poor lodging holding each other fast by the hand. Maggie's father and grandfather and great-grandfather had all worked in the Farley mills; they had left no heritage but work behind them for this orphan child; they had never been able to save so much that a long illness, a prolonged old age, could not waste their slender hoards away.

4

It would have been difficult for an outsider to understand the sudden plunge from decent comfort to actual poverty in this small mill town. Strange to say, it was upon the smaller families that the strain fell the worst in Farley, and upon men and women who had nobody to look to but themselves. Where a man had a large household of children and several of these were old enough to be at work, and to put aside their wages or pay for their board; where such a man was of a thrifty and saving turn and a ruler of his household like old James Dow in the cloth-hall, he might feel sure of a comfortable hoard and be fearless of a rainy day. But with a young man who worked single-handed for his wife and a little flock, or one who had an invalid to work for, that heaviest of burdens to the poor, the door seemed to be shut and barred against prosperity, and life became a test of one's power of endurance.

The agent went home late that noon from the counting-room. The street was nearly empty, but he had no friendly look or word for anyone whom he passed. Those who knew him well only pitied him, but it seemed to the tired man as if every eye must look at him with reproach. The long mill buildings of gray stone with their rows of deep-set windows wore a repellent look of strength and solidity. More than one man felt bitterly his own personal weakness as he turned to look at them. The ocean of fate seemed to be dashing him against their gray walls—what use was it to fight against the Corporation? Two great forces were in opposition now, and happiness could come only from their serving each other in harmony.

The stronger force of capital had withdrawn from the

league; the weaker one, labor, was turned into an utter help-lessness of idleness. There was nothing to be done; you can-not rebel against a shut-down, you can only submit.

A week later the great wheel stopped early on the last day of work. Almost everyone left his special charge of ma-chinery in good order, oiled and cleaned and slackened with a kind of affectionate lingering care, for one person loves his machine as another loves his horse. Even little Maggie pushed her bobbin-box into a safe place near the overseer's desk and tipped it up and dusted it out with a handful of waste. At the foot of the long winding stairs Mrs. Kilpatrick was putting away her broom, and she sighed as she locked the closet door; she had known hard times before. "They'll be wanting me with odd jobs; we'll be after getting along some way," she said with satisfaction.

"March is a long month, so it is—there'll be plinty time for change before the ind of it," said Mary Cassidy hopefully. "The agent will be thinking whatever can he do; sure he's very ingenious. Look at him how well he persuaded the di-rectors to l'ave off wit' making cotton cloth like everybody else, and catch a chance wit' all these new linings and things! He's done very well, too. There bees no sinse in a shut-down anny way, the looms and cards all suffers and the bands all slacks if they don't get stiff. I'd sooner pay folks to tind their work whatever it cost."

"'Tis true for you," agreed Mrs. Kilpatrick.

"What'll ye do wit' the shild, now she's no chance of pay, any more?" asked Mary relentlessly, and poor Maggie's eyes grew dark with fright as the conversation abruptly pointed her way. She sometimes waked up in misery in Mrs. Kilpatrick's warm bed, crying for fear that she was going to be sent back to the poorhouse.

"Maggie an' me's going to kape together awhile yet," said the good old woman fondly. "She's very handy for me, so she is. We 'on't part with 'ach other whativer befalls, so we 'on't," and Maggie looked up with a wistful smile, only half reassured. To her the shut-down seemed like the end of the world.

Some of the French people took time by the forelock and boarded the midnight train that very Saturday with all their possessions. A little later two or three families departed by the same train, under cover of the darkness between two days, without stopping to pay even their house rent. These mysterious flittings, like that of the famous Tartar tribe, roused a suspicion against their fellow countrymen, but after a succession of such departures almost everybody else thought it far cheaper to stay among friends. It seemed as if at any moment the great mill wheels might begin to turn, and the bell begin to ring, but day after day the little town was still and the bell tolled the hours one after another as if it were Sunday. The mild spring weather came on and the women sat mending or knitting on the doorsteps. More people moved away; there were but few men and girls left now in the quiet boarding-houses, and the spare tables were stacked one upon another at the end of the rooms. When planting-time came, word was passed about the Corporation that the agent was going to portion out a field that belonged to him a little way out of town on the South road, and let every man who had a family take a good-sized piece to plant. He also offered seed potatoes and garden seeds free to anyone who would come and ask for them at his house. The poor are very generous to each other, as a rule, and there was much borrowing and lending from house to house, and it was wonderful how long the people seemed to continue their usual fashions of life without distress. Almost everybody had saved a little bit of money and some had saved more; if one could no longer buy beefsteak he could still buy flour and potatoes, and a bit of pork lent a pleasing flavor, to content an idle man who had nothing to do but to stroll about town.

5

One night the agent was sitting alone in his large, half-furnished house. Mary Moynahan, his housekeeper, had gone up to the church. There was a timid knock at the door.

There were two persons waiting, a short, thick-set man and a pale woman with dark, bright eyes who was nearly a head taller than her companion.

"Come in, Ellen; I'm glad to see you," said the agent. "Have you got your wheel-barrow, Mike?" Almost all the would-be planters of the field had come under cover of darkness and contrived if possible to avoid each other.

"'Tisn't the potatoes we're after asking, sir," said Ellen. She was always spokeswoman, for Mike had an impediment in his speech. "The childher come up yisterday and got them while you'd be down at the counting-room. 'Twas Mary Moynahan saw to them. We do be very thankful to you, sir, for your kindness."

"Come in," said the agent, seeing there was something of consequence to be said. Ellen Carroll and he had worked side by side many a long day when they were young. She had been a noble wife to Mike, whose poor fortunes she had gladly shared for sake of his good heart, though Mike now and then paid too much respect to his often infirmities. There was a slight flavor of whisky now on the evening air, but it was a serious thing to put on your Sunday coat and go up with your wife to see the agent.

"We've come wanting to talk about any chances there might be with the mill," ventured Ellen timidly, as she stood in the lighted room; then she looked at Mike for reassurance. "We're very bad off, you see," she went on. "Yes, sir, I got them potaties, but I had to bake a little of them for supper and more again the day, for our breakfast. I don't know whatever we'll do whin they're gone. The poor children does be entreating me for them, Dan!"

The mother's eyes were full of tears. It was very seldom now that anybody called the agent by his christian name; there was a natural reserve and dignity about him, and there had come a definite separation between him and most of his old friends in the two years while he had managed to go to the School of Technology in Boston.

"Why didn't you let me know it was bad as that?" he asked. "I don't mean that anybody here should suffer while I've got a cent."

"The folks don't like to be begging, sir," said Ellen sorrowfully, "but there's lots of them does be in trouble. They'd ought to go away when the mills shut down, but for nobody knows where to go. Farley ain't like them big towns where a man'd pick up something else to do. I says to Mike: 'Come, Mike, let's go up after dark and tark to Dan; he'll help us out if he can,' says I—"

"Sit down, Ellen," said the agent kindly, as the poor woman began to cry. He made her take the armchair which the weaveroom girls had given him at Christmas two years before. She sat there covering her face with her hands, and trying to keep back her sobs and go quietly on with what she had to say. Mike was sitting across the room with his back to the wall anxiously twirling his hat round and round. "Yis, we're very bad off," he contrived to say after much futile stammering. "All the folks in the Corporation, but Mr. Dow, has got great bills run up now at the stores, and thim that had money saved has lint to thim that hadn't—'twill be long enough before anybody's free. Whin the mills starts up we'll have to spind for everything at once. The children is very hard on their clothes and they're all dropping to pieces. I thought I'd have everything new for them this spring, they do be growing so. I minds them and patches them the best I can." And again Ellen was overcome by tears. "Mike an' me's always been conthrivin' how would we get something laid up, so if anny one would die or be long sick we'd be equal to it, but we've had great pride to see the little gerrls go looking as well as anny, and we've worked very steady, but there's so manny of us we've had to pay rint for a large tenement and we'd only seventeen dollars and a little more when the shutdown was. Sure the likes of us has a right to earn more than our living, ourselves being so willing-hearted. 'Tis a long time now that Mike's been steady. We always had the pride to hope we'd own a house ourselves, and a pieceen o' land, but I'm thankful now—'tis as well for us; we've no chances to pay taxes now."

Mike made a desperate effort to speak as his wife faltered and began to cry again, and seeing his distress forgot her own, and supplied the halting words. "He wants to know if there's anny work he could get, some place else than Farley. Himself's been sixteen years now in the picker, first he was one of six and now he is one of the four since you got the new machines, yourself knows it well."

The agent knew about Mike; he looked compassionate as he shook his head. "Stay where you are, for a while at any rate. Things may look a little better, it seems to me. We will start up as soon as anyone does. I'll allow you twenty dollars a month after this; here are ten to start with. No, no, I've got no one depending on me and my pay is going on. I'm glad to share it with my friends. Tell the folks to come up and see me. Ahern and Sullivan and Michel and your brother Con; tell anybody you know who is really in distress. You've all stood by me!"

"'Tis all the lazy ones 'ould be coming if we told on the poor boy," said Ellen gratefully, as they hurried home. "Ain't he got the good heart? We'd ought to be very discrate, Mike!" and Mike agreed by a most impatient gesture, but by the time summer had begun to wane the agent was a far poorer man than when it had begun. Mike and Ellen Carroll were only the leaders of a sorrowful procession that sought his door evening after evening. Some asked for help who might have done without it, but others were saved from actual want. There were a few men who got work among the farms, but there was little steady work. The agent made the most of odd jobs about the mill yards and contrived somehow or other to give almost every household a lift. The village looked more and more dull and forlorn, but in August, when a traveling show ventured to give a performance in Farley, the Corporation hall was filled as it seldom was filled in prosperous times. This made the agent wonder, until he followed the crowd of workless, sadly idle men and women into the place of entertainment and looked at them with a sudden comprehension that they were spending their last cent for a little cheerfulness.

6

The agent was going into the counting-room one day when he met old Father Daley and they stopped for a bit of friendly talk.

"Could you come in for a few minutes, sir?" asked the younger man. "There's nobody in the counting-room."

The busy priest looked up at the weather-beaten clock in the mill tower.

"I can," he said. "'Tis not so late as I thought. We'll soon be having the mail."

The agent led the way and brought one of the directors' comfortable chairs from their committee-room. Then he spun his own chair face-about from before his desk and they sat down. It was a warm day in the middle of September. The windows were wide open on the side toward the river and there was a flicker of light on the ceiling from the sunny water. The noise of the fall was loud and incessant in the room. Somehow one never noticed it very much when the mills were running.

"How are the Duffys?" asked the agent.

"Very bad," answered the old priest gravely. "The doctor sent for me—he couldn't get them to take any medicine. He says that it isn't typhoid; only a low fever among them from bad food and want of care. That tenement is very old and bad, the drains from the upper tenement have leaked and spoiled the whole west side of the building. I suppose they never told you of it?"

"I did the best I could about it last spring," said the agent. "They were afraid of being turned out and they hid it for that reason. The company allowed me something for repairs as usual and I tried to get more; you see I spent it all before I knew what a summer was before us. Whatever I have done since I have paid for, except what they call legitimate work and care of property. Last year I put all Maple Street into first-rate order—and meant to go right through the Corporation. I've done the best I could," he protested with a bright spot of color in his cheeks. "Some of the men have tinkered up their tenements and I have counted it toward the rent, but they don't all know how to drive a nail."

"'Tis true for you; you have done the best you could," said the priest heartily, and both the men were silent, while the river, which was older than they and had seen a whole race of men disappear before they came—the river took this opportunity to speak louder than ever.

"I think that manufacturing prospects look a little brighter," said the agent, wishing to be cheerful. "There are some good orders out, but of course the buyers can take advantage of our condition. The treasurer writes me that we must be firm about not starting up until we are sure of business on a good paying margin."

"Like last year's?" asked the priest, who was resting himself in the armchair. There was a friendly twinkle in his eyes.

"Like last year's," answered the agent. "I worked like two men, and I pushed the mills hard to make that large profit. I saw there was trouble coming, and I told the directors and asked for a special surplus, but I had no idea of anything like this."

"Nine per cent. in these times was too good a prize," said Father Daley, but the twinkle in his eyes had suddenly disappeared.

"You won't get your new church for a long time yet," said the agent.

"No, no," said the old man impatiently. "I have kept the foundations going as well as I could, and the talk, for their own sakes. It gives them something to think about. I took the money they gave me in collections and let them have it back again for work. 'Tis well to lead their minds," and he gave a quick glance at the agent. "'Tis no pride of mine for church-building and no good credit with the bishop I'm after. Young men can be satisfied with those things, not an old priest like me that prays to be a father to his people."

Father Daley spoke as man speaks to man, straight out of an honest heart.

"I see many things now that I used to be blind about long ago," he said. "You may take a man who comes over, him and his wife. They fall upon good wages and their heads are turned with joy. They've been hungry for generations back and they've always seen those above them who dressed fine and lived soft, and they want a taste of luxury too; they're bound to satisfy themselves. So they'll spend and spend and have beefsteak for dinner every day just because they never had enough before, but they'd turn into wild beasts of selfishness, most of 'em, if they had no check. 'Tis there the church steps in. 'Remember your Maker and do Him honor in His house of prayer,' says she. 'Be self-denying, be thinking of eternity and of what's sure to come!' And you will join with me in believing that it's never those who have given most to the church who come first to the ground in a hard time like this. Show me a good church and I'll show you a thrifty people." Father Daley looked eagerly at the agent for sympathy.

"You speak the truth, sir," said the agent. "Those that give most are always the last to hold out with honest independence and the first to do for others."

"Some priests may have plundered their parishes for pride's sake; there's no saying what is in poor human nature," repeated Father Daley earnestly. "God forgive us all for unprofitable servants of Him and His church. I believe in saying more about prayer and right living, and less about collections, in God's house, but it's the giving hand that's the rich hand all the world over."

"I don't think Ireland has ever sent us over many misers; Saint Patrick must have banished them all with the snakes," suggested the agent with a grim smile. The priest shook his head and laughed a little and then both men were silent again in the counting-room.

The mail train whistled noisily up the road and came into the station at the end of the empty street, then it rang its loud bell and puffed and whistled away again.

"I'll bring your mail over, sir," said the agent, presently. "Sit here and rest yourself until I come back and we'll walk home together."

The leather mail-bag looked thin and flat and the leisurely postmaster had nearly distributed its contents by the time the agent had crossed the street and reached the office. His clerks were both off on a long holiday; they were brothers and were glad of the chance to take their vacations together. They had been on lower pay; there was little to do in the counting-room—hardly anybody's time to keep or even a letter to write.

Two or three loiterers stopped the agent to ask him the usual question if there were any signs of starting up; an old farmer who sat in his long wagon before the post-office asked for news too, and touched his hat with an awkward sort of military salute.

"Come out to our place and stop a few days," he said kindly. "You look kind of pinched up and bleached out, Mr. Agent; you can't be needed much here."

"I wish I could come," said the agent, stopping again and looking up at the old man with a boyish, expectant face. Nobody had happened to think about him in just that way, and he was far from thinking about himself. "I've got to keep an eye on the people that are left here; you see they've had a pretty hard summer."

"Not so hard as you have!" said the old man, as the agent went along the street. "You've never had a day of rest more than once or twice since you were born!"

There were two letters and a pamphlet for Father Daley and a thin handful of circulars for the company. In busy times there was often all the mail matter that a clerk could bring. The agent sat down at his desk in the counting-room and the priest opened a thick foreign letter with evident pleasure. "'Tis from an old friend of mine; he's in a monastery in France," he said. "I only hear from him once a year," and Father Daley settled himself in his armchair to read the close-written pages. As for the agent of the mills, he had quickly opened a letter from the treasurer and was not listening to anything that was said.

Suddenly he whirled round in his desk chair and held out the letter to the priest. His hand shook and his face was as pale as ashes.

"What is it? What's the matter?" cried the startled old man, who had hardly followed the first pious salutations of his own letter to their end. "Read it to me yourself, Dan; is there any trouble?"

"Orders — I've got orders to start up; we're going to start — I wrote them last week —"

But the agent had to spring up from his chair and go to the window next the river before he could steady his voice to speak. He thought it was the look of the moving water that made him dizzy. "We're going to start up the mills as soon as I can get things ready." He turned to look up at the thermometer as if it were the most important thing in the world; then the color rushed to his face and he leaned a moment against the wall.

"Thank God!" said the old priest devoutly. "Here, come and sit down, my boy. Faith, but it's good news, and I'm the first to get it from you."

They shook hands and were cheerful together; the foreign letter was crammed into Father Daley's pocket and he reached for his big cane.

"Tell everybody as you go up the street, sir," said Dan. "I've got a hurricane of things to see to; I must go the other way down to the storehouses. Tell them to pass the good news about town as fast as they can; 'twill hearten up the women."

All the anxious look had gone as if by magic from the agent's face.

Two weeks from that time the old mill bell stopped tolling for the slow hours of idleness and rang out loud and clear for the housekeepers to get up, and rang for breakfast, and later still for all the people to go in to work. Some of the old hands were gone for good and new ones must be broken in in their places, but there were many familiar faces to pass the counting-room windows into the mill yard. There were French families which had reappeared with surprising promptness. Michel and his pretty daughter were there, and a household of cousins who had come to the next tenement. The agent stood with his hands in his pockets and nodded soberly to one group after another. It seemed to him that he had never felt so happy in his life.

"Jolly-looking set this morning," said one of the clerks whose desk was close beside the window; he was a son of one of the directors, who had sent him to the agent to learn something about manufacturing.

"They've had a bitter hard summer that you know nothing about," said the agent slowly.

Just then Mrs. Kilpatrick and old Mary Cassidy came along, and little Maggie was with them. She had got back her old chance at doffing and the hard times were over. They all smiled with such blissful satisfaction that the agent smiled too, and even waved his hand.

Where's Nora?

1

"Where's Nora?"

The speaker was a small, serious-looking old Irishman, one of those Patricks who are almost never called Pat. He was well-dressed and formal, and wore an air of dignified authority.

"I don't know meself where's Nora then, so I don't," answered his companion. "The shild wouldn't stop for a sup o' breakfast before she'd go out to see the town, an' nobody's seen the l'aste smitch of her since. I might sweep the streets wit' a broom and I couldn't find her."

"Maybe she's strayed beyand and gone losing in the strange place," suggested Mr. Quin, with an anxious glance. "Didn't none o' the folks go wit' her?"

"How would annybody be goin' an' she up an' away before there was a foot out o' bed in the house?" answered Mike Duffy impatiently. "'Twas herself that caught sight of Nora stealin' out o' the door like a thief, an' meself getting me best sleep at the time. Herself had to sit up an' laugh in the bed and be plaguin' me wit' her tarkin'. 'Look at Nora!' says she. 'Where's Nora?' says I, wit' a great start. I thought something had happened the poor shild. 'Oh, go to slape, you fool!' says Mary Ann. "'Tis only four o'clock,' says she, 'an' that grasshopper greenhorn can't wait for broad day till she'll go out an' see the whole of Ameriky.' So I wint off to sleep again; the first bell was biginin' on the mill, and I had an hour an' a piece, good, to meself after that before Mary Ann come scoldin'. I don't be sleepin' so well as some folks the first part of the night."

Mr. Patrick Quin ignored the interest of this autobiographical statement, and with a contemptuous shake of the head began to feel in his pocket for a pipe. Every one knew that Mike Duffy was a person much too fond of his ease, and that all the credit of their prosperity belonged to his hard-worked wife. She had reared a family of respectable sons and daughters, who were all settled and doing well for themselves, and now she was helping to bring out some nephews and nieces from the old country. She was proud to have been born a Quin; Patrick Quin was her brother and a man of consequence.

"'Deed, I'd like well to see the poor shild," said Patrick. "I'd no thought they'd land before the day or to-morrow mornin', or I'd have been over last night. I suppose she brought all the news from home?"

"The folks is all well, thanks be to God," proclaimed Mr. Duffy solemnly. "'Twas late when she come; 'twas on the quarter to nine she got here. There's been great deaths after the winther among the old folks. Old Peter Murphy's gone, she says, an' his brother that lived over by Ballycannon died the same week with him, and Dan Donahoe an' Corny Donahoe's lost their old aunt on the twelfth of March, that gave them her farm to take care of her before I came out. She was old then, too."

"Faix, it was time for the old lady, so it was," said Patrick Quin, with affectionate interest. "She'd be the oldest in the parish this tin years past."

"Nora said 'twas a fine funeral; they'd three priests to her, and everything of the best. Nora was there herself and all our folks. The b'ys was very proud of her for being so old and respicted."

"Sure, Mary was an old woman, and I first coming out," repeated Patrick, with feeling. "I went up to her that Monday night, and I sailing on a Wednesday, an' she gave me her blessing and a present of five shillings. She said then she'd see me no more; 'twas poor old Mary had the giving hand, God bless

her and save her! I joked her that she'd soon be marrying
and coming out to Ameriky like meself. 'No,' says she, 'I'm
too old. I'll die here where I was born; this old farm is me
one home o' the world, and I'll never be afther l'avin' it; 'tis
right enough for you young folks to go,' says she. I couldn't
get my mouth open to answer her. 'Twas meself that was
very homesick in me inside, coming away from the old place,
but I had great boldness before every one. 'Twas old Mary
saw the tears in me eyes then. 'Don't mind, Patsy,' says she;
'if you don't do well there, come back to it an' I'll be glad to
take your folks in till you'll be afther getting started again.'
She hadn't the money then she got afterward from her cousin
in Dublin; 'twas the kind heart of her spoke, an' meself being
but a boy that was young to maintain himself, let alone a
family. Thanks be to God, I've done well, afther all, but for
me crooked leg. I does be dr'amin' of going home sometimes; 'tis often yet I wake up wit' the smell o' the wet bushes

in the mornin' when a man does be goin' to his work at home."

Mike Duffy looked at his brother-in-law with curiosity; the two men were sitting side by side before Mike's house on a bit of green bank between the sidewalk and the road. It was May, and the dandelions were blooming all about them, thick in the grass. Patrick Quin reached out and touched one of them with his stick. He was a lame man, and had worked as section hand for the railroad for many years, until the bad accident which forced him to retire on one of the company's rarely given pensions. He had prevented a great disaster on the road; those who knew him well always said that his position had never been equal to his ability, but the men who stood above him and the men who were below him held Patrick Quin at exactly the same estimate. He had limped along the road from the clean-looking little yellow house that he owned not far away on the river-bank, and his mind was upon his errand.

"I come over early to ask the shild wouldn't she come home wit' me an' ate her dinner," said Patrick. "Herself sent me; she's got a great wash the day, last week being so rainy, an' we niver got word of Nora being here till this morning, and then everybody had it that passed by, wondering what got us last night that we weren't there."

"'Twas on the quarter to nine she come," said Uncle Mike, taking up the narrative with importance. "Herself an' me had blown out the light, going to bed, when there come a scuttlin' a the door and I heard a bit of a laugh like the first bird in the morning" —

"'Stop where you are, Bridget,' says I," continued Mr. Quin, without taking any notice, "'an' I'll take me third leg and walk over and bring Nora down to you.' Bridget's great for the news from home now, for all she was so sharp to be l'aving it."

"She brought me a fine present, and the mate of it for yourself," said Mike Duffy. "Two good thorn sticks for the two of us. They're inside in the house."

"A thorn stick, indeed! Did she now?" exclaimed Patrick, with unusual delight. "The poor shild, did she do that now? I've thought manny's the time since I got me lameness how well I'd like one o' those old-fashioned thorn sticks. Me own is one o' them sticks a man'd carry tin years and toss it into a brook at the ind an' not miss it."

"They're good thorn sticks, the both of them," said Mike complacently. "I don't know 'ill I bring 'em out before she comes."

"Is she a pritty slip of a gerrl, I d' know?" asked Patrick, with increased interest.

"She ain't, then," answered his companion frankly. "She does be thin as a young grasshopper, and she's red-headed, and she's freckled, too, from the sea, like all them young things comin' over; but she's got a pritty voice, like all her mother's folks, and a quick eye like a bird's. The old-country talk's fresh in her mouth, too, so it is; you'd think you were coming out o' mass some spring morning at home and hearing all the girls whin they'd be chatting and funning at the boys. I do be thinking she's a smart little girl, annyway; look at her off to see the town so early and not back yet, bad manners to her! She'll be wanting some clothes, I suppose; she's very old-fashioned looking; they does always be wanting new clothes, coming out," and Mike gave an ostentatious sigh and suggestive glance at his brother-in-law.

"'Deed, I'm willing to help her get a good start; ain't she me own sister's shild?" agreed Patrick Quin cheerfully. "We've been young ourselves, too. Well, then, 'tis bad news of old Mary Donahoe bein' gone at the farm. I always thought if I'd go home how I'd go along the fields to get the great welcome from her. She was one that always liked to hear folks had done well," and he looked down at his comfortable, clean old clothes as if they but reminded him how poor a young fellow he had come away. "I'm very sorry afther Mary; she was a good 'oman, God save her!"

"Faix, it was time for her," insisted Mike, not without sympathy. "Were you afther wanting her to live forever, the poor soul? An' the shild said she'd the best funeral was ever in the parish of Dunkenny since she remimbered it. What could anny one ask more than that, and she r'aching such an age, the cr'atur'! Stop here awhile an' you'll hear all the tark from Nora; she told over to me all the folks that was there. Where has she gone wit' herself, I don't know? Mary Ann!" he turned his head toward the house and called in a loud, complaining tone; "where's Nora, annyway?"

"Here's Nora, then," a sweet girlish voice made unexpected

reply, and a light young figure flitted from the sidewalk behind him and stood lower down on the green bank.

"What's wanting wit' Nora?" and she stooped quickly like
a child to pick some of the dandelions as if she had found
gold. She had a sprig of wild-cherry blossom in her dress,
which she must have found a good way out in the country.

"Come now, and speak to Patrick Quin, your mother's
own brother, that's waiting here for you all this time you've
been running over the place," commanded Mr. Duffy, with
some severity.

"An' is it me own Uncle Patsy, dear?" exclaimed Nora, with
the sweetest brogue and most affectionate sincerity. "Oh, that
me mother could see him too!" and she dropped on her
knees beside the lame little man and kissed him, and knelt
there looking at him with delight, holding his willing hand in
both her own.

"An' ain't you got me mother's own looks, too? Oh, Uncle
Patsy, is it yourself, dear? I often heard about you, and I
brought you me mother's heart's love, 'deed I did then! It's
many a lovely present of a pound you've sent us. An' I've got
a thorn stick that grew in the hedge, goin' up the little rise of
ground above the Wishin' Brook, sir; mother said you'd mind
the place well when I told you."

"I do then, me shild," said Patrick Quin, with dignity; "'tis
manny the day we all played there together, for all we're so
scattered now and some dead, too, God rest them! Sure,
you're a nice little gerrl, an' I give you great welcome and the
hope you'll do well. Come along wit' me now. Your Aunty
Biddy's jealous to put her two eyes on you, an' we never
getting the news you'd come till late this morning. 'I'll go
fetch Nora for you,' says I, to contint her. 'They'll be tarked
out at Duffy's by this time,' says I."

"Oh, I'm full o' tark yet!" protested Nora gayly. "Coom on,
then, Uncle Patsy!" and she gave him her strong young hand
as he rose.

"An' how do you be likin' Ameriky?" asked the pleased
old man, as they walked along.

"I like Ameriky fine," answered the girl gravely. She was
taller than he, though she looked so slender and so young. "I
was very downhearted, too, l'avin' home and me mother,

but I'll go back to it some day, God willing, sir; I couldn't die wit'out seeing me mother again. I'm all over the place here since daybreak. I think I'd like work best on the railway," and she turned toward him with a resolved and serious look.

"Wisha! there's no work at all for a girl like you on the Road," said Uncle Patsy patiently. "You've a bit to learn yet, sure; 'tis the mill you mane."

"There'll be plinty work to do. I always thought at home, when I heard the folks tarking, that I'd get work on the railway when I'd come to Ameriky. Yis, indeed, sir!" continued Nora earnestly. "I was looking at the mills just now, and I heard the great n'ise from them. I'd never be after shutting meself up in anny mill out of the good air. I've no call to go to jail yet in thim mill walls. Perhaps there'd be somebody working next me that I'd never get to like, sir."

There was something so convinced and decided about these arguments that Uncle Patsy, usually the calm autocrat of his young relatives, had nothing whatever to say. Nora was gently keeping step with his slow gait. She had won his heart once for all when she called him by the old boyish name her mother used forty years before, when they played together by the Wishing Brook.

"I wonder do you know a b'y named Johnny O'Callahan?" inquired Nora presently, in a somewhat confidential tone; "a pritty b'y that's working on the railway; I seen him last night and I coming here; he ain't a guard at all, but a young fellow that minds the brakes. We stopped a long while out there; somethin' got off the rails, and he advised wit' me, seeing I was a stranger. He said he knew you, sir."

"Oh, yes, Johnny O'Callahan. I know him well; he's a nice b'y, too," answered Patrick Quin approvingly.

"Yis, sir, a pritty b'y," said Nora, and her color brightened for an instant, but she said no more.

2

Mike Duffy and his wife came into the Quins' kitchen one week-day night, dressed in their Sunday clothes; they had been making a visit to their well-married daughter in Lawrence. Patrick Quin's chair was comfortably tipped back against the wall, and Bridget, who looked somewhat gloomy, was putting away the white supper-dishes.

"Where's Nora?" demanded Mike Duffy, after the first salutations.

"You may well say it; I'm afther missing her every hour in the day," lamented Bridget Quin.

"Nora's gone into business on the Road then, so she has," said Patrick, with an air of fond pride. He was smoking, and in his shirt-sleeves; his coat lay on the wooden settee at the other side of the room.

"Hand me me old coat there before you sit down; I want me pocket," he commanded, and Mike obeyed. Mary Ann, fresh from her journey, began at once to give a spirited account of her daughter's best room and general equipment for housekeeping, but she suddenly became aware that the tale was of secondary interest. When the narrator stopped for breath there was a polite murmur of admiration, but her husband boldly repeated his question. "Where's Nora?" he insisted, and the Quins looked at each other and laughed.

"Ourselves is old hins that's hatched ducks," confessed Patrick. "Ain't I afther telling you she's gone into trade on the Road?" and he took his pipe from his mouth,—that after-supper pipe which neither prosperity nor adversity was apt to interrupt. "She's set up for herself over-right the long switch, down there at Birch Plains. Nora'll soon be rich, the cr'atur'; her mind was on it from the first start; 'twas from one o' them O'Callahan b'ys she got the notion, the night she come here first a greenhorn."

"Well, well, she's lost no time; ain't she got the invintion!" chuckled Mr. Michael Duffy, who delighted in the activity of others. "What excuse had she for Birch Plains? There's no town to it."

"'Twas a chance on the Road she mint to have from the first," explained the proud uncle, forgetting his pipe altogether; "'twas that she told me the first day she came out, an' she walking along going home wit' me to her dinner; 'twas the first speech I had wit' Nora. ''Tis the mills you mane?' says I. 'No, no, Uncle Patsy!' says she, 'it ain't the mills at all, at all; 'tis on the Road I'm going.' I t'ought she'd some wild notion she'd soon be laughing at, but she settled down very quiet-like with Aunty Biddy here, knowing yourselves to be going to Lawrence, and I told her stay as long as she had a mind. Wisha, she'd an old apron on her in five minutes' time, an' took hold wit' the wash, and wint singing like a blackbird out in the yard at the line. 'Sit down, Aunty!' says she; 'you're not so light-stepping as me, an' I'll tell you all the news from home; an' I'll get the dinner, too, when I've done this,' says she. Wisha, but she's the good cook for such a young thing; 'tis Bridget says it as well as meself. She made a stew that day; 'twas like the ones her mother made Sundays, she said, if they'd be lucky in getting a piece of meat; 'twas a fine-tasting stew, too; she thinks we're all rich over here. 'So we are, me dear!' says I, 'but every one don't have the sinse to believe it.'"

"Spake for yourselves!" exclaimed one of the listeners.

"You do be like Father Ross, always pr'achin' that we'd best
want less than want more. He takes honest folks for fools,
poor man," said Mary Ann Duffy, who had no patience at any
time with new ideas.

"An' so she wint on the next two or t'ree days," said Patrick
approvingly, without noticing the interruption, "being as quiet
as you'd ask, and being said by her aunt in everything; and
she wouldn't let on she was homesick, but she'd no tark of
anything but the folks at Dunkinny. When there'd be nothing
to do for an hour she'd slip out and be gone wit' herself for
a little while, and be very still comin' in. Last Thursday, after
supper, she ran out; but by the time I'd done me pipe, back
she came flying in at the door.

"'I'm going off to a place called Birch Plains to-morrow
morning, on the nine, Uncle Patsy,' says she; 'do you know
where it is?' says she. 'I do,' says I; ''twas not far from it I
broke me leg wit' the dam' derrick. 'Twas to Jerry Ryan's house
they took me first. There's no town there at all; 'tis the only
house in it; Ryan's the switchman.'

"'Would they take me to lodge for a while, I d' know?'
says she, havin' great business. 'What 'd ye be afther in a
place like that?' says I. 'Ryan's got girls himself, an' they're all
here in the mills, goin' home Saturday nights, 'less there's
some show or some dance. There's no money out there.'
She laughed then an' wint back to the door, and in come
Mickey Dunn from McLoughlin's store, lugging the size of
himself of bundles. 'What's all this?' says I; ''tain't here they
belong; I bought nothing to-day.' 'Don't be scolding!' says she,
and Mickey got out of it laughing. 'I'm going to be cooking
for meself in the morning!' says she, with her head on one
side, like a cock-sparrow. 'You lind me the price o' the fire
and I'll pay you in cakes,' says she, and off she wint then to
bed. 'Twas before day I heard her at the stove, and I smelt a
baking that made me want to go find it, and when I come
out in the kitchen she'd the table covered with her cakeens,
large and small. 'What's all this whillalu, me topknot-hin?'
says I. 'Ate that,' says she, and hopped back to the oven-
door. Her aunt come out then, scolding fine, and whin she
saw the great baking she dropped down in a chair like she'd
faint and her breath all gone. 'We 'ont ate them in ten days,'
says she; 'no, not till the blue mould has struck them all,

God help us!' says she. 'Don't bother me,' says Nora; 'I'm goin' off with them all on the nine. Uncle Patsy'll help me wit' me basket.'

"'Uncle Patsy 'ont now,' says Bridget. Faix, I thought she was up with one o' them t'ree days' scolds she'd have when she was young and the childre' all the one size. You could hear the bawls of her a mile away.

"'Whishper, dear,' says Nora; 'I don't want to be livin' on anny of me folks, and Johnny O'Callahan said all the b'ys was wishing there was somebody would kape a clane little place out there at Birch Plains,—with something to ate and the like of a cup of tay. He says 'tis a good little chance; them big trains does all be waiting there tin minutes and fifteen minutes at a time, and everybody's hungry. 'I'll thry me luck for a couple o' days,' says I; "'tis no harm, an' I've tin shillings o' me own that Father Daley gave me wit' a grand blessing and I l'aving home behind me."'"

"'What tark you have of Johnny O'Callahan,' says I.

"Look at this now!" continued the proud uncle, while Aunt Biddy sat triumphantly watching the astonished audience; "'tis a letter I got from the shild last Friday night," and he brought up a small piece of paper from his coat-pocket. "She writes a good hand, too. 'Dear Uncle Patsy,' says she, 'this leaves me well, thanks be to God. I'm doing the roaring trade with me cakes; all Ryan's little boys is selling on the trains. I took one pound three the first day: 'twas a great excursion train got stuck fast and they'd a hot box on a wheel keeping them an hour and two more trains stopping for them; 'twould be a very pleasant day in the old country that anybody'd take a pound and three shillings. Dear Uncle Patsy, I want a whole half-barrel of that same flour and ten pounds of sugar, and I'll pay it back on Sunday. I sind respects and duty to Aunty Bridget and all friends; this l'aves me in great haste. I wrote me dear mother last night and sint her me first pound, God bless her.'"

"Look at that for you now!" exclaimed Mike Duffy. "Didn't I tell every one here she was fine an' smart?"

"She'll be soon President of the Road," announced Aunt Mary Ann, who, having been energetic herself, was pleased to recognize the same quality in others.

"She don't be so afraid of the worruk as the worruk's afraid of her," said Aunt Bridget admiringly. "She'll have her fling for a while and be glad to go in and get a good chance in the mill, and be kaping her plants in the weave-room windows this winter with the rest of the girls. Come, tell us all about Elleneen and the baby. I ain't heard a word about Lawrence yet," she added politely.

"Ellen's doing fine, an' it's a pritty baby. She's got a good husband, too, that l'aves her her own way and the keep of his money every Saturday night," said Mary Ann; and the little company proceeded to the discussion of a new and hardly less interesting subject. But before they parted, they spoke again of Nora.

"She's a fine, crabbed little gerrl, that little Nora," said Mr. Michael Duffy.

"Thank God, none o' me childre' is red-headed on me; they're no more to be let an' held than a flick o' fire," said Aunt Mary Ann. "Who'd ever take the notion to be setting up business out there on the Birchy Plains?"

"Ryan's folks'll look after her, sure, the same as ourselves," insisted Uncle Patsy hopefully, as he lighted his pipe again. It was like a summer night; the kitchen windows were all open, the month of May was nearly at an end, and there was a sober croaking of frogs in the low fields that lay beyond the village.

3

"Where's Nora?" Young Johnny O'Callahan was asking the question; the express had stopped for water, and he seemed to be the only passenger; this was his day off.

Mrs. Ryan was sitting on her doorstep to rest in the early evening; her husband had been promoted from switch-tender to boss of the great water-tank which was just beginning to be used, and there was talk of further improvements and promotions at Birch Plains; but the good-natured wife sensibly declared that the better off a woman was, the harder she always had to work.

She took a long look at Johnny, who was dressed even more carefully than if it were a pleasant Sunday.

"This don't be your train, annyway," she answered, in a

meditative tone. "How come you here now all so fine, I'd like to know, riding in the cars like a lord; ain't you brakeman yet on old twinty-four?"

"'Deed I am, Mrs. Ryan; you wouldn't be afther grudging a boy his day off? Where's Nora?"

"She's gone up the road a bitteen," said Mrs. Ryan, as if she suddenly turned to practical affairs. "She's worked hard the day, poor shild! and she took the cool of the evening, and the last bun she had left, and wint away with herself. I kep' the taypot on the stove for her, but she'd have none at all, at all!"

The young man turned away, and Mrs. Ryan looked after him with an indulgent smile. "He's a pritty b'y," she said. "I'd like well if he'd give a look at one o' me own gerrls; Julia, now, would look well walking with him, she's so dark. He's got money saved. I saw the first day he come after the cakeens 'twas the one that baked them was in his mind. She's lucky, is Nora; well, I'm glad of it."

It was fast growing dark, and Johnny's eyes were still dazzled by the bright lights of the train as he stepped briskly along the narrow country road. The more he had seen Nora and the better he liked her, the less she would have to say to him, and tonight he meant to find her and have a talk. He had only succeeded in getting half a dozen words at a time since the night of their first meeting on the slow train, when she had gladly recognized the peculiar brogue of her own country-side, as Johnny called the names of the stations, and Johnny's quick eyes had seen the tired-looking, uncertain, yet cheerful little greenhorn in the corner of the car, and asked if she were not the niece that was coming out to Mrs. Duffy. He had watched the growth of her business with delight, and heard praises of the cakes and buns with willing ears; was it not his own suggestion that had laid the foundation of Nora's prosperity? Since their first meeting they had always greeted each other like old friends, but Nora grew more and more willing to talk with any of her breathless customers who hurried up the steep bank from the trains than with him. She would never take any pay for her wares from him, and for a week he had stopped coming himself and sent by a friend his money for the cakes; but one day poor Johnny's heart could not resist the temptation of going with the rest, and Nora had given him a happy look, straightforward and significant. There was no time for a word, but she picked out a crusty bun, and he took it and ran back without offering to pay. It was the best bun that a man ever ate. Nora was two months out now, and he had never walked with her an evening yet.

The shadows were thick under a long row of willows; there was a new moon, and a faint glow in the west still lit the sky. Johnny walked on the grassy roadside with his ears keen to hear the noise of a betraying pebble under Nora's light foot. Presently his heart beat loud and all out of time as a young voice began to sing a little way beyond.

Nora was walking slowly away, but Johnny stopped still to listen. She was singing "A Blacksmith Courted Me," one of the quaintest and sweetest of the old-country songs, as she strolled along in the soft-aired summer night. By the time she came to "My love's gone along the fields," Johnny hurried on to overtake her; he could hear the other verses some other time,—the bird was even sweeter than the voice.

Nora was startled for a moment, and stopped singing, as if she were truly a bird in a bush, but she did not flutter away. "Is it yourself, Mister Johnny?" she asked soberly, as if the frank affection of the song had not been assumed.

"It's meself," answered Johnny, with equal discretion. "I come out for a mout'ful of air; it's very hot inside in the town. Days off are well enough in winter, but in summer you get a fine air on the train. 'Twas well we both took the same direction. How is the business? All the b'ys are saying they'd be lost without it; sure there ain't a stomach of them but wants its bun, and they cried the length of the Road that day the thunder spoiled the baking."

"Take this," said Nora, as if she spoke to a child; "there's a fine crust of sugar on the top. 'Tis one I brought out for me little supper, but I'm so pleased wit' bein' rich that I've no need at all for 'ating. An' I'm as tired as I'm rich," she added, with a sigh; "'tis few can say the same in this lazy land."

"Sure, let's ate it together; 'tis a big little cakeen," urged Johnny, breaking the bun and anxiously offering Nora the larger piece. "I can like the taste of anything better by halves, if I've got company. You ought to have a good supper of tay and a piece of steak and some potaties rather than this! Don't

be giving yourself nothing but the saved cakes, an' you working so hard!"

"'Tis plenty days I'd a poorer supper when I was at home,"
said Nora sadly; "me father dying so young, and all of us
begging at me mother's skirts. It's all me thought how will I
get rich and give me mother all the fine things that's in the
world. I wish I'd come over sooner, but it broke my heart
whinever I'd think of being out of sight of her face. She looks
old now, me mother does."

Nora may have been touched by Johnny's affectionate
interest in her supper; she forgot all her shyness and drew
nearer to him as they walked along, and he drew a little
closer to her.

"My mother is dead these two years," he said simply. "It
makes a man be very lonesome when his mother's dead. I
board with my sister that's married; I'm not much there at
all. I do be thinking I'd like a house of my own. I've plinty
saved for it."

"I said in the first of coming out that I'd go home again
when I had fifty pounds," said Nora hastily, and taking the
other side of the narrow road. "I've got a piece of it already,
and I've sent back more beside. I thought I'd be gone two
years, but some days I think I won't be so long as that."

"Why don't you be afther getting your mother out? 'Tis
so warm in the winter in a good house, and no dampness
like there does be at home; and her brother and her sister
both being here." There was deep anxiety in Johnny's voice.

"Oh, I don't know indeed!" said Nora. "She's very wake-
hearted, is me mother; she'd die coming away from the old
place and going to sea. No, I'm going to work meself and go
home; I'll have presents, too, for everybody along the road,
and the children'll be running and skrieghing afther me, and
they'll all get sweeties from me. 'Tis a very poor neighborhood where we live, but a lovely sight of the say. It ain't often
annybody comes home to it, but 'twill be a great day then,
and the poor old folks'll all be calling afther me: 'Where's
Nora?' 'Show me Nora!' 'Nora, sure, what have you got for
me?' I 'ont forget one of them aither, God helping me!" said
Nora, in a passion of tenderness and pity. "And oh, Johnny,
then afther that I'll see me mother in the door!"

Johnny was so close at her side that she slipped her hand

into his, and neither of them stopped to think about so sweet and natural a pleasure. "I'd like well to help you, me darlin'," said Johnny.

"Sure, an' wasn't it yourself gave me all me good fortune?" exclaimed Nora. "I'd be hard-hearted an' I forgot that so soon and you a Kerry boy, and me mother often spaking of your mother's folks before ever I thought of coming out!"

"Sure and wouldn't you spake the good word to your mother about me sometime, dear?" pleaded Johnny, openly taking the part of lover. Nora's hand was still in his; they were walking slowly in the summer night. "I loved you the first word I heard out of your mouth, — 'twas like a thrush from home singing to me there in the train. I said when I got home that night, I'd think of no other girl till the day I died."

"Oh!" said Nora, frightened with the change of his voice. "Oh, Johnny, 'tis too soon. We never walked out this way before; you'll have to wait for me; perhaps you'd soon be tired of poor Nora, and the likes of one that's all for saving and going home! You'll marry a prittier girl than me some day," she faltered, and let go his hand.

"Indeed, I won't, then," insisted Johnny O'Callahan stoutly.

"Will you let me go home to see me mother?" said Nora soberly. "I'm after being very homesick, 'tis the truth for me. I'd lose all me courage if it wa'n't for the hope of that."

"I will, indeed," said Johnny honestly.

Nora put out her hand again, of her own accord. "I'll not say no, then," she whispered in the dark. "I can't work long unless I do be happy, and—well, leave me free till the month's end, and maybe then I'll say yes. Stop, stop!" she let go Johnny's hand, and hurried along by herself in the road, Johnny, in a transport of happiness, walking very fast to keep up. She reached a knoll where he could see her slender shape against the dim western sky. "Wait till I tell you; whisper!" said Nora eagerly. "You know there were some of the managers of the road, the superintendents and all those big ones, came to Birch Plains yesterday?"

"I did be hearing something," said Johnny, wondering.

"There was a quiet-spoken, nice old gentleman came asking me at the door for something to eat, and I being there baking; 'tis my time in the morning whin the early trains does be gone, and I've a fine stretch till the expresses are beginnin' to screech,—the tin, and the tin-thirty-two, and the Flying Aigle. I was in a great hurry with word of an excursion coming in the afternoon and me stock very low; I'd been baking since four o'clock. He'd no coat on him, 'twas very warm; and I thought 'twas some tramp. Lucky for me I looked again and I said, 'What are you wanting, sir?' and then I saw he'd a beautiful shirt on him, and was very quiet and pleasant.

"'I came away wit'out me breakfast,' says he. 'Can you give me something without too much throuble?' says he. 'Do you have anny of those buns there that I hear the men talking about?'

"'There's buns there, sir,' says I, 'and I'll make you a cup of tay or a cup of coffee as quick as I can,' says I, being pleased at the b'ys giving me buns a good name to the likes of him. He was very hungry, too, poor man, an' I ran to Mrs. Ryan to see if she'd a piece of beefsteak, and my luck ran before me. He sat down in me little place and enjoyed himself well.

"'I had no such breakfast in tin years, me dear,' said he at the last, very quiet and thankful; and he l'aned back in the chair to rest him, and I cleared away, being in the great hurry; and he asking me how I come there, and I tolt him, and how long I'd been out, and I said it was two months and a piece, and she being always in me heart, I spoke of me mother, and all me great hopes.

"Then he sat and thought as if his mind wint to his own business, and I wint on wit' me baking. Says he to me after a while, 'We're going to build a branch road across country to connect with the great mountain-roads,' says he; 'the junction's going to be right here; 'twill give you a big market for your buns. There'll be a lunch-counter in the new station; do you think you could run it?' says he, spaking very sober.

"'I'd do my best, sir, annyway,' says I. 'I'd look out for the best of help. Do you know Patrick Quin, sir, that was hurt on the Road and gets a pinsion, sir?'

"'I do,' says he. 'One of the best men that ever worked for this company,' says he.

"'He's me mother's own brother, then, an' he'll stand by me,' says I; and he asked me me name and wrote it down in a book he got out of the pocket of him. 'You shall have the place if you want it,' says he; 'I won't forget,' and off he wint as quiet as he came."

"Tell me who was it?" said Johnny O'Callahan, listening eagerly.

"Mr. Ryan come tumbling in the next minute, spattered with water from the tank. 'Well, then,' says he, 'is your fine company gone?'

"'He is,' says I. 'I don't know is it some superintendent? He's a nice man, Mr. Ryan, whoiver he is,' says I.

"'Tis the Gineral Manager of the Road,' says he; 'that's who he is, sure!'

"My apron was all flour, and I was in a great rage wit' so much to do, but I did the best I could for him. I'd do the same for anny one so hungry," concluded Nora modestly.

"Ain't you got the Queen's luck!" exclaimed Johnny admiringly. "Your fortune's made, me dear. I'll have to come off the road to help you."

"Oh, two good trades'll be better than one!" answered Nora gayly, "and the big station nor the branch road aren't building yet."

"What a fine little head you've got," said Johnny, as they reached the house where the Ryans lived, and the train was whistling that he meant to take back to town. "Goodnight, annyway, Nora; nobody'd know from the size of your head there could be so much inside in it!"

"I'm lucky, too," announced Nora serenely. "No, I won't give you me word till the ind of the month. You may be seeing another gerrl before that, and calling me the red-headed sparrow. No, I'll wait a good while, and see if the two of us can't do better. Come, run away, Johnny. I'll drop asleep in the road; I'm up since four o'clock making me cakes for plinty b'ys like you."

The Ryans were all abed and asleep, but there was a lamp burning in the kitchen. Nora blew it out as she stole into her hot little room. She had waited, talking eagerly with Johnny, until they saw the headlight of the express like a star, far down the long line of double track.

4

The summer was not ended before all the railroad men knew about Johnny O'Callahan's wedding and all his good fortune. They boarded at the Ryans' at first, but late in the evenings

"Nora had a good sisterly work-basket ready." Illustrated by A. I. Keller; *Scribner's Magazine,* 1898. Courtesy Dartmouth College Library.

Johnny and his wife were at work, building as if they were birds. First, there was a shed with a broad counter for the cakes, and a table or two, and the boys did not fail to notice that Nora had a good sisterly work-basket ready, and was quick to see that a useful button was off or a stitch needed. The next fortnight saw a room added to this, where Nora had her own stove, and cooking went on steadily. Then there was another room with white muslin curtains at the windows, and scarlet-runner beans made haste to twine themselves to a line of strings for shade. Johnny would unload a few feet of clean pine boards from the freight train, and within a day or two they seemed to be turned into a wing of the small castle by some easy magic. The boys used to lay wagers and keep watch, and there was a cheer out of the engine-cab and all along the platforms one day when a tidy sty

first appeared and a neat pig poked his nose through the
fence of it. The buns and biscuits grew famous; customers
sent for them from the towns up and down the long railroad line, and the story of thrifty, kind-hearted little Nora
and her steady young husband was known to a surprising
number of persons. When the branch road was begun, Nora
and Johnny took a few of their particular friends to board,
and business was further increased. On Sunday they always
went into town to mass and visited their uncles and aunts
and Johnny's sister. Nora never said that she was tired, and
almost never was cross. She counted her money every Saturday night, and took it to Uncle Patsy to put into the bank.
She had long talks about her mother with Uncle Patsy, and
he always wrote home for her when she had no time. Many
a pound went across the sea in the letters, and so another
summer came; and one morning when Johnny's train
stopped, Nora stood at the door of the little house and held
a baby in her arms for all the boys to see. She was white as
a ghost and as happy as a queen. "I'll be making the buns
again pretty soon," she cried cheerfully. "Have courage, boys;
'twon't be long first; this one'll be selling them for me on the
Flying Aigle, don't you forget it!" And there was a great ring-
ing of the engine-bell a moment after, when the train started.

5

It was many and many a long month after this that an old
man and a young woman and a baby were journeying in a
side-car along one of the smooth Irish roads into County
Kerry. They had left the railroad an hour before; they had
landed early that morning at the Cove of Cork. The side-car
was laden deep with bundles and boxes, but the old horse
trotted briskly along until the gossoon who was driving
turned into a cart-track that led through a furzy piece of
wild pasture-ground up toward the dark rain-clouded hills.

"See, over there's Kinmare!" said the old man, looking
back. "Manny's the day I've trudged it and home again. Oh, I
know all this country; I knew it well whin ayther of you wa'n't
born!"

"God be thanked, you did, sir!" responded the gossoon,
with fervent admiration. He was a pleasant-looking lad in a

ragged old coat and an absolutely roofless hat, through which
his bright hair waved in the summer wind. "Och, but the
folks'll be looking out of all the doors to see you come. I'll
be afther saying I never drove anny party with so rich a heart;
there ain't a poor soul that asked a pinny of us since we left
Bantry but she's got the shillin'. Look a' the flock coming
now, sir, out of that house. There's the four-legged lady that
pays the rint watchin' afther them from the door, too. They
think you're a gintleman that's shootin', I suppose. 'Tis Tom
Flaherty's house, poor crathur; he died last winter, God rest
him; 'twas very inconvanient for him an' every one at the
time, wit' snow on the ground and a great dale of sickness
and distress. Father Daley, poor man, had to go to the hospital in Dublin wit' himself to get a leg cut off, and we'd nothing but rain out of the sky afther that till all the stones in the
road was floatin' to the top."

"Son of old John Flaherty, I suppose?" asked the traveler,
with a knowing air, after he had given the eager children
some pennies and gingerbread, out of a great package. One
of the older girls knew Nora and climbed to the spare seat at
her side to join the company. "Son of old John Flaherty, I
suppose, that was there before? There was Flahertys there
and I l'aving home more than thirty-five years ago."

"Sure there's plinty Flahertys in it now, glory be to God!"
answered the charioteer, with enthusiasm. "I'd have no
mother meself but for the Flahertys." He leaped down to
lead the stumbling horse past a deep rut and some loose
stones, and beckoned the little girl sternly from her proud
seat. "Run home, now!" he said, as she obeyed: "I'll give you a
fine drive an' I coming down the hill;" but she had joined the
travelers with full intent, and trotted gayly alongside like a
little dog.

The old passenger whispered to his companion that they'd
best double the gossoon's money, or warm it with two or
three shillings extra, at least, and Nora nodded her prompt
approval. "The old folks are all getting away; we'd best give a
bitteen to the young ones they've left afther them," said Uncle
Patsy, by way of excuse. "Och, there's more beggars between
here and Queenstown than you'd find in the whole of
Ameriky."

It seemed to Nora as if her purseful of money were warm

against her breast, like another heart; the sixpences in her pocket all felt warm to her fingers and hopped by themselves into the pleading hands that were stretched out all along the way. The sweet clamor of the Irish voices, the ready blessings, the frank requests to those returning from America with their fortunes made, were all delightful to her ears. How she had dreamed of this day, and how the sun and shadows were chasing each other over these upland fields at last! How close the blue sea looked to the dark hills! It seemed as if the return of one prosperous child gave joy to the whole landscape. It was the old country the same as ever, — old Mother Ireland in her green gown, and the warm heart of her ready and unforgetting. As for Nora, she could only leave a wake of silver sixpences behind her, and when these were done, a duller trail of ha'pennies; and the air was full of blessings as she passed along the road to Dunkenny.

By this time Nora had stopped talking and laughing. At first everybody on the road seemed like her near relation, but the last minutes seemed like hours, and now and then a tear went shining down her cheek. The old man's lips were moving, — he was saying a prayer without knowing it; they were almost within sight of home. The poor little white houses, with their high gable-ends and weather-beaten thatch, that stood about the fields among the green hedges; the light shower that suddenly fell out of the clear sky overhead, made an old man's heart tremble in his breast. Round the next slope of the hill they should see the old place.

The wheel-track stopped where you turned off to go to the Donahoe farm, but no old Mary was there to give friendly welcome. The old man got stiffly down from the side-car and limped past the gate with a sigh; but Nora hurried ahead, carrying the big baby, not because he couldn't walk, but because he could. The young son had inherited his mother's active disposition, and would run straight away like a spider the minute his feet were set to the ground. Now and then, at the sight of a bird or a flower in the grass, he struggled to get down. "Whisht, now!" Nora would say; "and aren't you going to see Granny indeed? Keep aisy now, darlin'!"

The old heart and the young heart were beating alike as these exiles followed the narrow footpath round the shoulder of the great hill; they could hear the lambs bleat and the tinkling of the sheep-bells that sweet May morning. From the lower hillside came the sound of voices. The neighbors had seen them pass, and were calling to each other across the fields. Oh, it was home, home! the sight of it, and the smell of the salt air and the flowers in the bog, the look of the early white mushrooms in the sod, and the song of the larks overhead and the blackbirds in the hedges! Poor Ireland was gay-hearted in the spring weather, and Nora was there at last. "Oh, thank God, we're safe home!" she said again. "Look, here's the Wishing Brook; d' ye mind it?" she called back to the old man.

"I mind everything the day, no fear for me," said Patrick Quin.

The great hillside before them sloped up to meet the blue sky, the golden gorse spread its splendid tapestry against the green pasture. There was the tiny house, the one house in Ireland for Nora; its very windows watched her coming. A whiff of turf-smoke flickered above the chimney, the white walls were as white as the clouds above; there was a figure moving about inside the house, and a bent little woman in her white frilled cap and a small red shawl pinned about her shoulders came and stood in the door.

"Oh, me mother, me mother!" cried Nora; then she dropped the baby in the soft grass, and flew like a pigeon up the hill and into her mother's arms.

6

The gossoon was equal to emergencies; he put down his heavier burden of goods and picked up the baby, lest it might run back to America. "God be praised, what's this coming after ye?" exclaimed the mother, while Nora, weeping for joy, ran past her into the house. "Oh, God bless the shild that I thought I'd never see. Oh!" and she looked again at the stranger, the breathless old man with the thorn stick, whom everybody had left behind. "'Tis me brother Patsy! Oh, me heart's broke wit' joy!" and she fell on her knees among the daisies.

"It's meself, then!" said Mr. Patrick Quin. "How are ye the

day, Mary? I always t'ought I'd see home again, but 'twas Nora enticed me now. Johnny O'Callahan's a good son to ye; he'd liked well to come with us, but he gets short l'ave on the Road, and he has a fine, steady job; he'll see after the business, too, while we're gone; no, I couldn't let the two childer cross the say alone. Coom now, don't be sayin' anny more prayers; sure, we'll be sayin' them together in the old church coom Sunday.

"There, don't cry, Mary, don't cry, now! Coom in in the house! Sure, all the folks sint their remimbrance, and hoped you'd come back with us and stay a long while. That's our intintion, too, for you," continued Patrick, none the less tearful himself because he was so full of fine importance; but nobody could stop to listen after the first moment, and the brother and sister were both crying faster than they could talk. A minute later the spirit of the hostess rose to her great occasion.

"Go, chase those white hins," Nora's mother commanded the gossoon, who had started back to bring up more of the rich-looking bundles from the side-car. "Run them up-hill now, or they'll fly down to Kinmare. Go now, while I stir up me fire and make a cup o' tay. 'Tis the laste I can do whin me folks is afther coming so far!"

"God save all here!" said Uncle Patsy devoutly, as he stepped into the house. There sat little Nora with the tired baby in her arms; to tell the truth, she was crying now for lack of Johnny. She looked pale, but her eyes were shining, and a ray of sunlight fell through the door and brightened her red hair. She looked quite beautiful and radiant as she sat there.

"Well, Nora, ye're here, ain't you?" said the old man.

"Only this morning," said the mother, "whin I opened me eyes I says to meself: 'Where's Nora?' says I; 'she do be so long wit'out writing home to me;' look at her now by me own fire! Wisha, but what's all this whillalu and stramach down by the brook? Oh, see now! the folks have got word; all the folks is here! Coom out to them, Nora; give me the shild; coom out, Patsy boy!"

"Where's Nora? Where's Nora?" they could hear the loud cry coming, as all the neighbors hurried up the hill.

Bold Words
at the Bridge

1

"'Well, now,' says I, 'Mrs. Con'ly,' says I, 'how ever you may
tark, 'tis nobody's business and I wanting to plant a few
pumpkins for me cow in among me cabbages. I've got the
right to plant whatever I may choose, if it's the divil of a crop
of t'istles in the middle of me ground.' 'No ma'am, you ain't,'
says Biddy Con'ly; 'you ain't got anny right to plant t'istles
that's not for the public good,' says she; and I being so hasty
wit' me timper, I shuk me fist in her face then, and herself
shuk her fist at me. Just then Father Brady come by, as luck
ardered, an' recommended us would we keep the peace. He
knew well I'd had my provocation; 'twas to herself he spoke
first. You'd think she owned the whole corporation. I wished
I'd t'rown her over into the wather, so I did, before he come
by at all. 'Twas on the bridge the two of us were. I was stepping home by meself very quiet in the afthernoon to put me
tay-kittle on for supper, and herself overtook me,—ain't she
the bold thing!

"'How are you the day, Mrs. Dunl'avy?' says she, so mincin'
an' preenin', and I knew well she'd put her mind on having
words wit' me from that minute. I'm one that likes to have
peace in the neighborhood, if it wa'n't for the likes of her,

that makes the top of me head lift and clat' wit' rage like a pot-lid!"

"What was the matter with the two of you?" asked a listener, with simple interest.

"Faix indeed, 'twas herself had a thrifle of melons planted the other side of the fince," acknowledged Mrs. Dunleavy. "She said the pumpkins would be the ruin of them intirely. I says, and 'twas thrue for me, that I'd me pumpkins planted the week before she'd dropped anny old melon seed into the ground, and the same bein' already dwining from so manny bugs. Oh, but she's blackhearted to give me the lie about it, and say those poor things was all up, and she'd thrown lime on 'em to keep away their inemies when she first see me come out betune me cabbage rows. How well she knew what I might be doing! Me cabbages grows far apart and I'd plinty of room, and if a pumpkin vine gets attention you can entice it wherever you pl'ase and it'll grow fine and long, while the poor cabbages ates and grows fat and round, and no harm to annybody, but she must pick a quarrel with a quiet 'oman in the face of every one.

"We were on the bridge, don't you see, and plinty was passing by with their grins, and loitering and stopping afther they were behind her back to hear what was going on betune us. Annybody does be liking to get the sound of loud talk an' they having nothing better to do. Biddy Con'ly, seeing she was well watched, got the airs of a pr'acher, and set down whatever she might happen to be carrying and tried would she get the better of me for the sake of their admiration. Oh, but wa'n't she all drabbled and wet from the roads, and the world knows meself for a very tidy walker!

"'Clane the mud from your shoes if you're going to dance;' 'twas all I said to her, and she being that mad she did be stepping up and down like an old turkey-hin, and shaking her fist all the time at me. 'Coom now, Biddy,' says I, 'what put you out so?' says I. 'Sure, it creeps me skin when I looks at you! Is the pig dead,' says I, 'or anny little thing happened to you, ma'am? Sure this is far beyond the rights of a few pumpkin seeds that has just cleared the ground!' and all the folks laughed. I'd no call to have tark with Biddy Con'ly before them idle b'ys and gerrls, nor to let the two of us become their laughing-stock. I tuk up me basket, being ashamed then, and I meant to go away, mad as I was. 'Coom, Mrs. Con'ly!' says I, 'let bygones be bygones; what's all this whillalu we're afther having about nothing?' says I very pleasant.

"'May the divil fly away with you, Mary Dunl'avy!' says she then, 'spoiling me garden ground, as every one can see, and full of your bold talk. I'll let me hens out into it this afternoon, so I will,' says she, and a good deal more. 'Hold off,' says I, 'and remember what fell to your aunt one day when she sint her hins in to pick a neighbor's piece, and while her own back was turned they all come home and had every sprouted bean and potatie heeled out in the hot sun, and all her fine lettuces picked into Irish lace. We've lived neighbors,' says I, 'thirteen years,' says I; 'and we've often had words together above the fince,' says I, 'but we're neighbors yet, and we've no call to stand here in such spectacles and disgracing ourselves and each other. Coom, Biddy,' says I, again, going away with me basket and remimbering Father Brady's caution whin it was too late. Some o' the b'ys went off too, thinkin' 'twas all done.

"'I don't want anny o' your Coom Biddy's,' says she, stepping at me, with a black stripe across her face, she was that destroyed with rage, and I stepped back and held up me basket between us, she being bigger than I, and I getting no chance, and herself slipped and fell, and her nose got a clout with the hard edge of the basket, it would trouble the saints to say how, and then I picked her up and wint home with her to thry and quinch the blood. Sure I was sorry for the crathur an' she having such a timper boiling in her heart.

"'Look at you now, Mrs. Con'ly,' says I, kind of soft, 'you 'ont be fit for mass these two Sundays with a black eye like this, and your face arl scratched, and every bliguard has gone the lingth of the town to tell tales of us. I'm a quiet 'oman,' says I, 'and I don't thank you,' says I, whin the blood was stopped, — 'no, I don't thank you for disgracin' an old neighbor like me. 'Tis of our prayers and the grave we should be thinkin', and not be having bold words on the bridge.' Wisha! but I t'ought I was after spaking very quiet, and up she got and caught up the basket, and I dodged it by good luck, but after that I walked off and left her to satisfy her foolishness

with b'ating the wall if it pl'ased her. I'd no call for her company anny more, and I took a vow I'd never spake a word to
her again while the world stood. So all is over since then
betune Biddy Con'ly and me. No, I don't look at her at all!"

2

Some time afterward, in late summer, Mrs. Dunleavy stood,
large and noisy, but generous-hearted, addressing some remarks from her front doorway to a goat on the sidewalk. He
was pulling some of her cherished foxgloves through the
picket fence, and eagerly devouring their flowery stalks.

"How well you rache through an honest fince, you black
pirate!" she shouted; but finding that harsh words had no
effect, she took a convenient broom, and advanced to strike
a gallant blow upon the creature's back. This had the simple
effect of making him step a little to one side and modestly
begin to nibble at a tuft of grass.

"Well, if I ain't plagued!" said Mrs. Dunleavy sorrowfully;
"if I ain't throubled with every wild baste, and me cow that
was some use gone dry very unexpected, and a neighbor
that's worse than none at all. I've nobody to have an honest
word with, and the morning being so fine and pleasant. Faix,
I'd move away from it, if there was anny place I'd enjoy better. I've no heart except for me garden, me poor little crops
is doing so well; thanks be to God, me cabbages is very fine.
There does be those that overlooked me pumpkins for the
poor cow; they're no size at all wit' so much rain."

The two small white houses stood close together, with
their little gardens behind them. The road was just in front,
and led down to a stone bridge which crossed the river to
the busy manufacturing village beyond. The air was fresh
and cool at that early hour, the wind had changed after a
season of dry, hot weather; it was just the morning for a
good bit of gossip with a neighbor, but summer was almost
done, and the friends were not reconciled. Their respective
acquaintances had grown tired of hearing the story of the
quarrel, and the novelty of such a pleasing excitement had
long been over. Mrs. Connelly was thumping away at a handful of belated ironing, and Mrs. Dunleavy, estranged and soli-

"The road . . . led down to a stone bridge which crossed the river to the busy manufacturing village beyond." Illustrated by Maude and Genevieve Cowles; *McClure's Magazine*, 1899. Courtesy Dartmouth College Library.

tary, sighed as she listened to the iron. She was sociable by nature, and she had an impulse to go in and sit down as she used at the end of the ironing table.

"Wisha, the poor thing is mad at me yet, I know that from the sounds of her iron; 'twas a shame for her to go picking a quarrel with the likes of me," and Mrs. Dunleavy sighed heavily and stepped down into her flower-plot to pull the distressed foxgloves back into their places inside the fence. The seed had been sent her from the old country, and this was the first year they had come into full bloom. She had been hoping that the sight of them would melt Mrs. Connelly's heart into some expression of friendliness, since they had come from adjoining parishes in old County Kerry. The goat lifted his head, and gazed at his enemy with mild interest; he was pasturing now by the roadside, and the foxgloves had proved bitter in his mouth.

Mrs. Dunleavy stood looking at him over the fence, glad of even a goat's company.

"Go 'long there; see that fine little tuft ahead now," she advised him, forgetful of his depredations. "Oh, to think I've nobody to spake to, the day!"

At that moment a woman came in sight round the turn of the road. She was a stranger, a fellow country-woman, and she carried a large newspaper bundle and a heavy handbag. Mrs. Dunleavy stepped out of the flower-bed toward the gate, and waited there until the stranger came up and stopped to ask a question.

"Ann Bogan don't live here, do she?"

"She don't," answered the mistress of the house, with dignity.

"I t'ought she didn't; you don't know where she lives, do you?"

"I don't," said Mrs. Dunleavy.

"I don't know ayther; niver mind, I'll find her; 'tis a fine day, ma'am."

Mrs. Dunleavy could hardly bear to let the stranger go away. She watched her far down the hill toward the bridge before she turned to go into the house. She seated herself by the side window next Mrs. Connelly's, and gave herself to her thoughts. The sound of the flatiron had stopped when the traveler came to the gate, and it had not begun again. Mrs. Connelly had gone to her front door; the hem of her calico dress could be plainly seen, and the bulge of her apron, and she was watching the stranger quite out of sight. She even came out to the doorstep, and for the first time in many weeks looked with friendly intent toward her neighbor's house. Then she also came and sat down at her side window. Mrs. Dunleavy's heart began to leap with excitement.

"Bad cess to her foolishness, she does be afther wanting to come round; I'll not make it too aisy for her," said Mrs. Dunleavy, seizing a piece of sewing and forbearing to look up. "I don't know who Ann Bogan is, annyway; perhaps herself does, having lived in it five or six years longer than me. Perhaps she knew this woman by her looks, and the heart is out of her with wanting to know what she asked from me. She can sit there, then, and let her irons grow cold!

"There was Bogans living down by the brick mill when I first come here, neighbors to Flaherty's folks," continued Mrs. Dunleavy, more and more aggrieved. "Biddy Con'ly ought to know the Flahertys, they being her cousins. 'Twas a fine loud-talking 'oman; sure Biddy might well enough have heard her inquiring of me, and have stepped out, and said if she knew Ann Bogan, and satisfied a poor stranger that was hunting the town over. No, I don't know anny one in the name of Ann Bogan, so I don't," said Mrs. Dunleavy aloud, "and there's nobody I can ask a civil question, with every one that ought to be me neighbors stopping their mouths, and keeping black grudges whin 'twas meself got all the offince."

"Faix 'twas meself got the whack on me nose," responded

Mrs. Connelly quite unexpectedly. She was looking squarely at the window where Mrs. Dunleavy sat behind the screen of blue mosquito netting. They were both conscious that Mrs. Connelly made a definite overture of peace.

"That one was a very civil-spoken 'oman that passed by just now," announced Mrs. Dunleavy, handsomely waiving the subject of the quarrel and coming frankly to the subject of present interest. "Faix, 'tis a poor day for Ann Bogans; she'll find that out before she gets far in the place."

"Ann Bogans was plinty here once, then, God rest them! There was two Ann Bogans, mother and daughter, lived down by Flaherty's when I first come here. They died in the one year, too; 'tis most thirty years ago," said Bridget Connelly, in her most friendly tone.

"'I'll find her,' says the poor 'oman as if she'd only to look; indeed, she's got the boldness," reported Mary Dunleavy, peace being fully restored.

"'Twas to Flaherty's she'd go first, and they all moved to La'rence twelve years ago, and all she'll get from anny one would be the address of the cimet'ry. There was plenty here knowing to Ann Bogan once. That 'oman is one I've seen long ago, but I can't name her yet. Did she say who she was?" asked the neighbor.

"She didn't; I'm sorry for the poor 'oman, too," continued Mrs. Dunleavy, in the same spirit of friendliness. "She'd the expectin' look of one who came hoping to make a nice visit and find friends, and herself lugging a fine bundle. She'd the looks as if she'd lately come out; very decent, but old-fashioned. Her bonnet was made at home annyways, did ye mind? I'll lay it was bought in Cork when it was new, or maybe 'twas from a good shop in Bantry or Kinmare, or some o' those old places. If she'd seemed satisfied to wait, I'd made her the offer of a cup of tay, but off she wint with great courage."

"I don't know but I'll slip on me bonnet in the afthernoon and go find her," said Biddy Connelly, with hospitable warmth. "I've seen her before, perhaps 'twas long whiles ago at home."

"Indeed I thought of it myself," said Mrs. Dunleavy, with approval. "We'd best wait, perhaps, till she'd be coming back; there's no train now till three o'clock. She might stop here till the five, and we'll find out all about her. She'll have a very lonesome day, whoiver she is. Did you see that old goat 'ating the best of me fairy-fingers that all bloomed the day?" she asked eagerly, afraid that the conversation might come to an end at any moment; but Mrs. Connelly took no notice of so trivial a subject.

"Me melons is all getting ripe," she announced, with an air of satisfaction. "There's a big one must be ate now while we can; it's down in the cellar cooling itself, an' I'd like to be dropping it, getting down the stairs. 'Twas afther picking it I was before breakfast, itself having begun to crack open. Himself was the b'y that loved a melon, an' I ain't got the heart to look at it alone. Coom over, will ye, Mary?"

"'Deed then an' I will," said Mrs. Dunleavy, whose face was close against the mosquito netting. "Them old pumpkin vines was no good anny way; did you see how one of them had the invintion, and wint away up on the fince entirely wit' its great flowers, an' there come a rain on 'em, and so they all blighted? I'd no call to grow such stramming great things in my piece annyway, 'ating up all the goodness from me beautiful cabbages."

3

That afternoon the reunited friends sat banqueting together and keeping an eye on the road. They had so much to talk over and found each other so agreeable that it was impossible to dwell with much regret upon the long estrangement. When the melon was only half finished the stranger of the morning, with her large unopened bundle and the heavy handbag, was seen making her way up the hill. She wore such a weary and disappointed look that she was accosted and invited in by both the women, and being proved by Mrs. Connelly to be an old acquaintance, she joined them at their feast.

"Yes, I was here seventeen years ago for the last time," she explained. "I was working in Lawrence, and I came over and spent a fortnight with Honora Flaherty; then I wint home that year to mind me old mother, and she lived to past ninety. I'd nothing to keep me then, and I was always homesick afther America, so back I come to it, but all me old frinds and neighbors is changed and gone. Faix, this is the first welcome I've got yet from anny one. 'Tis a beautiful wel-

come, too,—I'll get me apron out of me bundle, by your l'ave, Mrs. Con'ly. You've a strong resemblance to Flaherty's folks, dear, being cousins. Well, 'tis a fine thing to have good neighbors. You an' Mrs. Dunleavy is very pleasant here so close together."

"Well, we does be having a hasty word now and then, ma'am," confessed Mrs. Dunleavy, "but ourselves is good neighbors this manny years. Whin a quarrel's about nothing betune friends, it don't count for much, so it don't."

"Most quarrels is the same way," said the stranger, who did not like melons, but accepted a cup of hot tea. "Sure, it always takes two to make a quarrel, and but one to end it; that's what me mother always told me, that never gave anny one a cross word in her life."

"'Tis a beautiful melon," repeated Mrs. Dunleavy for the seventh time. "Sure, I'll plant a few seed myself next year; me pumpkins is no good afther all me foolish pride wit' 'em. Maybe the land don't suit 'em, but glory be to God, me cabbages is the size of the house, an' you'll git the pick of the best, Mrs. Con'ly."

"What's melons betune friends, or cabbages ayther, that they should ever make any trouble?" answered Mrs. Connelly handsomely, and the great feud was forever ended.

But the stranger, innocent that she was the harbinger of peace, could hardly understand why Bridget Connelly insisted upon her staying all night and talking over old times, and why the two women put on their bonnets and walked, one on either hand, to see the town with her that evening. As they crossed the bridge they looked at each other shyly, and then began to laugh.

"Well, I missed it the most on Sundays going all alone to mass," confessed Mary Dunleavy. "I'm glad there's no one here seeing us go over, so I am."

"'Twas ourselves had bold words at the bridge, once, that we've got the laugh about now," explained Mrs. Connelly politely to the stranger.

A Landlocked Sailor

One morning early in June Doctor Hallett, a young assistant surgeon in the navy, took it into his head to go trouting. It was his second day of leave after a long sea-service, from which he had come straight inland to his old home. On this first morning of the visit he had happened to wake very early and find the sky overcast and the wind in the south, and yielded at once before a temptation to leave an affectionate household sound asleep, except the old coachman at the stable, who was always stirring with the first birds. It took only a moment to choose the best rod that was left in a boyish den above the carriage-house, then there was a hurried breakfast to be stolen, and off the Doctor tramped gayly to find his favorite haunt, the Dale Brook, and follow it up among the hills.

Nothing better can fall to the lot of a busy, much-companioned man than just such a chance of being alone in a piece of well-known country long unvisited. It was some years since John Hallett had followed the Dale Brook before, but neither appeared to have changed. The brook had often suffered in its conditions from drought and freshets, and so had the man, but both were in good condition on that June day; the Doctor at least had that comfortable sense of existence and continuance which made him, for the moment, know and understand himself. One possesses very seldom this unaffected sense of self, the rarely felt self-acquaintance that fell upon us first at the first conscious step we took out of infancy. Solitary and undisturbed, we are now and then aware of ourselves: not the person the world takes us to be, not the ideal person our hopes and ambitions are trying to evolve, but the real man. This is the clear self-consciousness that mirrors the surroundings of a happy solitude. One might say that such moments as these, such closeness to nature, are like a Sunday rest to all one's activities. "In it thou shalt do no work;" in it alone one may "listen to the voices" and receive what nature has to give and what man himself is hardly ever fit to receive.

The fern-filled crevices of the ledges were familiar to the young surgeon's feet. He wandered slowly up the great wooded slopes where the brook came swiftly down, turning now and then to look through the branches where there was a glimpse of the lower country, and toiled hastily across teasing bits of swamp where the alders were tangled overhead and the light was dim and the brook shallowed out into black mud and bright green grass and sopping clods of moss. Now and then the sun almost shone out and quickly clouded over again: it was a perfect morning for fishing. The brook was full and clear, and deep lay its flashing falls, where bubbles floated long and trout were hiding. There was a scent of new checkerberry leaves and bay on the high land, and of sweet-flag and mint in the swamps; overhead the cat-birds and yellow-hammers scolded together like disagreeing neighbors. Beyond the first long slope and the boggy strip of upland was a breadth of high, uneven farming country, where the best reaches of the little stream wound their crooked way; beyond this again rose the higher hills. The fisherman began to notice the pleasant weight of his basket as he tramped ahead towards the best pools of all, for although it was a good bit of distance even in his light-footed boyish days, he always made a point of going up to the very source of the brook in a cleft between the hills, — a tiny pond full of springs and shaded by noble oaks.

The strip of country which was about to be crossed was mostly taken up by sheep-pastures and tillage. At the edge of the woods, when Doctor Hallett was just pushing his grumbling way through a clump of alders and birches which

fringed the brook in a fashion most provoking to the calm-
est angler, he heard the bushes cracking and rustling not
very far off, and supposed his neighbor to be a wandering
cow, but presently, just at the edge of the open pasture, he
caught sight of the head and shoulders of a man. One is
fiercely jealous by instinct of a rival fisherman. He hitched at
his shoulder-strap with satisfaction at the weight of eight or
ten good trout which the basket held,—they were safe
enough at any rate; then the holiday surgeon stopped short
and looked sharply at his antagonist, whose figure was unexpected enough but quite familiar. For one dark instant he
was puzzled to recall the man's name; there was no rod in
his hand.

"Holloa, Mike!" he shouted the next moment,—having
rustled no bushes himself, out of respect to silence-loving
trout,—"Holloa, Mike! How in the world do you happen to
be here?"

"The divil may fly away wit' me if it ain't the Docther," said
Mike, coming straight through the brushwood as if it were
tall grass. "God bless you, sir; is it yourself, sir? I heard long
ago that this was your own country and your folks lived
down below there, but I thought you were on the say. Well,
well, Docther, I was often hoping for the day I'd see you again.
Any luck, sir?" and the Doctor swung round his creel in silence.

"Faix, they did all be waiting for you then," said Mike handsomely, shaking his officer's hand in a warm, determined
grasp, and looking at him with delighted eyes. "There do be
plinty folks thramps up the old brook and goes home as
impty as they comes. Dic'ration Day there wa'n't a b'y in the
country that wa'n't fishing in it, and—well, you've got a thrick
with the throut; that's plain, Docther."

"Those can find who know where to look," said the Surgeon, not displeased by such flattery, and they turned and
walked side by side into the shade of some little pines. The
sun was high and the morning was getting late, and the angler had begun to lose the first zest of pleasure.

Three years before, just when he was last ordered to sea,
Doctor Hallett had been stationed at one of the marine hospi-
tals, where Mike Dillon was brought one day with half a dozen
bones broken and generally out of repair by means of a fall

and bad crushing under a broken hoisting apparatus on board ship. They had known each other before as surgeon and patient on a long cruise, and it fell to Doctor Hallett's lot to mend him and patch him and pull him through his smart touch of surgical fever and at last send him out, a crippled man, into a careless world. He was pale with hospital bleach, and as weak as he was stout with rapid building up,—discharged for good, of course, and appealingly cheerful as they said good-by. The Doctor remembered well how he had wondered what the poor, good-natured, great fellow was going to do. He might turn into a shoemaker; but one couldn't force one's self to speak of it, for Dillon had the spirit of a rover. After the very best that could be done for him, one of his legs was a good deal shorter than the other. The Surgeon looked now to see how he managed with walking, and was pleased to notice that he seemed to be put to less inconvenience than had been feared.

"Mike," said he after they had recovered from a seizure of awkwardness born of mingled strangeness and old familiarity,—"Mike, you look as if you had turned into a farmer and got landlocked."

"Wasn't I born a farmer then, faith!" answered Mike. "County Wexford, sir, parish o' Duncannon. The first thing I remember, Docther, was riding home top of a barrow o' little pertaties and me father trundling me, God rest him! No, I wa'n't born on the say, sir," said Mike sweetly, "I'm a Wexford boy."

The former patient was something well above six feet in height if he stood on his long leg. There was the look of an old-fashioned New England farmer, like a kind of veneer, over his Irish sailorhood. Conformity and ready-made clothes were to blame for it. The Doctor stretched himself like a dog in the sun; the breeze sung in the pines and shone on the young birch leaves. "Oh, how good it is to feel the steady ground under you," he said. "Come, speak out, Dillon. You know I'm interested in your case. I should have as soon expected to meet old Parlow in a prayer-meeting as to come across you here in a pasture." Old Parlow was a hospital nurse.

"Sure he might forget himself an' talk very strange to the audience, sir," chuckled Mike. "He'd the most bad words of any man I ever talked with, but he'd a very tender hand with the sick. Parlow was like a mother to me some o' thim bad nights. He's dead, sir."

"Is Parlow dead?" exclaimed the Doctor.

"He is that indeed," answered Dillon with considerable solemnity. "I do be wondering sometimes if they've got it settled where they'd sind him,—there was good in Parlow,—but I suppose he'll be after getting his orders to one place or the other by now. Were you back at the old hospit'l lately, sir?"

"No," said the Doctor "not for more than three years. I'm just in from Valparaiso."

They were sitting together in a little open space at the woodland's edge where some fine sheep turf was just then well shaded, and near by were plenty of junipers and lamb-kill-laurel and low blueberry bushes. Just at the Doctor's back was a high-standing, fragile old pine-stump, where a great tree must have been cut in winter when the snow lay deep. He lay back against a knee of it with his feet stretched out over the soft grass, while Mike Dillon sat erect at his side, looking down affectionately now and then, and amusing himself by pulling great pieces off the powdery old wood, which sifted down, disclosing shiny black ants that hurried about in despair. Mike struck at them furiously or tossed the bits of rotten wood after a stray bird or butterfly, sprinkling his companion with brown and gray crumbs and chips and pieces of red-topped moss. Both the men had a comfortable, boyish feeling, but they were silent for a time; there may have been some sense of superior rank and old naval regulations, but the business of the man-of-war's man with the stump and the butterflies went steadily on.

"I suppose this was all pasture once," said the Surgeon at last, "for all these birches and young stuff have come up within a few years; they ought to be cleared. This turf is the best sort; good sheep-pasture, isn't it, through all this region?"

"You're right there, sir," said Dillon, clearing his throat deliberately, as if there were need of further comment and explanation, but he said nothing more.

"This must have been an enormous white pine," said the Doctor. "It's a very old stump and all worn away by weather, but it must he a good four feet across now at the butt."

"Pretty close to it," said Dillon, turning to regard the ruin. "I does be minding some old story they tell about this stump; 'twas a known tree at any rate."

"How far do you live from here?" inquired the Doctor by way of leading question.

"In the old Dale place itself, sir, or up to Dillon's, as they say now," answered Dillon proudly. "I was walking me finces, having a little spare time."

"Good for you," said Doctor Hallett with large sympathy; but there was a pause in the conversation, and presently he went on:

"I left the old Minerva in Brooklyn only yesterday; she's likely to be there all summer. I think she's worse below decks than they were ready to believe."

"She'd more leaks than a basket this spring four years ago when I was aboard of her," asserted Dillon. "The innocint inspictors was ch'ated in a lot of copper sh'athing, and there was black-hearted conthractors retired from business soon after to live 'asy on their means." Dillon spoke with an air of complete assurance. "There was rats in her the size of dogs, though, an' we knew by that she'd float longer, or we'd all gone ashore together. I always remimbered those rats for the biggest I was ever acquainted with. Anybody does be having great knowledge of rats that stays long in the service. My wife 'on't believe me when I speak of the size of them."

"Your wife?" interrupted the Surgeon with renewed interest. "I know all about those rats, but I never heard of your being married."

"Well, now I'm feeling homesick for the old days from seeing you, sir, I'm as well to be telling you honest, sir, but 'tis true for me I'm well married and settled since I was to the hospit'l," answered Mike with an air of pride. "Look here, Docther, let me pit the fish out here a bit further in the cool bushes. They're fine trout, an' it's growing warm." He got to his feet a little clumsily, took the basket from beneath a clump of juniper, and carried it down towards the brook, where he could be heard tearing off handfuls of birch leaves to cover them, and letting the young tree-tops swish back. The Doctor got his matchbox out and a handful of cigars. When Mike returned he sat down a trifle further away than at first, so that he and the Doctor faced each other. The Doctor sud-

denly became aware that he personified for the moment all
the delights of sea-going friendship, that he was a kind of
embodiment of the service. Mike was looking squarely in
his face and had lost all self-consciousness: they were only
two sailors together.

"I ain't seen a navy man this long time to have a word
with," said Dillon. "I does be thinking of the b'ys a good deal,
sir. No, keep it yoursilf, Docther; you'll want to be smoking a
bit as you're going home, an' I've got me pipe in me pocket'll
do for me. I don't know did you happen to see the old crew
of the Lion was paid off last week, home from Gibraltar? I
gets what I can on the papers, but that's not much," and
Mike gave a sigh. "I was born a farmer, but I never thought I'd
die one, sir."

The tobacco was well lighted; the desired moment for
the narrative of Mike's adventures seemed to have come.

"God bless us! I'll have to tell you all," said Mike; "'tis a
great story for a sayman that was always glad to be off shore.
Whin I got left out o' hospit'l that time by yourself and Parlow
I felt grand to be going; yourself knows how I'd been t'asing
as if for me liberty out of jail, for all I had great kindness
from every one there. I was none too strong, sir; there was
no strington in me legs, an' they so surprised with being
mismated altogether. Aff I wint wit' me bowld air, but I didn't
get far down the road on me leg that's too short an' me leg
that's too long till I felt as if the two of 'em was punching
through at me shoulders an' a great pain grinding in me back,
so I had to go sit down in the side o' the road. I tried would
I lay down, an' I tried would I sit up, an' I couldn't contint
myself wit' neither one till I cried me heart out there in the
dead leaves, an' a bird come an' lighted on a bush and made
me swear wit' her little song that begun new every time and
stopped short in the middle. I'd been light-hearted as a b'y,
faith I had, for all me hurts, an' now me life was broke in
two for me, an' I looked at me legs an' says I, 'Where'll you
go now, Mickey lad, an' what'll you do whin you get there?
You've got thim two damn legs an' a stiffness in your lift
elbow; an' just feel o' your poor back and your side how
they ache,' says I to myself, making the worst of everything.
'You're no sailor now,' says I, 'an' 'on't be a sailor again while

the world lives, an' that's the only fag ind of a trade you've got. Look at that now for you,' says I."

"Poor fellow!" said the Doctor.

"I thought the sky'd turned dark, I did indeed, sir," said Mike; "I wished I was back in the old hospit'l; I thought I'd creep back and beg lodgings for what work I'd do about the place, an' then I minded how old Parlow'd lift me in his arrums and I knew I'd no stringth to do that for a sick man nor anything else, and I'd got sick of the smell of the medicines, besides being ashamed to go back to it after me coming away so bold. I'd been allowed a taste of somethin' to stringthen me by Parlow when I was l'aving, and my heart was wake in me wit wanting more. I felt in me pocket for an ould knife Parlow gave me, mine being lost in the pocket of me bloody clothes the time I got hurted. I couldn't count the times I'd cursed Parlow as well as I knew how an' he paying me back the same way, but I cried for him thin wit' the knife in me hand for company, an' I in the side of the bushes by the fince. I never blamed any man since if I saw him a coward. 'Twas intirely from walking the first mile away from the hospit'l whin I'd only been loafin' round the garden of it before."

"You had to start some time or other," said the Surgeon kindly. "I remember it was a good day, a little too warm perhaps. Picked up your strength pretty fast, didn't you, Dillon?"

"I'll tell you the truth, Docther: it wasn't the week's ind before I wouldn't take a bould word from anny one. My head was as high as ever, and I feeling pretty well and 'ating like the birdie that pays the rint, an' me pains didn't trouble me where me bones was minded. The weather was fine and smiling, and I kept on through idleness far up the country. Says I to myself, 'We'll take a hand wit' the planting for a while.' I heard great tark in the towns that help was very scarce on the farms, and I thought I'd go footing it along as slow as I liked and see all the places, and pick me a nice, 'asy corner where I'd stay for a while an' hear from me pinsion. I'd plinty of money first, thanks be to me frinds, to go in the cars, but 'twas fine to be out and always hungry, so I took time enough to fill me up, but I never could, sir, and I thought I'd get me poor legs used to travelling together. The green

fields looked fine to me, I'd been so long at sea. I got lodgings handy to the road all the while, and I'd sometimes get a
lift in a team from pity on me legs an' love for me buttons,
and so I worked mesilf along, and I was very proud-feeling
at first, but at the end I came to want, and I couldn't suit
anybody's needs on the road. I'd no chance wit' the farmers,
you'll see; they'd look me over, for all I was sure I could plant
and hoe wit' any man, and they'd till me I might go to the
women folks and get me dinner, or else they'd say I might
get out of it an' they wanted no tramps. So the weather come
hot an' I got surly, an' was as bad as troops on the march
with rags and dirt after I'd had two weeks more travel. I'd
spint me money, Lord knew whin I'd have me pinsion, and
everywhere I wint 'twas full before I come; an' I wont tark all
day, Docther, but I'd fallen in great trouble. How'd I got there I
d'know, an' howd I get back I d'know, an' so I lost heart altogether or I was ready to fight the whole road by turns. Now
I'm goin' to tell you me story—"

"Take a cigar; your pipe's out now, Dillon," said the Doctor encouragingly, and Dillon looked doubtful for a moment,
then laid his pipe on the grass beside him, turned the cigar
in his fingers, and after a moment of reflection cheerfully
accepted a light.

"I was toiling up the gravelly road below here a mile or a
mile an' a half, sir," he went on, with a fresh breeze in the
sails of his story. "You'll mind how there's a long hill comes
up this side of the old school-house, and beyant there's a
little t'read of a brook that comes into this; there's trout in it
too, in a place I'll be showing you where it's dammed by a
tree or two across; I own woods there, sir; 'tis two miles
from here, but the fish do be crowded in the wather."

"Good for you, Mike," said the Surgeon in a brotherly tone.

"Yes, sir; 'tis true for me, sir; I remimber thim old days in
the hospit'l, sir. I don't be much for fishin' anyways mesilf.
Well then," said Mike gallantly, "I was coming up that long hill
an' I was as hungry as a saint's dog. I'd no pinny left in me
pocket; 'twas noontime, an' I'd a mind if school was keeping
to ask the childer at the school-house for a bite of bread an'
cheese, an' I'd tell them a story to pl'ase them. 'Twas Saturday intirely, an' I'd forgot it, an' the door was shut. I looked
round in the grass an' I saw the crust of a piece of pie, an' I

picked it up as if 'twas money and ate it down and looked everywhere for another. That part of the country is very poor-looking land, and I sat awhile on the school-house steps thinking of the size of me for a fool. I didn't know what made me go so far from the salt water, or how would I get anybody to write a letter for me or give me a cint for a card to sind to a frind that would help me out. An' where was any frind I'd write to with the ship gone to sea, yourself having sailing orders with the rest, an' Parlow having told me he was going to the old country for a holiday. I come near makin' another whillalu over meself: me head was the last ind of me to get well, there's the truth, but that was the last day it ever felt hollow on me as it did then, an' the school-house hopped up and down when I tried to look at it to keep me steady. Oh, I'm too long wit' it all, sir, but I wa'n't so bad as the first time in the bushes. 'Go wash your face,' says I, 'an' get dacint, and go up to the top of this hill,' says I; ' there's sometimes fine land on the top of gravelly hills like this, and then, if you don't find annything, turn round an' come back;' an' so I got laughing, an' there was courage in me crust of pie that I d found, and I stepped meself on up the hill.

"Docther Hallett," continued Mr. Dillon with much so-lemnity, "whin I was on the top what did I see, an' I looking ahead to seek me fortune, but a fine figur' of a woman comin' out from a little white house beyant, an' she running whoop-ing down the road towards me, as if she was expecting the likes of me all day; but she stopped by some bars and I walked on the best I could to meet the lady and tell her I was after being there intirely, and thin I saw what she was after. 'Twas not meself, but the crows that were pulling up her young corn by the roots and 'ating it. She'd run to and fro in her field like a boy, an' she yelling and shaking her apron. 'Lord be good to me,' says I, 'here's me chance! Me shirt wants buttons as bad as me inside wants bread, — 'tis a tidy-look-ing house; I wish I'd pl'ase the lady.'

"'Let me do that ma'am,' says I. 'I'll stand still in the field and them little birds'll take me for a scarecrow.'"

"What did she say to that?" asked the Surgeon with interest.

"'I don't want no tramps about me place,' says she, as many another had said before her.

"'A lady like you,' says I (Dillon repeated the conversation in persuasive tones), oughtn't to be sp'iling her perty skin,' says I, 'out driving crows in the hot sun.' She was not young, sir, but she had good looks, an' I minded that the first thing. 'Go in, ma'am,' says I very gintle-spoken, — 'go in, ma'am, an' rest 'asy; for here's a man, though but a poor one, 'll scare the crows in your stead an' be thankful for the kind privilege!'

"'They do trouble me bad,' says she. 'I don t want you round,' says she, very plain and hearty, 'but I'm baking pies the day, an I'm all alone.' Then she caught herself up an' was sorry for having let on to me that she was all alone.

"'Don't mind me, ma'am,' says I; 'I'll defind you to the last drop of me blood before anny one shall lay a finger on you!' and she turned to me wit' a laugh an saw I had the right feelings, and we tarked a little more, an' she wint in the house and I drove thim crows like a crazy windmill an' watched the blue smoke coming out of the chimney, and by the time the sun got over me head she come out by the fince an' set me down a fine plate heaped up three stories high with a Frinch roof, an' I ate every crumb that was there and set the plate down with a finer polish than was on it before. I niver thought of Parlow nor how would I get back to the hospit'l from that time."

The Doctor began to say something appreciative of the situation, but Dillon did not stop to listen.

"I got me plateful again for supper an' I thought out me course. It wa'n't best to do anything but go away out of sight that night, for fear she'd be plain with me that I couldn't stop at all, an' the gates of Heaven would be shut by me own fault. So I says good-night whin the sun dropped an I goin' by the house, an' she come out an' offered me fifty cints for me throuble, but I says no; she'd given me in food an' kindness all the work was worth; an' so she invited me very wishful to stop an' see her if I come that road again, an' she hoped me leg would get better an' all them things. There was some navy buttons still left on me to show me trade, an' when I looked back she was lookin' after me too out o' the windy; but I wint down the road like the tramp I'd fallen to be, and when it came dark I stole back an' got into her tidy barn and I slept well there in the hay."

"Was she young?" asked the Surgeon, as if to gratify a neighborly curiosity.

"I'm afther telling you, sir, that she wasn't young. I should think she might be sixty years of age at the time or a little less, but a fine, smart lady, sir. No, she wa'n't sixty, I suppose, but she was that kind you wouldn't think how old was she, but only a fine shape of a woman, an' good-hearted looking. 'Twas your first thought of her that she was good-looking, and not old nor young."

The Surgeon could not help glancing up with a suspicious smile. Mike was not above forty, and his eyes and forehead and his curly hair had not lost their boyishness, and the Doctor smiled broadly, but Mike looked serious and innocent as he proceeded.

"The next morning was Sunday you'll see, sir, from the day before having been Saturday, an' I was out very early with the sun just blazing up. ''Twill be a fine hot day,' says I, 'an' the old lady'll be vexed wit' them crows, an' she'll want to l'ave home to be goin' to church, an' there's nobody to l'ave the crows wit' but me,' an' I see two or three black old thieves in the air that minute; an' I took a turn t'rough the orchard an' come up the road, so if she was looking out she'd think I'd spint the night far beyant. An' I dealt very bowld wit' thim birds, Docther, for I could see thim roosting all in the archard-edge and among the young pines overright it, one here and one there, keeping watch would I go away an' they'd all light down together. But I rose no noise; she'd had a hard day's work, the cr'atur', an' I says, 'Let her get her Sunday sleep; and whin breakfast-time arrives,' says I to my stomach that was complainin' o' me walking the field to and fro an' it empty, says I, 'she'll remember you an' no fears o' that, me darlin'.' An' I wint on blowing a foul curse at the crows wit' me finger ends an' walkin' the field's deck till I thought she'd got a stroke or something, sir; the house looked like she was dead in it; an' of a sudden I saw the door fly open and up wint every crow into the air with a great flutter out of the trees. There wa'n't a black feather of them from the field. And she looked sharp an' saw me in the impty place, an' how the birds had all been sitting round as if they mint to pick me bones, an' I dead wit' the hunger, an' I heard her burst out laughing, an' she shut the door an' wint in. An' in a minute the smoke come out of the chimney as if 'twas the nose of a gun, an' I sat down and waited by the field side. 'Twas a good breakfast, sir. I got me willin' poor legs to carry me to it, an' 'twas by the kitchen table inside I was, sir, an' herself mindin' the crows from the door."

The story had reached a climax of triumph, and Mike and his surgeon both laughed, while the latter signified an eager desire to hear more.

"She wint to church the day, sir. I advised her to it, the weather being fine, an' after me iligant breakfast I'd stop till night an' welcome, before I wint on, the next day being Monday; and she wint away down the road like a gerrl with her house-key in her pocket. I was aisier with the crows for a while at noon, the sun being very hot an' she'd locked up her well in the shed, from not being sure of me characther, so I could get no drink unless I wint far down the hill for it, an' I was most bate with the heat, I having always in the worst of times stopped off the road in the middle of the day. I'd a mind to go on, once, and l'ave the crows in to their dinner, but for the lady thrusting me, an' so I stayed on till she come hurrying home looking an' looking to see would I be still there an' everything safe. I watched through the fince and rose up as she came by. 'I was afraid you'd gone,' says she before she took thought, an' I says, 'I gave me word to a lady,' I says; 'an' you've misthrusted the wrong man,' an' she was very pleasant intirely. 'Don't mind the crows anny more for a while,' says she. 'Look at thim then,' says I, an' threw one o' me stones into a tree an' up they wint with a great clack and squawking into the air. 'I'd lost half me corn but for you, sir,' says she.

"'I'd best mind 'em for a day yet,' says I; 'they've come out of the whole country into the one field,' says I. I'd respict to her being a lone woman an' very helpless wit' 'em, Docther, and havin' nobody to call on for help."

"Of course," said the Doctor gravely.

"Wit' her l'ave, thin, I made me a fine little shady hut by the field gate out of some inds of old boards, a sintry-box you might call it ashore, an' I wint on duty there, an' she give me a large hand-bell and I made a little heap of stones, and wit' me pipe an' a song I'd a fine afternoon there, an' the good company o' mesilf whilst I was making a clapper I'd often seen at home whin all the boys do be out minding the crows for the farmers, and before long I was raising a great noise with it if a crow would fly down. 'Twas that same night I got the invitation in to drink tay with herself, and I cl'aned me old clothes the best I could, though I was outrageous-like for a man-o'-war's man, I was indeed, but she was very r'asonable, and I told her me story, and other thravels of meself and frinds by land and say; and the evening was as short as the day was long, an' she had great pity on me throubles, and I got a bottle from her for me lame legs: to rub the short one so it would grow or to reef the lingth of the long one, I forget which it was mint to do, for neither leg was the better of it. And she saw how well I could help her round the place, and that me heart was honest and me luck very bad, and I having been started at home a farmer's boy. Herself was disappointed wit' a man that had promised to come and work, and she'd all her land planted, and no cour-age how would she ever get through the s'ason.

"'Twas very hard for the lady, an' I'd seen it all from the beginning, and me arms were pretty good, an' the farm all being on a side hill in respict to me legs was a great con-vanience. So she said I'd best stay till she minded up me clothes, I being a sailor and having served the country, sir, and hersilf having a young brother once that ran away to say and was lost. Betune it all we got on very well. I'm there yet, sir."

"Good harborage for you," said the Doctor warmly. He could not help thinking how much better it was for the hearty, good-natured fellow than to have drifted into the miserable idleness of a sailors' refuge to waste his days in drinking and foolishness. Dillon wore an air of authority and looked very prosperous for a country farmer and a limping, disabled man.

"How soon did you get married?" the Doctor asked with interest, wishing to hear more of this seaman's pastoral.

The two men were on their feet now, but Mike had an air of wishing to make further confidence.

"Deed, then, I've been married two years and two months," said he. "I never thought I'd die on the land. We're fine and happy, sir, as the days are long, and they're very long too, this time of the year on the hills. I'd like to kape to the watch on an' off, as it is on board ship. Yes, I'm married,

Docther—you see the old lady's very sharp with the work an' 'twas very expinsive for her wit' me wages, so she made us no throuble."

"The old lady?" repeated the Doctor doubtfully, a little puzzled by Mike's tone.

"Oh, coom now, sir!" exclaimed Mr. Dillon with consternation. "Sure, Docther, 'tisn't hersilf; 'tis the niece I married, a fine, pretty girl, one that she took very small to bring up and of late years promised the farm to her if she'd get a good husband. I'm that indeed, sir, too; their only fright is I might run away to sea. And we all drives the crows together!"

The Doctor laughed until Mike began to laugh too, and went away, still smiling, to get the creel from its cool hollow. His romance had taken such a sudden and unexpected turn that the listener resorted to professional interests at last to cover his amusement.

"You might have come out of that accident a good deal worse," he said. "You've done well, Mike: nobody in the world would think of hiring you for a scarecrow now."

Mike nodded. "Coom up wit' me to the house," he urged; "we'll thry the cider an' I'll drive you home in the cool of the afternoon, sir,—'tis too hot for you to be tramping t'rough the woods."

"All right," said Doctor Hallett, as Dillon went on ahead in the narrow sheep-path they were following. "You're a lucky fellow, Mike."

"Tis the thruth for you, I'm lucky, thin," agreed Mike, looking over his shoulder. "I've got the beautiful wife, 'tis yoursilf'll say so from having seen her, an' the Lord is good to me legs in respict to its being a hill country. The old lady's a mother to me. But I made bowld to slip away from it for a while the day; 'twas thinkin' of salt wather and the gay old times wit' the b'ys I was whin I caught sight of yourself comin' t'rough the brush."

Elleneen

There was a cheerful noise within the house that mid-winter day, but Mary Ann Dunn looked up innocently from her ironing as her pretty younger sister opened the door and came in. Ellen had only arrived from Ireland in the late autumn; she was still a greenhorn, in spite of the first snow, and several weeks' steady work in the cotton mills of the next town, and even in spite of a fine American hat which waved its feathers in a sort of angry incoherence.

Mary Ann's two babies were playing with a puppy, and the three young creatures seemed to cover the whole floor. There was a door open behind them into a comfortable bedroom, and a bright clean oilcloth on the floor of the kitchen; there was a gay little clacking clock on the high chimney shelf above the stove, with a pair of shining lamps. Everything was cheerfully clean and thrifty in the warm little place, and Mary Ann herself looked as if she were able to keep her housekeeping up to the highest standard.

"Well, there now!" she exclaimed with an almost ostentatious air of hospitality. "How are ye the day, Elleneen? I was after wishing you here a minute ago; how come you out?"

"I'm loafing for the afternoon," said the guest disconsolately. "There was something stopped wit' the machine-ry. I wish fast enough I was out altogether. I'll never get learnt, anyway; me mind ain't on it."

"Oh, go 'way!" responded Mary Ann vigorously.

"'Tis thrue for me. I'm getting pay now only for their being so short-handed; but me mind ain't on it nor in it, so it ain't."

Mary Ann made an inarticulate sound signifying contempt.

"I t'ought I'd come over an' give yez a lift wit' the houseworrk," ventured Ellen somewhat timidly.

"Well, I'm obliged to your kindness," said Mary Ann amiably. "I've enough to do, 'tis thrue for me. That biggest one, Hinry there, was roaring all night wit' the ear-ache, an' I'd small chance to sleep."

"Coom, Hinry, coom an' see aunty Ellen," said the visitor, who was still standing, and turned now to show an interest in the three playmates. "Well, I'll go lay me hat in on the bed; they might be picking off all me feathers if our backs 'ould be turned."

"No, no, give it here to me; that Hinry 'd be on the bed after it aisier than anny place," exclaimed Mary Ann anxiously. "Give me your jacket too, an' I'll put them here, see, on the hook behind the door. Sit down wit' yourself by the stove an' rest a while till we tark a bit. What's all the news?"

"I'd rather be doin' something," protested Ellen.

"Well, I've me ironing most done," answered Mary Ann, "an' I'll be thinking what I'd best do next. Faix, I've enough of it. Hinry, there, ain't got a whole frock nor a dacint petticoat to put on. He's the torment, annyway."

The smiling Henry toddled over to his young aunt, and made an attempt at familiar speech.

"'Tis sweeties he do be asking for," explained the intelligent mother. "No more sweeties 'll he get, the day, I can tell him!"

"Did you get nice sweeties the day, darlin'?" asked Ellen with ready sympathy as she lifted the solid, unwilling little shape to her lap, whence he promptly slipped to the floor again, to stand facing her at a safe distance, and begin a second series of perfectly unintelligible remarks.

"Pity for you, you 'ont learn to tark like a Christian; a great man of a shild like you!" scoffed his mother with assumed severity. "See how well your aunty can't get the sense of a word you say! 'Tis of the nice grocer man he bees tarking, that niver comes inside the door 'less there's a sweetie in his pocket for Hinry. Well, then, you should have the pride to tark like other folks, as I'm always advising you."

Henry had not more than reached the age of two years,

but he was evidently animated by a fiery spirit that served him well in the place of experience. He now stamped his little foot and protested loudly, but his elders went on talking over his head with perfect indifference, and presently he returned, not in the least sulky, to the lively company of the smaller baby and their friendly little dog.

"I'm sorry enough that I ever come out," Ellen announced regretfully, after a pause.

"Ain't you the big fool!" remarked the elder sister, who was well married and settled in a good tenement, which even afforded a best room and a magnificent piano lamp with a yellow silk shade, a wedding present given by her man's associates at the gas-house. "I never saw the half day I wanted to go back," she continued; "I might like just to see the folks an' make a little visit of two-t'ree weeks. Himself was having great tark last night about his own old folks, and sometime he'd get a couple of months off an' we'd go home. He'd like well to show Hinry there to his fader. 'What tark you have of goin' home like a lord,' says I to him; 'for mesilf I'd rather the money was well in the bank than spending it on them dirty ships goin' home.' I'd like well enough to see me mother too," she added more softly; "but John's a great boy to spend his money if I wa'n't sharp wit' him. I've deceived him that a good deal wint to pay the grocer's books that's safe in the bank this minute. Only last night he come home wit' a suit o' clothes for Hinry there, that was a good three sizes too big. I'm all put back wit' me ironin'; I had to go carry 'em back to the store this morning soon as me dishes was done."

"'Tis better than the stingy kind," sighed Ellen.

"Ain't you downhearted the day?—Loafin' ain't good for you," said Mary Ann as she came briskly to the stove for a hot iron and stood for a moment holding it near her cheek. "Whisper now; what kind of a b'y was Danny, John's next brother, the one that they kept at home on the land? John has great tark of him bein' so smart; but he's far too foolish about his own folks, we all know."

"Oh, he's the lovely b'y; he's twice as handsome as John— I ain't sayin' but John's good-looking too," responded Ellen with a lively blush. "Oh, I thinks very often o' poor Danny," she added softly. "We parted very angry, too, wit' each other."

Ellen grew rosier still, and the tears shone in her pretty eyes and were winked away, and then they came back again at once. "'Twas all me own fault," she managed to say.

"Well, there's no harm done," Mary Ann insisted kindly. "There's smart b'ys enough to be choosing—pretty b'ys, too. Jerry Callahan was walking wit' you last Sunday."

"He's a great lout, so he is," said Ellen with sudden fury. "I turned down a street to get rid of his company. Great omadhaun!"

"An' Phil Carroll's a good fellow that come away from Mass wit' you on the Sunday before. Oh, there's little birds tells me everything; an' all the b'ys said you was the prettiest girl on the floor last Saturday's dance a week ago."

But Ellen would not be cheered. "'Tis aisy tarking, then," she answered gloomily. "'Tis all them fools has to tark about, is other people and what they does."

"John says his brother Dan's got his mind on some girl now; I don't know who it was told him—"

"Oh, 'tis that tall Desmond girl at home, that lived on this side the road beyond Donnelly's. She always wanted him," said Ellen after a strange little pause, but the color all left her bright cheeks. Mary Ann did not look round, but seemed more than usually intent on her ironing work.

"She had money too, hadn't she?" Mary Ann persisted.

"Folks said it of her; 'twas from an old aunt in Dublin that she got named after. Some said it was forty pounds—there was conversation about nothing else an' I coming away."

Ellen spoke slowly as if with much effort.

"What come between you an' Danny, then, if you liked him?" asked Mary Ann with the authority and directness of an elder sister and a married woman.

"'Twas me own foolishness; there ain't a day but I says it," answered Ellen mournfully. "I never thought of anny one but poor Danny, an' I never was satisfied till I'd find some way to tease him. He'd them honest eyes like John's, that'd be lookin' at you all the time like an old dog, and he'd take every word a girl said for the thruth, an' I wint too far wit' telling him he'd no wish for anny one but the Desmond girl since she got her money."

"Most like 'twas but forty shillings in the stead o' pounds," said Mary Ann consolingly. "Well, an' what happened then?"

"I'd given him no promise," said Ellen, more sadly still, "except 'twas in me own heart. I think I'll never see anny one in the world like Danny; an he had the lovely patience wit' me for a grand while, till I plagued him too far an' we had a smitch o' tark that day on the road. All the way we didn't stop a bird from singing, we were so quiet ourselves, till I t'ought I'd tease him; an' he pled with me then like a priest— would I turn away from him altogether and misthrust him so? An' I don't know ever since why didn't I give in, but I didn't, an' I turned an' walked off down the road from him, an' I thought ivery step I took he'd be after me, till I'd changed me mind so much I demeaned meself to look over me shoulder, an' he wasn't stopping where I left him at all, but going off like a soldier, most out o' sight. An' he wouldn't look back, an' thin I called loud enough to him, and afterward I went back of the furze bushes, so none o' the market folks would see me, an' I cried till all me tears was gone. So that's the ind; and I ain't the first girl, either, that was such a fool, but I wish I'd be the last."

"An' what made you come off then an' l'ave him? All the while since you come out I've said to John you wa'n't happy; 'twa'n't Ameriky displeased you, but something of your own was on your mind. You might have had the sinse to speak," said Mary Ann, with awful severity; "an' John makin' things worse with writin' home what admiration all the b'ys had for your looks an' your dancing."

"I was full to the head o' me wit' pride an' sorrow, an' I wouldn't let on I'd got hurted," said Ellen, "an' I come out to hide away from ivery one there, an' now I've told all. Ah, 'tis all done an' over. Folks would try to tease me, an' there was those would both fetch a lie an' carry one, an' fan the fire o' throuble. I listened for him whistling by night whin 'twas fine an' dark, as he'd always done when he'd waited a while after our little pets before, an' I'd run out to him then, an' we'd make up lovely what throubles had been between us. But this time he'd no whistle left, an' they told me he was seen a good deal up to Desmond's, an' all that. Sometimes I'm glad I come away, an' sometimes me heart's broke that I was iver such a fool. He'd never speak to me again anny way; but I don't blame 'im ayther."

Ellen had now come to the point where she couldn't do without the help of a much fumbled little handkerchief. "He didn't come with all the neighbors to say good-by to me, an' I was lookin' for him to come an' stop me from it, an' I pretindin' to be full of laugh and very gay-hearted, so nobody'd carry him word, an' I thought the first month I was here I'd be getting a letter from him ivery day, or a word in somebody's letter to wish me luck; two or t'ree times I sint word to him with the rest, wishing him happiness and not making anny joke at all."

"You were the big fool," pronounced Mary Ann coldly, as she tried another iron with her wetted finger; "I've got no word meself but that for yez." She tried to look harshly at poor Ellen, who still sat crying. "Coom now, Elleneen, don't feel too bad; don't cry, Elleneen dear. This is the last iron, an' then we'll sit down an' make Hinry his two little petticoats when I've done me last pieces here, an' I'll make the tay early for the two of us. You'd better think of some o' the other b'ys, now that's all past." But Ellen only cried the more.

"'Tis plain enough now he don't care very much for anny one," said Mary Ann with cold decision.

There was a sudden noise in the room beyond, as if somebody protested at the last remark.

"Run quick for me, Elleneen," exclaimed Mary Ann; "'tis the little dog in there tipping everything over."

Elleneen ran, and Henry toddled after her, and the innocent puppy after him. There was a shriek of joy and the sudden appearance of a big, hearty young man with bright curly hair and a wistful face. Danny had been waiting all the time, a suffering captive in the inner room.

"She saw you coming," humbly explained the lover to his happy Elleneen a minute later. "'Twas Mary Ann seen you coming on the street, sure, whin I was just getting me directions how I'd go find you. An' she said if I come out before she'd give me l'ave, she'd have me heart's blood. I t'ought ivery nixt minute she'd break the news for us. Sure I worked iver since to get the money for me passage. Don't mind me harkin' to all the poor little sorrows, darlin'; sure 'tis meself only loves you the more. Don't mind me for stayin' in the room."

"Ah-h!" said Ellen, returning to her old sports as soon as she could speak, "'twas just like a stupid man! Sure, I'd been out o' me cage like a wild blackbird the minute I got sound o' your voice. Anny way, I've got the lovely pinance after me confession."

And Elleneen hid her face again in the rough frieze coat, which still carried a homelike fragrance of turf smoke, though mixed with the duller and more recent odors of tobacco and the salt sea.

JACK MORGAN teaches at the University of Missouri-Rolla. He has published in the areas of American literature, folklore, Irish literature and studies, ethnicity, and film. His Irish and Irish-American work has appeared in *Irish University Review, Notes on Irish Literature, Éire-Ireland,* and *The Irish Literary Supplement.*

LOUIS A. RENZA is a professor of English at Dartmouth College. He is the author of *"A White Heron" and the Question of Minor Literature.*